A BAD AND DANGEROUS MAN

ADVANCED PRAISE

A Bad and Dangerous Man

BY BRETT LOVELL

"***A Bad and Dangerous Man*** is a taut, gripping novel about a simpler time that isn't simple at all in the hardscrabble landscape of the Virginia mountains. This debut is packed with all the elements of a great, Southern burner: greed, murder, and an unforgettable cast of moonshiners and outlaws."

—**Scott Blackburn,** author of ***It Dies With You***

"In Brett Lovell's ***A Bad and Dangerous Man***, family ties become snares that pull an entire community apart. A simple flirtation lights a fuse that culminates in the historic shootout at the Carroll County Courthouse. As Payne, a detective fresh out of union-busting for the mining companies, pursues Sidna Allen and his nephew, he realizes what the reader gets from the start. There are no "good guys," but neither are the bad ones so very "bad and dangerous." Even knowing some of the major historical moments, I couldn't turn away from the cat-and-mouse pursuit. In some ways the inevitably of the shootout made it an even more compelling read. Lovell delves deep into the inner world of the Allen family—men and women, their community allies, and their political rivals, bringing the blood-soaked past to life in rich and compelling detail."

— **Sarah Warburton**, author of ***You Can Never Tell***

"In ***A Bad and Dangerous Man***, Lovell weaves an intricate history of outlaws, betrayals, and vengeance, of blood spilled and binding, with the precision of an architect and the grace of a poet."

—**Megan Lucas**, author of ***Here in the Dark***

(MORE PRAISE)

"Brett Lovell skillfully navigates the ruthless real-world events of the 1912 Hillsville, Virginia Massacre to create a compelling novel filled with revenge, violence, and — ultimately — redemption. ***A Bad and Dangerous Man*** marks the debut of a powerful new voice in Appalachian fiction."

—**Bobby Mathews**, author of ***Living the Gimmick***

"Brett Lovell's debut historical fiction novel is well-paced, beautifully written, and chock-full of intriguing mountain lore. ***A Bad and Dangerous Man*** will quickly suck you in and ferry you into the twisting mines and hollers of Appalachia—straight through to its heartbreaking conclusion. You will remember Wesley, Sidna, Floyd, and Claude long after the final scene. If you're a fan of Appalachian fiction, you need this book on your bookshelf!"

—**C.W. Blackwell**, author of ***Hard Mountain Clay***

BRETT LOVELL

A BAD AND DANGEROUS MAN

A NOVEL
BASED ON THE
HILLSVILLE
COURTHOUSE
SHOOTOUT

2023

A BAD AND DANGEROUS MAN

This book is a work of fiction. Names, characters, places, and incidents either are products of the author's imagination or are used fictitiously.

Any resemblance to actual persons, living or dead, events, or locales is entirely coincidental.

Published by **Shotgun Honey Books**

215 Loma Road
Charleston, WV 25314
www.ShotgunHoney.com

Cover Design by Ron Earl Phillips.

First Printing 2023.

ISBN-10: 1-956957-21-9
ISBN-13: 978-1-956957-21-1

9 8 7 6 5 4 3 2 1 23 22 21 20 19 18

For Abby

A Bad and Dangerous Man

PART I

A RED EAR OF CORN
AUTUMN 1911

ONE

WESLEY EDWARDS

Wesley Edwards hitched his black quarter horse to a weathered fence post and walked up the dirt path to Hubbard Easter's barn. Two dozen young men and women were gathered around a heap of corn. It was just before sunset and the shadow of the Virginia Blue Ridge was fading into the Carolina Piedmont. A bonfire raged on the edge of the gathering. He stopped and warmed his hands against the chill of fall. A string band picked by the corner of the barn and flatfoot dancers kicked their feet fast and close to the dirt in time with the banjo. He spotted Maude Iroler sitting on the ground around the mound of corn, shucking, and laughing with her friends. Maude's long dress was spread across the grass and her hair was bunched on her head in a loose bun that left a few strands dangling down across her cheek. He decided right then, if he found a red ear of corn, he would kiss Maude. It was rare to find a red ear of corn and the rules were simple, shuck a red ear and you're entitled to steal a kiss from another participant.

Wesley's cousins Claude Allen and Friel Allen, sons of different maternal uncles, were sitting on wooden chairs around the pile of corn catty-corner to Maude. Claude was sitting with his long legs stretched out in front of him and Friel was bent over a large bushel basket shucking corn. Wesley kicked a jig past the flatfoot dancers and continued to where his cousins were sitting.

"What do you say?" Friel asked.

"I'm give out. Been working on the farm all day and I ain't too excited about shucking all that corn," Wesley said.

"Good food and unattached women should make the work bearable," Friel said.

Wesley laughed and said, "What do you know about unattached women?"

Friel was the son of Jasper "Jack" Allen. He was eighteen, two years younger than Wesley and four years younger than Claude. He was also the smallest of the three cousins, in height and frame.

Wesley reached into his inside coat pocket and pulled out a flask of moonshine. The dull tin flask was scratched and dented. Claude popped off his chair, snatched the flask from Wesley's hand, and took a drink.

"Good gracious," Claude said, shaking his head against the burn.

"Found a red ear yet?" Wesley asked.

"Not yet. But there's bound to be one or two in the pile," Claude said.

"You ate yet?" Wesley asked.

"Yea, but I could again," Claude said.

Claude was the son of Wesley's Uncle, Floyd Allen. Claude was tall and his face was bisected by dark eyebrows that joined above his nose. Wesley had always wanted to take a razor to the middle of Claude's brow.

The three cousins went inside the small lean-to barn where the hosts Hubbard Easter and his wife Essie stood behind a small table packed with food. Hubbard wore denim overalls over a loose red-checkered shirt that hid his sturdy frame and Essie Lou had her hair beneath a white bonnet. They had arranged a feast for their guests. A slow-roasted pig carcass was splayed open in the middle of the table surrounded by a bowl of beans, whole roasted potatoes, biscuits, and a jug of vinegar barbeque sauce.

"I smoked that pig all day. He's nice and tender. Pick ya a bite," Hubbard said.

Wesley stuck his hand into the open cavity and tore off a chunk of meat that released in juicy strings. He took a bite and the tender pork fell apart in his mouth.

"That'll eat," Wesley said.

Wesley covered his plate with a large portion of each dish. He said thanks and placed his hand on the old farmer's heavy shoulder and carried his plate to where Maude was sitting.

"Is this spot taken?" Wesley asked.

Maude said no and Wesley sat down and waved Claude and Friel over and they filled the gap in the circle around the pile of corn. He cleared his plate in silence and then approached the heap of corn. He filled a weaved bushel basket and returned to his spot next to Maude. Maude whispered and giggled with the girl beside her, and Wesley wondered if they were talking about him. After a while, she stood, and Wesley kept his eyes on her while she refilled her empty basket. She was almost as tall as him with long dark hair and looked like one of the Gibson Girls Wesley had seen in the pictures hanging in his uncle's general store. He had known Maude since they were both students in the one-room schoolhouse and they had always shared a close connection. There was an easiness between them that he had not experienced with other girls.

Claude elbowed Wesley in the ribs.

"Get back to work," Claude said.

Wesley reached into his basket and removed an ear that was

slightly smaller than the others. He tore off the upper husk and revealed a patch of red speckled with yellow dots. He ripped off the remaining husk like a child unwrapping a present and jumped up.

"I found a red ear!" Wesley yelled.

Everyone cheered and clapped. The band stopped playing and the crowd grew quiet waiting for Wesley to make his decision. Wesley stood and turned toward Maude and extended his right hand out to her.

"Miss Iroler, may I have a kiss?"

She accepted his hand and stood. Wesley watched her cheeks flush. He closed his eyes as his lips met hers. He pulled away after a short peck and she stood there with her eyes closed looking like she wanted more. He leaned in again for another kiss. Her lips were firm and slick, and he lingered for longer than he should have. The crowd laughed and clapped and Claude and Friel hooted and hollered. The band started playing a brisk banjo tune as Wesley and Maude sat back down and continued shucking. They shucked in companionable silence while they watched the flames and listened to the string band and recovered from the embarrassment of their public kiss. Wesley broke the awkward quiet between them before it went on for too long.

"What have you been into lately?"

"Nothing fun at all. Working chores around the farm. Doing my apprenticeship."

"Apprenticeship, for what?"

"For being a farmhouse wife," Maude said with disdain.

"What do you really want to do?"

"I think I want to be a teacher."

"You should do it then. What do you have to do to be one?"

"Go to college. I applied to the Radford Teacher's School for Women's study-by-mail program," Maude said.

"That's great."

"What have you been up to since you left school?"

Wesley gave her a crooked smile and said, "No good."

"I believe it."

"Where is Will Thomas tonight?" Wesley asked.

"I don't know."

The girl beside Maude spoke up. "She is going to break it off with him. He just don't know it yet."

Wesley was not surprised by the news. He had heard of Maude courting at least two other young men in the past year. He wondered if he could settle her wandering nature. They continued husking the corn from their woven baskets. Wesley hummed along with the string band as the banjo player sang "Poor Ellen Smith" and hit the high notes in his mountain twang. The mound of corn diminished. People started leaving. Maude shucked the last ear in her basket and pointed over to a horse and buggy.

"My father is here to pick me up," Maude said.

"It was good to see you again. I enjoyed talking with you. Can I come calling at your house sometime?"

"Yes. That would be nice."

Wesley escorted her to her father's horse-drawn buggy. Maude's father glared down at Wesley, expressionless, and Wesley decided against helping her up into the buggy. She took her father's hand and climbed up. Her soft cotton dress rippled in the breeze and clung to her slender legs. She sat down and her father snapped the reins and the buggy bounced down the rutted dirt road. Wesley watched the buggy disappear around a bend and hoped he would see her again.

TWO

WESLEY

His Primitive Baptist congregation used the one-room schoolhouse in Fancy Gap as a house of worship. The rectangular schoolhouse had a gabled entrance on the short side and a simple bell tower protruding from the roof. Wesley removed his bowler hat and entered the schoolhouse. The wide floorboards creaked as he eased up the aisle in the same dirty boots that he had worn the night before. At least fifty people were crammed into the small schoolhouse. His Uncle Garland was the reverend, and Wesley was related to half of the congregation. Wesley nodded to his cousin Friel as he walked towards the front and took a seat with his mother. The reverend's agenda for the sermon was written on the blackboard next to the previous Friday's multiplication tables. Wesley had attended school there until the age of twelve when he was forced to quit after his father died. He traded grammar and arithmetic for farmwork and never finished his studies.

Garland Allen stood behind the podium in a black wool suit. Garland never stood still while preaching, and he immediately began pacing back and forth across the room in front of the blackboard.

"Welcome. I am so glad that you are all able to join me here this morning. Please turn your hymnal to page 2-5."

The worshipers stood and started singing the opening hymn. Wesley belted out the words in his smooth tenor over the entire congregation. Halfway through the song someone tapped him on the shoulder. He turned and saw Will Thomas poking his head through the cracked front door. Will pointed his finger at Wesley and motioned for him to come outside. Wesley didn't hesitate. He kept singing with the congregation as he stood and slid past his mother. Friel gave him a confused look and Wesley responded with a swift nod of his head to indicate it was fine. He strutted down the aisle to the front door and out into the gray morning light.

Will Thomas and three other young men stood shoulder to shoulder in the yard. Will was tall and lanky. His hat pressed down on his large ears and gave him a childish appearance. Wesley recognized one of the other boys as Will's younger brother. Will's brother was shorter than him but had the same big ears and lanky limbs. The two other young men were the McCraw brothers. Wesley couldn't remember their first names. They were smaller but stocky and stout looking. One of the McCraw boys held a set of brass knuckles in his right hand. The McCraw boy opened and closed his fingers around the thick chunk of metal and glared at Wesley.

"I want to talk to you about last night," Will said.

"It looks like you want to do more than talk."

"I don't want to hear of you coming around Maude again. You get near her again and I swear there'll be hell to pay. She wouldn't go for a no-'count son of a bitch like you anyway."

"I don't know, Will. I think she liked it. The way she leaned into that kiss. I could have taken her up in the woods if I wanted. But I'm a gentleman."

Wesley could see the rage swelling in Will's eyes. Way he reckoned, he had to strike first, or he didn't stand a chance against the four of them. It felt like his heart might beat out of its cage. He picked up a baseball-sized rock from the schoolyard. The rock was coated in dry earth that wicked away the nervous sweat from his palm. He went for the one with brass knuckles first. He cocked his arm and charged. The one with the knuckles bent over and tucked his head towards his knees as Wesley ran forward. The others stood still with wide eyes as Wesley slung the rock. The rock struck the back of the McCraw boy's head. The McCraw boy slumped to his knees and Wesley continued forward. Wesley plowed his knee into the boy's forehead. Will lunged forward and threw a wide punch at Wesley's head. Wesley easily ducked the loopy punch and rose in one graceful motion and hit Will under the chin. Will fell onto the rocky schoolyard. Wesley backed off and waited for the counterattack. The other two looked at each other in disbelief and helped their brothers up. Will struggled to stand upright and leaned on his brother's shoulder. Wesley heard footsteps on the gritty ground behind him and he jumped around thinking another one had snuck up on him. It was his cousin Friel. He was relieved to have Friel at his back.

"You boys, get on outta here," Friel said.

Wesley picked up another rock and tried to ignore the pain in the knee that had collided with the poor McCraw boy's head. Wesley and Friel stood their ground and watched Will Thomas, his brother, and the McCraw brothers retreat down the dirt road. Wesley dropped the rock and limped back into church with Friel. He hobbled down the aisle and joined the congregation at the end of the Lord's Prayer, "forgive us our trespasses, as we forgive those who trespass against us, and lead us not into temptation, but deliver us from evil."

THREE

WESLEY

Wesley rocked in a chair on the front porch with his mother five days after his trouble with Will Thomas. He thumped the rocking chair over the uneven slats in time with the melody of the hymn his mother hummed. She'd given him her gray eyes and dark hair and a smooth singing voice, but that was about all she'd given him. A fine, misty rain flew across the orchard. Wesley tilted his head and gazed up at the fog-covered mountain. The obscured mountaintop appeared to stretch endlessly up through the clouds. Living at the foot of Fancy Gap Mountain was like living in geographic purgatory. The geography matched that of the land across the border in the North Carolina Piedmont, rolling foothills that appeared to stretch on forever with slightly different cultures and accents. Wesley's family was from on top. It was where he had gone to school, where most of his friends lived, and where the center of gravity for the county resided in Hillsville. Virginia always pulled him up the mountain.

He was resting for a spell in between shifts of working odd jobs on the farm before burning his still later that night. He kept a small still at the back of his property in the woods on the side of the mountain. He didn't want to make a career out of either one, but he would choose illegal liquor over farming if he was obliged to pick one over the other. The back of their thirty-acre farm butted up to the bottom of the mountain. Half of the land rose sharply up the mountainside and the other half was a small field with an orchard on the hillside in front of the house. Most of their land was tangled and rocky and not suitable for growing crops or raising livestock. They squeezed all that they could out of their small farm and eked out just enough to sustain themselves.

A man on a horse popped over the hill in front of the house. Wesley squinted and made out a skinny man with wispy hair on a large chestnut horse. The man rode over the hill and down through the orchard. Wesley did not recognize him, but it was clear that the man represented the law. The drab brown overcoat and the stitched county seal on the breast pocket gave it away as the deputy got closer to the house. The deputy had one hand on the reins and the other on the handle of his holstered pistol that stuck out from his right hip. Wesley's heart raced thinking about the still he had hidden in the rocky woods behind the house. The only people who knew about the still were his Uncle Floyd and his cousin Claude. If this was a raid, wouldn't they send more than one skinny lawman? He couldn't think of anything else illegal that he had done lately. The deputy rode the horse right up to the high porch and did not dismount. The Deputy had a strange pink spot about the size of a quarter on the right side of his face. Wesley wondered if it was a birthmark.

"Wesley Victor Edwards?" the deputy asked.

The deputy stayed on his horse and stretched out his hand holding a tri-folded bunch of papers.

"I'm Deputy Samuels and these are papers saying that you are charged with assault and disrupting a church service. You must appear in court on the date indicated."

The Deputy turned the neck of his horse away from the porch, tipped his cap, and rode back through the orchard. Wesley opened the papers and read the details.

"What's it say?" his mother asked.

He continued reading and folded the paper back up when he was done and stuffed it into his coat pocket. He didn't answer his mother. He jumped off the high porch and started walking to the barn.

"It's nothing," Wesley said over his shoulder. "I was supposed to do some work for Floyd after supper and I'm already late. I'll be back later tonight."

"Boy, you better not be in trouble with the law."

He felt her eyes on his back. He picked up his pace and jogged to the barn and threw a saddle over his black quarter horse. He jumped on and pushed her hard south from the base of the mountain across the narrow dirt road to his Uncle Floyd's house. Hillsville was the seat of power for the county, but Floyd ruled below the mountain where the county officials either didn't take the time to visit or didn't want to visit. Floyd was deputized as the special peace officer for his district. Floyd would know what to do.

FOUR

WESLEY

Floyd's house was on the main road to Mount Airy across from the general store he owned. Wesley tied his horse to a low branch that jutted off the sprawling oak tree in the front yard. He removed his hat and knocked on the front door. Half minute later his Aunt Frances opened the door.

"Is Uncle Floyd around?"

"He's laid up in the bed with the gripe. I'd let him be."

"I really need to talk to him. I'm in trouble with the law."

His Aunt raised her eyebrows at him as she wiped her hands on the apron covering the front of her long navy-blue dress.

"What did you do?"

"Nothing. I was just defending myself."

Frances took a deep breath and pushed the air back out through her teeth as she motioned for Wesley to come inside. Wesley followed her into the house. Frances was a kind and gentle woman. Wesley figured she had to be to counterbalance Floyd's petulance. Floyd's short temper was notorious and had bought him lots of enemies. But Floyd was also as loyal as an old coon dog. You were either his bitter enemy or his best friend with not many people in between.

The bedroom was just to the right of the foyer. His aunt knocked on the door and Floyd let out a low grunt from inside the bedroom. Wesley followed his aunt into the dark room. The windows were covered with unevenly hung quilts fashioned up to block the afternoon sun. The room smelled medicinal, but Wesley couldn't exactly place the bitter smell. It smelled like someone had boiled some unknown weed and the steam had permeated the entire room. Floyd was propped up on his back, sweating like a pale sow in midsummer. Floyd cultivated a bushy mustache that had turned almost full gray, streaked with strands of black like his salt and pepper head of hair. The mustache completely covered his mouth like his nose was the handle of a broad paintbrush. It was the type of mustache that made Wesley wonder if Floyd grew it just to keep his wife from kissing him.

"Floyd, your nephew Wesley is here to talk to you," Frances said.

"Don't get too close. You don't want this shit. What's on your mind?" Floyd asked.

Frances left the room and pulled the door shut but didn't latch it, leaving a thin crease of light coming through the crack at the door frame.

"I'm in trouble with the law, Uncle Floyd."

"What branch?"

"Huh?"

"Town or county?"

"County. I think."

"What for?"

Wesley held his hat against his sternum and started telling his story. He stared at the floor when he finished and braced for Floyd's fury, but his fury never came, just a long silence before Floyd flew into a coughing fit. The coughing went on for an awkward amount of time before Floyd finally spoke again.

"Well, that don't surprise me much at all. This is exactly what happens when you cross the crooked republicans in this county. That courthouse clique of republicans, Goad, Foster, and Sheriff Webb ain't going to grant you any quarter. They'll throw the book at you because of your familial connections," Floyd said.

Wesley didn't know much about how Floyd's feud with Dexter Goad and William Foster started. It had something to do with a petty election dispute that happened when Floyd was a County Commissioner. Wesley wasn't about to ask about it now, or ever, else he himself might feel the weight of Floyd's wrath.

"When are you due in court?" Floyd asked.

"A week from Tuesday."

Floyd tried to talk but started coughing again and grabbed a soiled rag from his nightstand, covered his mouth with the rag and winced between the harsh-sounding coughs.

"What's today?" Floyd asked.

"Friday."

"Go hide out in Carolina. I've got some things I need to tend to in Hillsville. I'll go up there and post your bond when I get better. Go see Mr. Taylor at Mount Airy Grocery. Tell him that you're my nephew and he will give you a job and a place to stay for a few days."

"Don't I have to show up for the indictment next week?"

"No. Just skip it. You ain't going to get fair treatment up there."

"Why not? I didn't do anything wrong. I was just standing up for myself."

"Because you're my nephew and those goddamn inbred republicans have it out for us."

Floyd started on another coughing fit. Wesley backed closer

to the door. Floyd removed the sullied rag from his mouth and nose.

"Just listen to me, boy, I don't feel like arguing with you right now. You came here seeking my advice and that's it."

"Yes, sir."

Floyd opened his bedside table drawer, pulled out his bill-fold, and handed Wesley a fifty-dollar bill. Wesley accepted the money.

"Hope you get feeling better soon," Wesley said.

Floyd burst into an uncontrollable coughing fit and Wesley backed out of the room.

FIVE

SIDNA ALLEN

Sidna Allen stood behind the long display cabinet in his general store. Canned goods lined the shelves behind him. Glass jars packed with candy filled the counter around the bulky cash register. He squinted at the thick ledger open on the counter in front of him. The front door flew open and broke his concentration from the matrix of numbers in the ledger. The bell above the door rang three beats longer than usual. His brother Floyd barged through the entrance. Floyd trounced down the middle aisle and weaved around the barrels full of dried beans and grains that occupied the open space in front of the counter. A young woman named Betty Ayers was in the back changing room trying on consignment dresses. She poked her head out from the changing room curtain. Sidna smiled at her and she closed the curtain. He peered out over round spectacles perched on the end of his nose. Floyd's blue eyes burned like hot flames.

"I need your help, brother. Two Hillsville deputies arrested Wesley in North Carolina. They have him trussed up to the back of a wagon like a dog, dragging his ass up the mountain. This won't stand," Floyd said.

Sidna had been expecting the capture of his nephew, Wesley Edwards. Wesley had been on the run from the law for two weeks. It was a wonder Wesley evaded capture for as long as he had.

"They've already captured him. Surely you don't intend to release him. Let me talk to the deputies and try to persuade them to release Wesley. Maybe I can talk them into letting him ride up in the wagon instead of being dragged around like a beast," Sidna said.

"I already tried talking," Floyd said. "I was just up in town today to see about posting bond for him. I met the deputies with Wesley at the foot of the mountain on my way back home. I asked them to release him and let him ride on a horse or in the wagon and they refused. I asked them for their extradition papers for bringing him across the state line and they couldn't produce any papers. I continued home but the more I thought about it, the madder I got, and I had to turn around. I kept thinking about the helpless look Wesley gave me when I rode off. They are trying to humiliate us, and I won't allow our family to be disrespected like this. Why do you think they brought him up this way through Fancy Gap instead of Ward's Gap? They are coming this way to parade Wesley through our part of the county, right in front of our faces."

Sidna walked over to the window and looked out as the wagon crested the hill a hundred yards from his storefront. Wesley was chained to the back of the wagon by his wrists, escorted by two Carroll County Deputies. One deputy drove the wagon and the other walked behind Wesley. Sidna could see that Wesley was struggling to keep pace. Sidna watched the wagon drag Wesley down the hill. Over and again, the chain stretched, the wagon jerked him forward, and then the chain went slack, he fell behind, and the wagon jerked him onward.

"They're coming down the hill," Sidna said.

Sidna turned back to see Floyd fiddling with his revolver.

Floyd opened the cylinder and loaded each chamber, slammed it shut, and slid the gun into his left inside breast pocket.

"We don't need any guns," Sidna said.

"I ain't going out there without it," Floyd said.

Floyd was an irascible man and Sidna felt the tug of his anger. There was no talking Floyd down once he got that vicious look in his eyes. Not until whatever affronted him was resolved, usually with violence.

"Just take it calm and let me do the talking," Sidna said.

Floyd grunted. Sidna opened the door as the wagon passed by the storefront. He squinted against the fall sun, low in the sky, as he rushed down to the road. Sidna stopped twenty paces in front of the horse, threw both hands up, and yelled, "Whoa, whoa!"

The driver pulled the reins to turn the team left and tried to continue going around Sidna. The horses didn't respond. They stopped in the middle of the road and refused to go around Sidna. The deputy on the road approached Sidna with his right hand on the handle of his holstered gun. The persistent breeze across the windy plateau made the deputy's hair splay across his short forehead like one of the shaggy horses pulling the wagon. Sidna noticed a strange mark on the right side of the deputy's face, a strawberry-colored birthmark.

"Afternoon, deputy. I'm Sidna Allen. That's my nephew you have chained up. I don't think his crime fits this punishment. Why don't you let him ride up in the back of the wagon?"

"I had to chain him up. He resisted. Anybody that interferes will also be arrested. Let us get on down the road," commanded the scrawny deputy.

"Why don't you just let him go and we'll take him the rest of the way to Hillsville? We can post bond for him and make sure he shows up for the trial. You can even go with us. Just unshackle the poor boy and treat him with some decency," Sidna said.

"What about them other boys, Pinky? Have y'all charged them for starting what Wesley finished?" Floyd asked.

Sidna knew that Floyd never cared about the law except on the few occasions when he had been deputized. He considered himself the law in his end of the county. Most went along with it because they were scared to tell him otherwise.

"Alright, y'all keep your britches on," Sidna said, trying to break the tension. Both men ignored him.

"I'm just doing my job. You can take it up with the sheriff," Pinky said.

"Do you also have orders to bring him along this route?" Floyd asked.

The deputy didn't answer. Floyd continued. "I won't allow you to drag this poor boy all the way to Hillsville."

Sidna walked over to the deputy and extended his hand. The deputy shook Sidna's hand. "You don't sound like you're from around here. Where are you from?"

"I'm from Greenville, South Carolina."

"Greenville?" Sidna asked. "What in the hell are you doing up here?"

"I had a connection with the sheriff."

Floyd rolled his eyes and said, "Republican nepotism."

"Do you really go by Pinky or is that some put-down nickname my clever brother has laid on you?" Sidna asked.

"Most people call me Pinky. My daddy started calling me that when I was a baby on account of this pink birthmark. My real name is Paul Samuels."

"Alright Pinky. How about you let us put Wesley in the back of that wagon and we will all go to Hillsville together? You can do your job and deliver your prisoner and we can post his bond," Sidna said.

"I'm sorry. I can't do that. Now let us pass or I'll arrest both of y'all."

"I ain't going to allow this. I'm a sworn peace officer for this district, a keeper of the peace deputized with all the rights and responsibilities of the law and sworn in by Judge Massie. I ain't never seen a prisoner handled like this," Floyd said.

Deputy Samuels drew his pistol and leveled it at Floyd. Floyd didn't flinch.

"The sheriff's orders overrule yours. Let us pass," Pinky said.

Sidna watched from the side of the road. Wesley had fallen to his knees with his head hunched over in exhaustion. It was another six miles to Hillsville. Wesley would be broken by the time he reached town. Floyd had that look in his eyes. Sidna had seen that look many times, like a cornered animal. Years of knowing Floyd had taught him that there was no going back once he got that look in his eyes. He wanted to stop Floyd, go grab him by the two ends of his mustache and drag him back up the road. Instead, he stood by and watched Floyd ease up to the deputy. Floyd left his pistol holstered. The deputy kept his gun pointed at Floyd. Floyd stopped two feet from the gun. Then, in an instant, Floyd ducked his head down while moving to his left and reached up and snatched the gun from the deputy's hand. The deputy looked stunned and stood with his mouth open as Floyd opened the chamber, removed the bullets, and threw them into the grass. Floyd wasn't finished with the deputy. He turned the gun around and held it by the barrel so that the bottom of the grip faced out like the head of a hammer and raised it toward the deputy. Sidna flinched as Floyd struck Pinky again and again with the end of the handle until

Pinky was curled up in a ball on the ground like a distressed wooly worm.

"You never had it in you to shoot nobody. Give me the goddamn keys, Pinky. I aim to release him," Floyd said.

Pinky dug in his pocket and handed the keys to Floyd. Floyd tossed the keys to Sidna. Floyd smashed the deputy's pistol on a large rock by the roadside. The cylinder separated from the frame, and Floyd threw the broken revolver into the tall weeds. Pinky moaned in pain on the ground, his face marbled with streaks of bright red.

"I think he's had enough," Sidna said.

Floyd didn't listen and walked back over and kicked Pinky in the forehead with the end of his black boot. Pinky rolled down into the roadside ditch. Floyd turned to the other deputy who had not budged from the wagon bench. The deputy driving the wagon looked like he might have to change his britches.

"You tell Sheriff Webb we'll bring him in ourselves," Floyd said.

Sidna helped Wesley up from the rocky road and removed the shackles from his bloody wrists. The knees of Wesley's britches were shredded and damp with blood.

"We'll get you up to the house and bandaged up," Sidna said.

The other deputy jumped down from the wagon and grabbed Pinky under the arms and dragged him up into the back of the wagon. Sidna watched as the deputy pulled the reins and the horses made a sharp turn to avoid Floyd who was still standing in the middle of the road. The deputy drove the wagon halfway off the road to avoid Floyd and bounced over the hill toward town.

SIX

SIDNA

Sidna and Floyd carried Wesley between their shoulders up the dusty road to Sidna's house. Wesley struggled to bear his own weight and his feet left a pair of long, curvy trails up the dirt road. They lifted him up the stairs onto the front porch.

Sidna yelled through the front door, "Bettie! We need some help!"

Sidna's wife walked into the foyer with a book in her hand. She gasped when she saw Wesley. The housekeeper poked her head out of the dining room and Bettie waved her off.

"What happened to him?" Bettie asked.

"The town deputies arrested him and dragged him up the mountain chained to the back of a wagon," Sidna said.

Wesley's wrists had been rubbed raw by the handcuffs and blood was trickling from his nose into the corner of his mouth. Bettie squinted and drew her mouth down into a slight frown.

"And why is he here now if the deputies arrested him?" Bettie asked.

"We tried to talk them into letting him ride in the back of the wagon. They refused and Floyd took it upon himself to release Wesley," Sidna said.

Bettie pried Wesley's arm away from Floyd's and pushed

Floyd out of the way. Floyd backed toward the front door. She glared at Floyd.

"Watch the girls for me while I tend to him."

Bettie pointed at the girls and motioned with her round face toward the front door. Floyd followed the girls out to the front porch. Sidna and Bettie helped Wesley to the bathroom. They sat Wesley down on the toilet. Bettie inspected his injuries and opened the medicine cabinet looking for supplies.

"I'll tend to him and let you know if I need any help. It looks like scratches and fatigue. You go back out and watch the girls…and Floyd," Bettie said.

"You sure?" Sidna asked.

"She's right," Wesley said. "I'm just nicked up and exhausted. I'll be alright if I can just rest a spell."

"Alright."

Sidna left them in the bathroom and walked back into the foyer and stopped at the bottom of the stairs. He put his hand on the thick railing that rested on heavy balusters and sat down on the curved steps below the large stained-glass window set in the wall separating the foyer and kitchen. Light passed through the stained glass from the kitchen and illuminated the orange, yellow, and green panels in the window. His hand trembled with a palsy-like shake that had started after Floyd released Wesley. He steadied his hand and took a deep breath to calm his nerves. He took his time. The girls were fine. He heard their shrieks of joy and giggles in the front yard.

The foyer still smelled like new wood. Ornate crown molding, intricate baseboards, and rich wood paneling filled the open entrance. They had lived in their dream home for less than a year. The house was in the Queen Ann style. It had a wraparound front porch with a gazebo under a conical roof on the left side that gave the house an asymmetrical beauty.

Ionian columns supported the porch roof. A tower under another conical roof rose out of the center of the house. He built the house from the finest materials he could procure. People said it was built with funds obtained from a nefarious blend of counterfeiting and moonshining. Others spread a rumor that he had struck gold in 1898 during the rush to the Klondike. The truth was that he bought it with hard work and patience. It was one of the finest homes in Carroll County. He and Bettie had planned and designed the home themselves. Bettie planned the interior and Sidna designed the exterior. It had eight rooms with a large living room, a separate formal dining room, and parlor. The house was a marvel compared to his neighbors' humble cabins and boringly efficient farmhouses. It had indoor lights lit by acetylene gas and the water for indoor plumbing was pumped with power provided by a tall windmill that towered over the back of the house. The house wasn't perfect. It didn't have a basement or a crawlspace. It was built directly on the ground. He and Bettie had opted to use the money that a basement would cost to cover the opulent fixtures and finishes. It was a house built for show.

Thinking about the beautiful home he and Bettie had built calmed his nerves. He stood and walked out onto the porch and took a seat in one of the white rocking chairs beside Floyd. The house faced west and was positioned on the highest point of the plateau with views of the Virginia Blue Ridge in every direction. He watched his little girls frolic in the fading light as the sun set behind the blue-tinged mountains. The view did not calm his fury at Floyd.

"Damn it, Floyd. What in the hell were you thinking down there? They won't let this slide. You just can't keep it down, can you? Now we are all going to pay for your recklessness."

Floyd stared back with contempt. Floyd wasn't used to

people talking to him like that. Sidna knew that he was about the only person around who had the nerve to stand up to Floyd. His courage came from a lifetime of arguments and forgiveness and brotherhood.

"Dexter Goad and William Foster and Sheriff Webb and those goddamn inbred republicans can kiss my ass. They were asking for trouble by dragging him up the mountain and through our part of the county," Floyd said.

"They won't see it that way Floyd. They will see this as an opportunity to finally get you under their thumbs. They control all the major elected positions in the county now and the new state-appointed judge won't see things our way as easily as the county judges used to. We need to return Wesley this evening," Sidna said.

"I ain't going back to town today. We can wait and take him in tomorrow morning, or you can go tonight if you want," Floyd said.

"Alright. I will take him in after dinner. The longer we wait the worse this will look. It will look like we planned it. It will make our case better if we take him back now and show that we were just releasing him from that cruel deputy's chains and not trying to interfere with the legal process," Sidna said.

"Fine then."

Floyd stood and stretched his arms up to the haint blue porch ceiling.

"I need to take a piss," Floyd announced as he reached for the front doorknob.

"Oh, you'll have to use the outhouse. I'm afraid that our indoor plumbing isn't working right now. The windmill that powers the water pump is not working. The wind can be strong up on the highpoint of this tableland and the windmill has been in a continuous state of repair. I am eventually doing away with the windmill and putting in a spring-fed water system that will be pumped from a hydraulic ram. I am going to build a reservoir and send water all over the property."

"Always tinkering with something, aren't you? Never satisfied with things as they are. I still can't get used to going inside of the house anyway. I prefer to do my business in the outhouse," Floyd said.

"You better get with the times, Floyd. Some things are changing for the better," Sidna laughed.

"I don't know why anybody would want to take a shit inside their house. I'd rather go to the outhouse and do my business and leave the stink outside."

"It's right nice once you get used to it, especially on cold nights."

Floyd disappeared around to the back of the house. Sidna's hands were still shaking from the confrontation. He tried again to slow his breathing and steady his nerves. Floyd appeared undisturbed by the encounter and didn't seem to have any lingering effects. Floyd had always traded easily in violence. Floyd was quick to throw a punch without thinking about the consequences. Sidna recalled numerous times when he was a child watching their mother tie Floyd up to the staircase bannister as he flailed away like a rabid raccoon. Pauline ran up the porch stairs and stretched out her hand offering a rock. Sidna took the rock from her tiny hand.

"Daddy, look at these rocks I found. This is the daddy rock, this is the mommy rock, and this is the sister rock. Here you can be the daddy."

Pauline ran back down the steps and into the front yard to look for more rocks. She appeared oblivious to his anxiety. He leaped off the porch and chased Marguerite and Pauline around the front yard. Pauline stopped running and fell onto the ground and curled up in a ball. He pounced on her and started tickling her torso. She howled with laughter, yelled stop, and jumped up and ran away shrieking with joy. Ten-year-old Marguerite took off around to the back of the house and five-year-old Pauline followed. He chased them around the back of the house and watched them start a game of hide and seek. They had the look of their mother. They both had her round face and light blue eyes. He had missed too many of these moments in his daughters' short lives. Between managing his general store and his sawmill and his large farm, it didn't leave much time for him to be a dad to his little girls. If his afternoon hadn't been disturbed by Wesley's capture, then he would still be working at the store all the way up until suppertime. Some nights he worked through supper and missed the girls' bedtime. There was never an end to all the work on his list. He had figured it would slow down when they finished their house but after moving into their dream home the jobs had kept piling up.

"Girls! It's time to go inside and wash up for supper," Sidna bellowed.

They ignored him and kept playing. He yelled again in a louder, more stilted tone. It was a tone he had developed in his early twenties over two years as a teacher in a one-room schoolhouse. The serious tone halted the girls' play, and they ran past Sidna into the house.

SEVEN

WESLEY

After supper, Wesley followed his Uncle Sidna to the stable. The smell of horse manure and wet hay hit his nostrils when they walked into the barn. The late-evening light filtered through the cracks in the wallboards and illuminated dust motes that hung in the stale air. Wesley leaned against the wall and watched Sidna wrap the harness around the torso of a dirty blond pony. His legs ached under the tight bandages that Aunt Bettie had used to cover his gashed knees and his wrists were still raw from the tight handcuffs that had attached him to the back of the wagon that pulled him up Fancy Gap Mountain.

"I reckon you would prefer riding in the buggy rather than in the saddle of a horse after that brutal treatment," Sidna said.

Wesley frowned and nodded in agreement. Sidna led the old pony over to the small buggy parked along the outside of the barn, tethered the pony to the buggy, and placed an extra pillow on top of the bench for Wesley to sit on. Sidna climbed up into the two-seater bench and then offered his hand to Wesley. Wesley eased up onto the buggy.

"How are you feeling?" Sidna asked.

"Like an overworked mule after a hard day plowing a crooked field."

"You're young. You will heal quickly. I'm sorry that you may have to heal in a jail cell," Sidna said.

"Why don't you just let me run on back to Carolina? I'll do a better job hiding this time," Wesley said.

Sidna laughed. "You couldn't hide out if your life depended on it. You'd get the itch for pussy and liquor and we'd be right back here in a fortnight. Except with more trouble to our names."

Wesley grunted, half in agreement with his uncle's crude statement. Sidna clicked his tongue against the roof of his mouth, pulled the harness, and said, "Let's go, old girl." The pony started them off across the plateau toward town. The mountain road rose and fell over rolling hills with long stretches of dense woods and thickets of brush broken up by segments of open pastureland that stretched up the mountainsides.

"I wish the State would get off their ass and upgrade these roads for mechanized vehicles. I'd already own a Model T if the roads could handle automobile traffic. The time from Fancy Gap to Hillsville would be shortened considerably once the infrastructure was upgraded. I'd start doing all my business down in Mount Airy."

Wesley didn't say anything. He was still trying to figure out how he had gone from hiding out in North Carolina that morning to being dragged up the mountain, released by his raging Uncle Floyd, and then back on his way to jail with his Uncle Sidna that evening. Sidna turned his head and looked Wesley in the eyes.

"No more burning the still, you hear me. That won't lead you anywhere but to where we are heading right now and that is no way to start your life. I know it's hard these days for a man who doesn't own any land. You either push your way into the competitive lumber business, move out of the county to look for work in a more industrialized place, or endure a lifetime of hard labor as a low-wage farmhand. None of those seem like good options. A man would have to scrimp and save just to have enough money to buy twenty or thirty acres of rocky land. I know it seems like the only opportunity is on the outside of the law, but I just dabbled in it, and that was years ago. I never made enough money to build up my current businesses. I built my life with hard work, discipline, and determination. And I didn't bring any gold back from the Klondike, contrary to the rumors. I think that you have plenty of potential and I'll tell you what. You've got a job as my shadow when all this blows over. We'll call it an apprenticeship. You can help me run the businesses. What do you say?"

"Deal."

EIGHT

SIDNA

It was dark when they reached the outskirts of Hillsville. Wesley started to fidget when they crossed the town limits. The main street was deserted. Soft light bloomed out from inside a few of the buildings that lined the main street. Sidna turned the buggy left a block before the courthouse and drove into the hitching lot next to the Hillsville Jailhouse.

Sidna left Wesley in the buggy and walked up to the front door of the Sheriff's Office. He tried the door handle. It was unlocked. Sidna was suddenly aware of the pistol concealed in the holster under his coat. He wore a concealed weapon so frequently on his trips to town that most of the time he was unaware it was on his body. It made him feel safer on the dark ride through the sparsely populated countryside between Fancy Gap and Hillsville. If a keen observer paid attention to his habits, they would know that he sometimes carried large amounts of cash on the eight-mile journey into town. Sections of the little mountain road meandered through large stretches of secluded woods and large thickets of bush in between segments of open farmland dotted with the occasional farmhouse here or there. Like a watch or a pocketknife, he was hardly aware of the tool until it was needed. He opened the door and a deputy greeted him from a desk in the back-right corner of the room. The weak-chinned deputy had a bushy mustache that accentuated the severity of the angle between his mouth and neck. Sidna introduced himself and told the deputy who he was bringing in and what happened. The deputy's beady eyes got smaller as he squinted at Sidna, looking like he might also throw Sidna in jail with Wesley.

"I ought to arrest you right here and now for what you all did to Pinky," the deputy said.

Sidna retorted back with as much force as he could muster.

"You don't know a damn thing about what happened out there. I suggest we all talk to our lawyers before we go making accusations," Sidna said.

"Sheriff Webb already knows, and he will be talking to the Commonwealth's attorney tomorrow. There ain't nothing I can do until then, except take back custody of our prisoner."

"We want to post bond and take Wesley back home," Sidna said.

"Oh, there ain't no way he will be released on bond. We consider him a flight risk. He already ran once. He will be held in the county jail until his trial. My guess is that by the time his trial comes around, if he is found guilty then he will be released on time served," the deputy said.

"And how long will that be?"

"Well, I ain't a prosecutor but my guess is thirty to sixty days, if he's on his best behavior." The lanky deputy stood. "Where is he?"

"Out front."

Sidna led the deputy out to the buggy. Sidna helped Wesley climb down. Wesley moved gingerly like an old man about to buckle over in pain. The deputy grabbed Wesley by the wrists and cuffed his hands behind his back.

"Come on, boy," the deputy said.

Sidna watched the deputy move behind Wesley. The deputy put one hand on Wesley's shoulder and the other hand on the chain that linked the handcuffs on Wesley's sore wrists. Wesley winced in pain as the deputy pushed him toward the jailhouse.

NINE

DEXTER GOAD

Judge Massie cracked the gavel and adjourned court for the day. Dexter Goad stayed seated at his desk behind the bar. The courtroom was nearly empty except for William Foster, the Commonwealth's Attorney, Sheriff Webb, a deputy acting as bailiff, and the horse thief who had just pleaded guilty. Dexter organized the documents strewn out in front of him and filed them in his brown briefcase. The deputy bailiff shackled and escorted the horse thief out of the courtroom. Sheriff Webb hovered behind the bar. Dexter could feel the sheriff's eyes on his back. Dexter could sense that the sheriff was waiting for the right time to approach. Dexter was an important man and he had grown accustomed to people hovering and staring and trying to determine the right time to interrupt his concentration.

Dexter picked up an unimportant piece of paper and pretended to read. He didn't need to read the document, but it made him look busy and kept Sheriff Webb waiting a little longer. His official duties as Clerk of Circuit Court were largely administrative and he had two deputy clerks, one was his daughter Jezebel, to handle the mundane paperwork like filing wills and marriage licenses and recording deeds and deeds of trust and powers of attorney and real estate transactions.

If it had anything to do with running the court, he touched it. After a half minute, he filed the unimportant paper in his briefcase, buttoned it up, shouldered the strap, and looked over to acknowledge the sheriff. Sheriff Webb moved quickly towards him with pursed lips and spoke.

"I need a few minutes," Sheriff Webb said.

"Alright, Sheriff. I'm in a hurry. I have a meeting with the Commonwealth's attorney. We can talk on the way down there."

Dexter left the courtroom and went down the stairs that led to the front veranda of the redbrick courthouse. The sheriff followed behind and started briefing Dexter.

"We've had some trouble with Floyd Allen," Sheriff Webb said.

"What happened?" Dexter asked.

"Well, you know that nephew of his, Wesley Edwards. The one who fled when we charged him with disrupting a church service and assault. The sheriff down in Surry County captured him and two of our deputies met them at the border yesterday to exchange custody. Wesley resisted during the transfer at the border and my deputies chained him up behind the wagon and transported him up the mountain. Floyd didn't appreciate my deputies having chained Wesley up. Floyd intercepted them on the road in front of Sidna Allen's store. He assaulted my deputies and released the boy."

Dexter stopped on the veranda beside of one of the massive Greek columns that framed the front of the courthouse. He grinned through the left side of his mouth and chuckled. He hesitated for a moment and allowed a group of men to walk by and pass out of earshot. He placed his hand on the sheriff's shoulder.

"Is the boy still at large?"

"Sidna turned him in last night."

"Alright. That is great news. Go ahead and charge Floyd and Sidna with assault and illegal rescue of a prisoner. I'll inform the Commonwealth's attorney in our meeting here in a few minutes. I'm sure he will agree with me. We can't let this opportunity slide. Now is our time to put them in their place. Floyd and Sidna must face the consequences for their lawlessness."

"I have my deputies working on the case as we speak. We are getting statements from the deputies and looking for other witnesses. We should have the evidence ready soon."

"Okay, we'll go ahead and file charges against Floyd and Sidna for assault, interfering with official police business, and illegal seizure of a prisoner. I'll drop the charges against the other boys involved in the fight with Wesley. Our investigation into that crime was inconclusive and we couldn't prove that the other boys did anything wrong," Sheriff Webb said.

"Good man. We run this county now and they aren't getting away with this shit anymore. I'll push hard for the maximum sentence," Dexter said.

"Floyd Allen ain't going down without a fight," Sheriff Webb said.

"I know. We just have to push him a little and then set back and watch him flail," Dexter said.

They clasped hands and Sheriff Webb started walking down the courthouse steps and across the muddy street. Dexter stood under an archway and looked up at the sky. He savored the news. The headstone-gray sky defied his mood and he walked to his next meeting with a spring in his gait.

TEN

WESLEY

A deputy held open the back door of the jail and said, "Come on through." The cold wind hit Wesley's face and went through his thin coat like he wasn't wearing one. It was the same coat he'd worn when Sidna dropped him off two months prior. The deputy slammed the door behind Wesley. He was free. He squinted against the wind that blew from the southwest and looked out into the hitching lot behind the jail and saw his cousins Claude and Friel. Claude was leaning up against a post with an extra horse tied to his black-and-white Appaloosa.

"It done turned cold," Wesley said.

"You want me to see if they can take you back into the warm jailhouse?"

"Hell no."

"It's a little warmer below the mountain. Let's get down before the sun sets."

Claude handed Wesley a black wool coat and the three cousins galloped out of town.

ELEVEN

WESLEY

Maude's family farm was just up Mount Airy Road from his Uncle Floyd's house. Wesley turned his horse off the road and led it down the narrow, rutted path that cut through a large orchard filled with bare apple and cherry trees. The cold weather had confined him indoors ever since he was released from jail, like some higher power had seen fit to tack additional time onto his sentence. He had started his apprenticeship with Sidna as soon as he was released from jail and the nights had been so cold and the working hours so long that he had taken to sleeping on a cot in the middle of the general store next to the little black stove. He'd gone straight from jail to a different kind of prison, the cramped and cluttered confines of the general store. But at least he was getting paid and learning something in his current reformatory. Sidna had given him the afternoon off, and it was the first day the mercury had registered above the freeze line since his eight-week stint in jail ended. Wesley took it slow and savored the freedom of being outside. He had a flask of blueberry brandy in his pocket and Maude on his mind. He thought of Maude constantly when he was locked behind those steel bars. He tried to picture her pleasant face, sweet eyes, and soft lips during those long nights on the hard jail-cell cot.

It was a good-sized farm. He figured it was two-hundred acres or more and he could see the roof of a large barn rising over the orchard. He passed the back end of the orchard and the farm opened into flat grazing pasture revealing a humble two-story farmhouse surrounded by a craggy split-rail fence flanked by a large gambrel-roofed barn. A large man walked out of the barn with a pitchfork in his hand, strings of hay stuck in the long teeth. A middle-aged woman was sweeping off the front porch of the house. She stopped sweeping and watched him approach the barn.

"Good afternoon, sir. Are you Mr. Iroler, Maude's father?" Wesley asked.

"I am."

"I'm Wesley Edwards. I'm here to call on your daughter."

"You Floyd Allen's nephew?"

"Yes, sir."

"She ain't here."

"Can you please tell her that I was here to visit?"

"I'll tell her when she gets back."

"Thank you. You've got a pretty place here. You need any help? I can help you while I wait for Maude to return."

"No thank ye. We've got enough help. You can just get on up the road."

Maude's father turned his back and strode into the barn. Wesley looked toward the house hoping that Maude's mother might wave him up, but she had disappeared. He clicked his tongue on the roof of his mouth and steered the horse back down the path to the main road. He pulled the horse to a stop when he reached the road and turned his head down the tree-lined path leading back to Maude's house. He wondered when he would see her again. It was foolish to even think that her family would approve of her marrying a young man with scant land and few prospects. He clicked his tongue and kicked his horse up the road. The rocky dirt road sped by underneath his horse. Then, when he was fifty yards up the road, he heard someone yell his name. It was the strained voice of a woman off in the distance. He jerked the rein to a stop and swiveled his head back down the road toward the entrance to Maude's farm. He swiveled his head back behind him and saw a horse trotting fast towards him with a female riding sidesaddle. It was Maude. She closed the distance quickly. Her long dress flapped against the left flank of the chestnut colored horse.

"Hidey," she said.

"Hidey."

"What are you doing over here?"

"Just passing by. Thought I would swing by on my way home."

"I'm glad that you did," Maude said with a smile.

He moved his horse closer to hers. He grabbed her horse's throatlatch and drew their horses together. He leaned over and kissed her. It was a short kiss. Nothing more than a peck. Her horse moved and pulled them apart. She nudged her horse back closer to his and leaned in for another kiss. Her lips were firm and slick. They kissed, longer this time, until their horses pulled them apart again.

"I've been thinking about doing that ever since the corn shucking," Wesley said.

They dismounted and tied their horses to a weathered fence post and sat under an old oak tree beside the road. Their horses started eating grass between the wooden fence and the road.

"How have you been doing?" Maude asked.

"Better, now that I'm out of jail. My Uncle Sid gave me a job as his apprentice. Doing the day-to-day chores in his general store and learning how to run a business."

"That's great. When did you get out of jail?"

"'Bout two weeks ago."

"You picked a good time to be incarcerated. It has been a cold winter and I don't think we would have been able to see each other that much," Maude said.

"There ain't never a good time to be incarcerated. You can't even imagine the boredom and loneliness I felt while in that tiny room. I know one thing, I ain't never going back."

"I still can't believe they put you in jail for that. It seems too harsh for the crime," Maude said. "And Will Thomas and those other boys weren't charged with assault. They should be charged with something too, right? I mean, they started it and you were just defending yourself."

"I don't know about them. I ain't heard if they have. Floyd said that their daddies have political connections with the courthouse clique. I don't know. Half the stuff Uncle Floyd says is that everybody is out to get us. I shouldn't have run off to Carolina."

"Why didn't you just turn yourself in after they charged you?" Maude asked.

"Floyd told me that I wouldn't get a fair trial in Hillsville. He said that I should hide out in Mount Airy until he could sort it out with the authorities. So, I listened to him. They found me after two weeks on the run and the Surry County Sheriff turned me over at the border. They claimed I resisted, I didn't, and they strung me up behind the wagon and towed me up the mountain. That is when Floyd intercepted them and released me."

"When is Floyd's trial?"

"March 11th is when his trial starts. I reckon I'll be there to support him. He'll either be found not guilty or there will be hell. He is not too optimistic about winning the case. He says he ain't going to lay over and surrender without a fight."

There was a long pause between them. They sat under the tree and watched their horses pick through the dormant grass on the edge of the road.

"Anyway, how have you been?" Wesley asked.

"Good. I got into that teacher school I was telling you about, the Radford Teacher's School for Women's study-by-mail program."

He could hear the excitement in her voice. "That is fantastic. When do you start?"

"I'm not sure yet. My parents still aren't convinced it's a good idea. I'm not sure if I'll enroll in the program."

Wesley caught movement on the road out of the corner of his eye. He looked down the road and saw Maude's mother was walking towards them. He cringed and waited for an earful. Maude took after her father. Her mother was short and plump. Maude stood almost a head taller than her mother.

"Maude, I hate to break up your conversation, but I need help getting supper on the table and you need to finish the laundry."

Maude's mother started walking back down the road. Maude took a deep breath and exhaled slowly. Wesley could see the disappointment on her face. He didn't want to leave, and he sensed that she didn't either. Then he had an idea.

"What if?" Wesley asked. He paused and said, "Never mind."

"What?" Maude asked.

"What if...?" Wesley asked but trailed off like he wasn't sure about the idea.

"What?" Maude asked again, annoyed.

"Nah, never mind. It was good to see you again. I hope we can get together again soon."

"Tell me. What?"

"Well. I was thinking that I could head down the road and loaf at the store for a while and come back later tonight."

"Okay. I can ask Mama if you can join us for supper."

"No. I was thinking after dark and somewhere we can be alone. Like I said, never mind. It's a bad idea."

"I would like that." Maude didn't hesitate. "Although, I'm not sure if I can sneak out past my sister, we share a bedroom, but I'll try. There's an old tobacco shed in the middle of the orchard before you get to the road. It has a little cozy interior room."

"Eleven?" Wesley asked.

"See you then."

Wesley mounted his horse and watched Maude lead her horse down the road. He reached into his coat pocket and pulled out a small can of tobacco snuff, dipped out the fine powder with his little wooden dipper, and sniffed it up into his right nostril. The smell of the sweet tobacco supplanted Maude's perfume. He placed the can of tobacco snuff back in his coat and kicked his horse down the road.

TWELVE

MAUDE IROLER

The laundry nook was in the narrow entryway between the kitchen and the back porch. Maude had spent countless hours there since she graduated from secondary school the previous summer. She grabbed another pair of her father's filthy britches, the bottom of the legs caked in a foul mixture of mud, dried grass, and cow manure. She knelt over the large bucket of hot, soapy water and vigorously rubbed up and down the ribbed metal washboard. She rung them out over a bucket and hung them on the drying rack and pulled another pair from the top of the dirty pile. She loathed the idea of spending her whole life stuck in the endless loop of farmhouse chores. She missed school, it had been her sanctuary, her chance to get away from the long summers on the farm. She especially missed her last few years of school when Miss McAllister had allowed her to help with the younger children. She developed a love of teaching. Seeing the little ones' eyes light up when a lesson sunk into their permeable young brains became her passion. Now she spent her days trapped with her mother learning how to run a proper farmhouse. That included seasonal chores such as maintaining the backyard garden in the spring and summer, preserving the harvest in late summer and early fall, cleaning the house in the early spring, mending fabric, or stringing tobacco bags in the winter, and the day-to-day chores of cooking, cleaning house, and washing clothes.

"Supper's almost ready," her mother hollered from the kitchen.

Maude left the pile of laundry that she had dwindled throughout the afternoon and walked into the dining room. Her family was already seated. A small feast was spread across the table; fried salt ham, biscuits, green beans from their garden, fried apples from their orchard, and a pyramid of biscuits stacked high on a plate in the middle. She built herself a plate and started eating.

"I saw Ken Marsh's mother after church the other day. She said that he enjoyed visiting with you and would like to see you again soon," her mother said.

Maude smiled in acknowledgment but didn't respond. The only sound was chewing and swallowing and clanking of forks and knives on plates. She pushed her beans around the plate and tried not to look up at her mother. Ken Marsh was nice enough. He was pleasant to look at and always treated her with warmth and respect. He also came from one of the wealthiest families in the county. If she had to endure a life as a farmer's wife, then Ken's big family farmhouse was the best place to settle. However, two things gave her pause about Ken, her attraction to Wesley and Ken's reaction when she had told him that she had been accepted into the Radford Teacher's School for Women. Ken wanted a wife to tend to the house while he worked the farm and he had scoffed at her dream of being a schoolteacher when she told him. Marrying Ken meant continuing the endless cycle of tedious seasonal chores. She didn't know if Wesley was the one, but there was something about him that made her believe he could be. He was kind and gentle, but with a wild glint in his eyes that beckoned her to follow.

"Your father and I were just trying to set you up with someone from a respectable family. Ken can provide a very secure future for you. Do you really want to be with a man who has already had a stint in the jailhouse prior to his twentieth birthday? That kind of track doesn't give me much confidence in his future," her mother said.

"Wesley comes from a respectable family too," Maude said.

The table was silent while her father finished chewing his last bite. Her sister, Elizabeth, continued eating with a little smile, like she was enjoying the awkwardness of the conversation. Her father finished chewing and spoke with anger hinged in the back of his throat.

"That depends on who you ask. Do you know the rumors about how his uncles got their wealth? They are into moonshine and other underground activities. It looks like he is on that same path," her father said.

"From what I hear, Will Thomas is the one who should be in jail," Maude said.

"I heard it the other way," her father said. "You only heard it from Wesley. He's just telling you what you want to hear."

"He is changing, doing an apprenticeship with his Uncle Sidna, and helping run Sidna's businesses. That ought to count for something."

"Does he own any land or stand to inherit any land?" her father asked.

"I don't know."

"There is no opportunity around here for a young man who doesn't have any land. There may have been opportunity twenty years ago when I was making my way, but these mountains are getting more crowded and they ain't making any more land. You can do better than him and his family. I don't never want to see that little peckerwood around here again. I best never see the two of you together. His family ain't no count and I won't be associated with them. Sidna is just as bad as Floyd. He dabbles in moonshine and was charged and tried for counterfeiting just last year in Greensboro. Midnight trades are the only things that boy will learn from Sidna Allen."

Maude wanted to scream but she stopped herself. She stood and shoved the chair backwards with her legs and took the stairs two at a time up to her bedroom, even more intent on sneaking out later that night. The cold couldn't keep her inside. She would be there waiting for him.

THIRTEEN

MAUDE

She kept still in her bed and listened for her sister's breathing. She waited for the slow deep breaths of sleep to set in. Elizabeth was a light sleeper and Maude was careful not to wake her. She gently pulled the top quilt off her bed, folded it up, pinned it under her left arm, and grabbed the little oil lamp from her nightstand. The pinewood floor creaked as she walked toward the door and the latch clicked when she turned the knob.

"Where are you going?" Elizabeth asked.

"I can't sleep. I think I drank too much coffee today. I'm going downstairs to read. Go back to sleep."

Her sister rolled over and Maude left the room. She eased down the stairs being careful not to wake her father and mother as she walked by their room that was just off the hallway by the front door. It was a dark night and she stopped halfway through the front yard and listened for some unknown danger. She chuckled and huffed out loud at herself and continued through the orchard feeling silly for still being afraid of the dark. Her mother had always told her that she need not worry about monsters or wild beasts getting her, it was other humans you needed to be wary of. She rounded the corner of the small lean-to barn and ran into Wesley. She jumped and let out a shriek and quickly covered her mouth to dampen the sound.

"I didn't mean to startle you," Wesley said.

"You're early. It's not quite eleven yet. How long have you been waiting?"

"Oh, I've been here for about an hour. I couldn't wait at the store anymore. They closed down at dark and run me off. I was hoping that you might get here early too."

"My parents would have a conniption if they knew I was here with you right now."

"I brought my pistol if your dad gives me any trouble again."

His smile betrayed the cruelty of the statement. Maude led the way under the awning. Wesley opened the door to the shed. They walked across the dirt floor over to the smaller room in the back-left corner of the shed. Maude, her sister, and mother usually used the little room to keep warm in the fall when they were grading and bundling the small amounts of tobacco that her family's farm produced. The sweet smell of the dried tobacco from the last harvest lingered in the cold air. She lit the oil lamp and set it on top of the small stove in the corner. Then she bent down and opened the stove. Ash dust puffed up out of the stove and she pointed to the pile of kindling stacked in the corner of the room and said, "Let's start a fire."

"I don't think we need that. This will keep us warm," Wesley said as he pulled out a flask from his inside pocket.

"What is that?"

"Blueberry brandy. Homebrew aged with sugar and blueberries and other ingredients. My secret recipe."

"You trying to get me all liquored up?"

"Maybe."

He flashed his cocky grin and offered her the flask. She took a sip expecting it to burn like hell, but it was surprisingly sweet and smooth. She was still on edge from sneaking out of the house and the drink calmed her nerves. The flask hit her lips again and then she handed it back to Wesley.

"If that don't keep us warm then we can keep each other warm," Wesley said.

She splayed the blanket out over the wide wooden floor planks. He offered the flask again and she took another sip. It warmed her core and her courage. He kept his eyes fixed on hers. The reflection of the small flame from the lamp burned in his dilated pupils. She stayed still and he moved closer. His chin touched the top of her head when they hugged, and his broad shoulders felt strong and comforting. She felt his hand on the small of her back. The fear of her father or her sister barging through the door melted away in Wesley's embrace.

FOURTEEN

WESLEY

He couldn't think of a more boring job than facing and blocking shelves of canned goods. The pay was decent at ten dollars a week, but he was being treated more like a stock boy than an apprentice. He was trying to be patient, at least for the moment. He bent down, reached to the back of a low shelf, and pulled a few cans of soup to the front and rotated the cans to make sure the label was facing out. He stopped and pulled a small can of tobacco snuff from his pocket and sniffed the fine powder into his nostril and went back to blocking the shelves.

It was quiet inside of the store. He was the only person inside with it being close to dinnertime. Sidna was out front loafing with a couple of old men, regulars who would sit out front for hours hollering at people riding by on horses and buggies and chatting up customers as they came and went. He could hear the low mumble of their voices through the thin front door. Their conversation was sometimes interrupted by laughing or good-natured cursing. The front door opened, and Sidna walked in with a customer.

Sidna led the man down the aisle past Wesley. A musty odor drifted from the man, a conglomeration of sweat, tobacco smoke, and whiskey. The man wore a tattered and patched overcoat with brown work britches frayed at the boot.

The customer's face was boney, and his thick brow shaded his weary eyes. Sidna extended his hand, gave the man a wide smile, and introduced himself. The customer removed his hat and smiled back, exposing missing and jagged teeth. Wesley kept stocking and listened to the interaction.

"I'm Jack Akers. Live just over the ridge in Snake Creek."

"Where at in Snake Creek?" Sidna asked.

"Over the ridge on this side of the creek. Right at the fork in the road that goes over to Willis Gap. I need some food and supplies for the winter. Me and my wife were sick some this summer and didn't produce much of a crop. I need some cornmeal, salt, sugar, flour, and a little coffee if you have any in stock. Maybe some liquor?" His voice trailed off in question. "Would you be willing to help me out with some store credit?"

"I will certainly try to help you. I have some rules for store credit, though. The maximum amount I will give on credit is thirty dollars. I don't sell liquor on store credit. My policy is to give everyone store credit once and then decide on future store credit when the debt has been paid. Go pick out what you need, and I'll get my credit logbook."

"Thank you, Mr. Allen. I appreciate it. I promise I'll pay you back shortly."

Wesley kept his eye on Jack as he perused the store. Jack finished selecting his items and approached the glass counter. Sidna opened the credit book and squinted through his round spectacles as he recorded Jack's items.

"The credit is due in ninety days. You will be eligible for store credit again after you have paid your debt. Your account will go into collection after ninety days. Sign here."

Sidna handed Jack the pencil and Jack held it awkwardly like it was a foreign instrument.

"You need a poke?" Sidna asked.

"Yeh."

Sidna reached down under the counter and pulled out a paper bag. Sidna bagged the items. Jack said thanks and shuffled out the door.

"Wesley," Sidna said. "Come up here for a minute."

Wesley stood and approached the counter.

"That man is a notorious deadbeat. Other local merchants have warned me about him. He has reneged on debts at several other local businesses. I figure you and I will have to pay him a visit in ninety days to collect what he owes us."

"Why did you give him credit if you know he can't pay you back?"

"Everyone deserves one chance, Wesley. He will never forget that I helped him and if he ever gets himself straight then I'll have a customer for life."

Sidna pointed to the open credit account book in front of them on the counter. The debt was recorded as twenty and a half dollars along with Jack Akers' name and the date. Jack had scrawled a shaky X in the signature box in the last column.

"In case I'm not here and someone asks for store credit. Always check to find their name in this book. If they have any outstanding credit, then I usually don't let them take out more unless I know they are good for it. If I'm not here, then just use your judgment and don't let anyone have more than thirty dollars outstanding at any one time."

Sidna closed the book and went back outside to continue shooting the shit with the two old men out front. Wesley kept on facing the shelves. He could hear the muffled voices of Sidna and the old men talking outside. After fifteen minutes, the talking stopped for longer than usual and then a different man said y'all get on out of here in a high tenor that sounded familiar. Wesley walked down the narrow aisle toward the front door and peeked outside. He saw Dexter Goad perched on a large horse. The horse was all black save for the strip of white between its eyes stretching down to its nostrils. Wesley's mind immediately went back to the day in court a few months before when Dexter gleefully watched as he was found guilty and sentenced to two months in jail. Dexter sat erect on the horse hiding under a wide-brimmed hat and a long black wool coat that stretched over most of the horse's hindquarters. The old men who had been talking with Sidna were slowly walking away from the front of the store toward the road. Wesley cracked open the front door and peered out. Sidna was sitting on the wooden bench to the left of the front door with his right leg crossed over his left thigh. Wesley must have had a concerned look on his face because Sidna waved his hand at him like it was alright. Sidna turned his head back to Dexter Goad who was still sitting high in the saddle.

"Why don't you get down from your horse and sit for a spell?" Sidna asked.

"I'll stay where I am," Dexter said.

"How can I help you?"

"Floyd's trial is next week. Your trial is going to be set soon. I've come to offer you and Floyd my goodwill and a chance to get past your terrible deeds without tarnishing your…." Dexter paused. "Tarnishing what's left of your reputation."

"What's your offer?" Sidna asked.

"If you publicly back me in the next election, I'll have all the charges dropped. You can go about your life like you never illegally rescued that'n," Dexter said, pointing at Wesley.

"No thanks. I'm not interested," Sidna said. "I can't speak for Floyd. You'll have to go down and ask him yourself."

"I don't have time to go down there to the nether regions of the county. You can tell him yourself if you are interested. If not, then I'll see to it that you and Floyd spend some quality time together in the penitentiary."

Dexter scrunched up his left nostril after he spoke. Wesley recognized it as the same arrogant snarl that Dexter had flashed towards him in the courtroom before he was sentenced.

"We might be able to cut a deal and work together," Dexter said.

"Work together on what?" Sidna asked.

"Things that men like you and I do when the world ain't looking," Dexter said.

"I don't work in those trades," Sidna said.

"That's not what the federal court down in Greensboro says. I know they tried you last year for counterfeiting and now you have another trial pending down there for perjury."

"I was acquitted on the counterfeiting. It was a misunderstanding with an associate and now that associate is serving his time and I was found innocent. And rightly so. I'm innocent until otherwise proven on the perjury charge."

Dexter's horse got impatient and turned a hundred and eighty degrees away from the front of the store. Dexter swiveled his head back around and pulled the reins at the same time. His long coat flapped in the wind as the horse swung back around and he made one last appeal.

"I know you've been counterfeiting. How else can you afford that house up there?"

"I brought all that gold back from the Klondike. Haven't you heard the rumors?"

Wesley stepped forward. "That's enough. Why don't you get on out of here?"

Dexter laughed and his horse spun around again. He righted it and the horse high-stepped closer toward Wesley and Sidna.

"Just think about it," Dexter said.

Dexter turned his horse away and headed down the road. He was at a full gallop by the time he passed the two old men taking their time down the dirt road. Sidna stood and opened the front door of the store and motioned for Wesley to go inside.

"There's your first life lesson as my apprentice. Never trust a man who ain't willing to get off his horse and look you square while he's offering you a deal," Sidna said.

FIFTEEN

DEXTER

The judge's office door was closed when Dexter arrived. Muffled voices escaped through the thick wooden door. Judge Massie had hastily called a meeting with the sheriff and the Commonwealth's attorney. The Judge hadn't said what the meeting was about, just that it was urgent, but Dexter knew the reason. It was two days before Floyd Allen's trial and the entire courthouse was on edge with anticipation. He opened the door and walked into the judge's spacious office. The walls and floors were all wood and the large wooden desk reflected glossy light. Sheriff Webb stood off in the corner of the room against the wall, his right ankle crossed over his left foot, toothpick sticking out of the corner of his mouth. Judge Massie was reclined back in his large black leather chair reading a single piece of paper that had been tri folded. Dexter took a seat beside of William Foster in one of the two chairs in front of the judge's large desk and waited for the judge to break the silence.

"Good evening, Mr. Goad. Thank you for meeting us here at such a late hour," the judge said.

Judge Massie folded the letter and stood and handed the letter across the desktop to Dexter.

"William received a disturbing letter in the mail regarding

the Floyd Allen trial. There was no return address, and the letter was unmarked," the judge said.

Dexter unfolded the letter and read the single sentence:

If you find Floyd Allen guilty you will die.

Dexter folded the letter up and handed it back to the judge. They all stared back at him, waiting for him to speak.

"This does not surprise me. The Allens have operated like this for decades. Floyd knows we've got him this time and he's scared. This is exactly why we need to see this through to the end," Dexter said.

"It can't be proven, but it is clear to me that Floyd Allen, or one of his kin, is the author of this letter. He is trying to intimidate the court into a favorable decision or into dropping the case altogether," Foster said.

"It is also a crime to threaten or intimidate officials of a court prior to trial. We should move to include this as additional evidence in the trial," Dexter said.

Judge Massie held up the letter in his only hand and shook it. Some unknown farm accident had taken half of the judge's left hand when he was a child. Dexter had never inquired about the accident out of respect and reverence for the judge.

"We can't prove that Floyd or any other Allen sent this letter. I will not allow this as evidence in a trial unless there is conclusive proof that the letter was personally drafted by Floyd. Anyone could have written this letter," Judge Massie said.

"But we should consider this as a credible threat to the court. I think we should put additional armed deputies in the courtroom during the trial and search everyone entering the courtroom for weapons. No weapons should be allowed in the court during the trial," Foster said.

Judge Massie shifted to the other side of the large chair and easily crossed his left leg over his right. Dexter always marveled at the judge's sharp memory. His brain was like one of the rabbit traps Dexter had used as a kid. Once a rabbit got caught up in that steel cage it was not getting out. Judge Massie could instantly recall obscure court rulings and specific Virginia Codes, the index number, and the subject matter. However, Dexter often wondered if the Judge had the common sense to apply those random facts.

"Mr. Foster, thank you for bringing this letter to my attention. We shall continue as if this is an ordinary trial. Increased security would be cowardly. My court will not be swayed by intimidation or threats. The authority of the Commonwealth of Virginia is sufficient to dissuade any acts of violence," Judge Massie said.

"But, sir, are you familiar with their history?" Dexter asked.

"I am aware of their history of violence, but I will not be bullied into displaying excessive force in my courtroom. I am also aware that Floyd was named a special deputy peace officer just last September. I trust that he will respect the law since he himself has been an officer of the law," Judge Massie said.

"They've got their own idea of justice below Fancy Gap Mountain. Ideas that are outside of the law. I have been trying to rein them in ever since I, we, the republicans, took over the county. In the days of the county judges, before the Circuit Court, the Allens got used to getting away with these things because of the county judge. Judge Bolen lived out there near them and he was either in cahoots with them or scared of them because he failed to even have a trial on several occasions, no matter how horrific the crimes," Dexter said.

William Foster squinted his eyes in question. "What was the name of that man they broke out of the jail cell and shot?"

"Howlett. Mack Howlett," Dexter said.

"Yeah, that's the one. Floyd's cousin Carr Allen was shot

and killed in some silly dispute. Carr's honor must have been questioned or something, you know how these disputes usually start around here. A man named Mack Howlett and his brother were arrested and being held in the jail for Carr's murder. The night before the grand jury was to be convened, a group of masked men showed up at the jail and dragged Mack and his brother out into the street. They strung them up and shot them and left them dead in front of the jailhouse. Now, who do you think did that? The Allens of course. No doubt led by Floyd," Foster said.

"I remember that. The county-appointed judge didn't do anything. The judge disbanded the grand jury. No one was ever charged for the murder of Mack Howlett and his brother," Sheriff Webb said.

"Oh, I've got a better one," Dexter said. "Remember the time that Floyd and his brother Jack got into a shootout over the inheritance of their father's illegal liquor stash."

"What?" Foster asked. He bellowed out a laugh from the bottom of his gut. "You can't make this shit up."

Judge Massie sat in his bulky chair and stared back, stone-faced. Dexter figured the judge had heard it all and wasn't impressed by their outlandish crime stories. Dexter continued with the story anyway.

"Jack was the executor of their father's estate, which apparently included a few batches of that nasty corn liquor they make, and Floyd wanted it as part of his stash. They quarreled over it for a while and eventually Floyd ended up shooting at Jack when they got into it one night. Floyd's petulance is legendary in these parts, so of course you know Floyd shot first. Struck his brother Jack in the forehead. It glanced off that old hardheaded son of a bitch. Then Jack started shooting back, shot Floyd three times. One of the bullets struck Floyd in the side. He was laid up in bed for a couple months. Their younger brother Sidna was in the Klondike with gold fever, looking to get rich, and wasn't here to talk them down like he usually does."

"I guess Jack ended up with the liquor," Sheriff Webb said.

"Sure did," Dexter said. "The county-appointed judge let 'em both off without a trial. Called it an eye for an eye."

They all sat around the judge's room in silence like they all were letting those stories linger in their minds. Dexter silently recalled the time that Floyd Allen was accused of murdering a black man for supposedly trespassing on his property. Dexter almost brought up that story to the group, but then he realized that none of the men present in the room would have been charged for that crime, given that they were all white men with the right connections and social standing.

Judge Massie stood and walked over to the closet beside of the door. He removed his black robe with dexterity, despite his missing hand, and placed the robe in the closet. The judge placed the letter in the inside pocket of his robe and put on his heavy winter coat. March had come in like a lion and it was bitter cold. Spring felt off in some distant future. Judge Massie stopped at the door.

"Those unfortunate incidents occurred too often under the old county-appointed judges. I've seen my share of those episodes throughout my career, as an attorney and judge. Sometimes only after the locals have taken matters into their own hands. An accused child molester disappears and is never seen again, a cattle thief gets his barn burnt down, an accused rapist gets held down while the daddy of the girl castrates him. Those are just a few examples of what they called mountain justice. That changed when the State General Assembly amended the Constitution in 1902. Individual communities with their arbitrary, subjective, and often biblical forms of justice no longer have power in the courts. We are the vanguard of the new criminal justice system in Virginia. A court that is not beholden to local ties, one that is independent, and one that is modern and civilized. I will not be intimidated by threats of violence. I cannot be intimidated. The Commonwealth of Virginia and its courts will not be bullied by the threats of Floyd Allen or anyone else who tries to defy its authority. Our job is to prosecute, not persecute. Good evening, gentlemen."

The Judge buttoned up his coat, one handed, and strode out of his office leaving Dexter alone with William Foster and Sheriff Webb. They both stared back at Dexter in disbelief.

"It is simply incomprehensible to him that someone would try to defy the State," William said.

"There is no doubt in my mind who sent that letter. Hell, Deputy Pinky Samuels has left town to avoid testifying against Floyd and Sidna. You know that Floyd has probably already threatened Pinky into not testifying," Dexter said.

"We still have a strong case even without Pinky as a witness. I'm not dropping this case for any reason. No matter how many threats we receive. Their threats and intimidations do nothing but strengthen my desire to see this through," William said.

"Floyd Allen and his kin have gotten away with things like this for far too long. They can't handle being brought to justice. They're like spoiled kids returning from a long stay at Grandma's house. The parents always need to bring them back in line. We run this county now. We need to be prepared for the worst. I am not entering that courtroom with Floyd Allen unless I have my pistol strapped to my side," Dexter said.

"I'll be armed too. We must be armed, or we will be sitting

ducks. That letter says it all for me," William said. "What about you Sheriff?"

"I agree. I make it a point to not carry a weapon with me while on duty. Somebody has to set an example for all of these men who won't even go to the outhouse to take a shit without a gun. I don't even have a firearm issued to me from the department. I'll bring one though. I'll have to borrow a gun from one of my deputies," Sheriff Webb said.

"Let's meet at my house the day before the trial. My farmhouse, not my house in town. We can kick back and discuss strategy and practice our aim," Dexter said.

"Three o'clock in the afternoon sound good?" William asked.

"Alright with me," Dexter said.

SIXTEEN

DEXTER

Dexter lined up a rusty old coffee can, an empty coke bottle, and a little green glass bottle of elixir along the top rail of the fence that separated his backyard from the pasture. It was ten minutes until the Commonwealth's attorney and Sheriff Webb were scheduled to arrive for target practice. He walked over to a big oak stump and sat down. He bent over and rested his elbows on his knees. The temperature was just above freezing, and the gray sky aggravated the cold. Little wispy clouds danced low along the mountainsides like scouts looking for places for the bigger clouds to drop their rain. He fiddled with his Colt automatic pistol and pushed the button on the side of the blued steel frame to release the empty magazine. He opened a box of cartridges and inspected the brass casings and loaded them into the magazine and pushed the loaded magazine up into the pearl handle and pulled back on the slide, loading the chamber. He put the Colt back into the leather holster fixed to his belt.

Floyd Allen's trial was set to start the next morning. Dexter was giddy about the prospect of reading a guilty verdict and watching Floyd squirm in his shackles. This was finally his chance to bring down Floyd and his clan. Floyd was the reason Dexter had started his political career in the first place. Their feud had started a decade prior when Dexter was the United States Commissioner for Carroll County. Floyd found out that Dexter had been making blockade whiskey and selling it out of his office and Dexter was forced to resign. It was an embarrassment, caught for selling homemade whiskey out of the very office that was supposed to enforce the federal liquor laws. He never forgave Floyd for ratting him out. It should have ended Dexter's career as a public servant, but then he started meeting with the local Republican Party. Floyd was a Democrat and so Dexter went the other way. He learned their positions and platforms until he could recite and debate their ideas more articulately than they could. He didn't care about republican views or values, he cared about power and using that power to enrich his family and exact revenge on his enemies. He won office and slowly consolidated his power within the party and eventually began hand selecting candidates for other elected positions. Sheriff Webb and William Foster walked around the side of the house and knocked Dexter out of his vengeful daydream. The sheriff and the Commonwealth's attorney owed him their allegiance.

"You ready to take some target practice?" Sheriff Webb asked.

"I've got the targets all lined up and ready. You want to go first?" Dexter asked.

"How about you go first? It looks like you're ready," Sheriff Webb said.

Dexter walked ten paces out from the stump and aimed his Colt at the rusty coffee can set up on the fence rail. He slotted the sights, pulled the trigger, and missed. The sheriff chuckled and said try again. Dexter aimed at the can again and gently squeezed the trigger. The rusty coffee can fell to the ground and Dexter immediately aimed at the Coke bottle and shattered it with the next shot. He aimed at the smallest target, pulled the trigger and the little green bottle of elixir burst into a hundred pieces. Then he emptied the magazine into the old coffee can on the ground.

"Not bad shooting," Sheriff Webb said. "You better watch out or I'll deputize you one of these days."

"I'm not made for policing. Your turn."

Dexter placed more targets on the fence. The sheriff fiddled with the slide mechanism on his semiautomatic pistol. The slide was hung open, and the sheriff couldn't get it to slide back.

"You know how to operate that thing?" Dexter asked.

"My deputy gave me a short tutorial this morning, but I've never fired one of these semiautos."

The sheriff pulled back hard on the slide, and it sprung back into place, chambering a round. The sheriff aimed, fired, and missed. Then aimed, fired, and missed again. He fired a third time and grazed the side of a coffee can. Dexter was uncertain if that had been the can the sheriff had been aiming at, or if he had been aiming at one of the others and made a lucky miss. The can rattled around and stayed put on the fence rail.

"Looks like you needed the practice," Foster said from behind them.

"Might help if we had a picture of Floyd's head up there," Sheriff Webb said, laughing at his own joke.

"You must be sitting behind the desk too much and not getting your hands dirty. You got your deputies ready for tomorrow?" Dexter asked.

"I told them to come armed. There's no way I'm going in that courtroom tomorrow without a few armed deputies and a pistol strapped to my hip. The judge is naïve to think that

Floyd and his clan won't try something to defy the court. We know better than that and we will be ready."

"Good," Dexter said. "We've hand selected a jury that should be partial to the state. Floyd is not going to like their decision."

"I've already told my wife that I might not be coming home tomorrow, and I've made peace with it," Foster said, taking aim at the targets with his revolver. "There is nothing we can do now except be prepared for the worst."

Dexter stuck his fingers in his ears and Foster emptied the contents of the cylinder and left the targets strewn across the ground. Dexter replaced the targets along the fencerow and walked back toward the sheriff and Commonwealth's attorney with a smile on his face and his hands held up like don't shoot.

"It's not too late to be lenient on him," Sheriff Webb said. "I think pushing for the maximum sentence of one year in the penitentiary is too harsh. Floyd won't accept it."

"You aren't having second thoughts, are you?" Dexter asked and kept talking before the Sheriff could answer his question. "I'm the reason that both of you got elected. If you aren't going to go along with my plan then I'll damn sure find some other, more pliable, men to take your places when the next election comes around."

"I ain't saying that he is innocent, but we can't let revenge get in the way of what's right and what's in accordance with the law," Sheriff Webb said.

"Revenge has nothing to do with it. This is about upholding the law and bringing those who defy it to justice. Sidna's trial is next, and we will push for the maximum sentence for him as well," Dexter said.

Dexter pulled his pistol back out of its holster. He dropped the empty magazine and loaded another full magazine and glared at the Sheriff and Commonwealth's Attorney. Sheriff

Webb nodded back in acceptance. Dexter knew that the dark path he was traveling down was illuminated by vengeance and no one, not even himself, could stop what he had set in motion. He turned toward the targets and shot through each one with three dead eye shots.

"Fellows, we get through tomorrow, we're made," Dexter said.

SEVENTEEN

SIDNA

The first day of Floyd's trial was uneventful. The jury had failed to reach a verdict and the judge adjourned until the next morning. Sidna's ass ached from sitting on the hard bench all day and his tailbone welcomed the fitted leather saddle on his horse. He wanted to push his horse hard through the rain, but Floyd's pace lagged. Sidna's wide-brimmed hat amplified the sound of the rain. It was a six-mile ride across the dormant winter landscape from Hillsville to his house in Fancy Gap. They didn't pass a single soul on the road back to Fancy Gap. The sun had already set over the mountains and the evening light was fading. Floyd was languishing in the miserable weather, reluctant to reach the next destination, grudgingly riding toward the day that would seal his fate.

They rode up the last hill to his house. The interior shone through the night like a beacon of serenity. Sidna and Floyd rode their horses down the path around the back of the house to the stable. They led their horses into the barn, soaped down the tack, and hung their saddles on the hooks on the outside of the stalls. Sidna wiped down both horses and set them up with water and feed for the night. The rain had picked up while they were inside the barn and his feet sloshed as he shuffled through the mushy grass from the barn to the back door of the house. He took off his rain clothes and hung them up on the hooks inside the entrance to the kitchen and pulled off his wet boots and peeled off his wet wool socks. He removed his pistol and placed it in the drawer of the little wooden table beside the back door and locked it up for the night. He'd felt uncomfortable sitting in the courtroom all day with the gun tucked under his suit coat, but he knew he wasn't the only one concealing a weapon.

Floyd rushed by Sidna out of the rain and went straight into the kitchen, dripping wet, without taking off his rain clothes. Floyd pried off his wet overcoat and boots and held them out in his right hand as a puddle formed on the pristine hardwood floors.

"Let me put those wet clothes away for you," Bettie said.

She shot an annoyed look toward Sidna.

"What's for dinner?" Floyd asked. "Smells like you've got something good in the oven."

"Pintos, pork, and cornbread," Bettie said. "Have a seat and I'll fix you a plate."

"You got any coffee?" Floyd asked. "I ain't going to be able to sleep much tonight anyway. Might as well warm up with some coffee."

Marguerite and Pauline jumped down from the kitchen table and rushed over to Sidna shrieking, "Daddy's home, Daddy's home!"

Sidna squeezed both girls together and picked them up at the same time, one in each arm, and carried them back to the table. Floyd took a seat at the small kitchen table, reached under his black suit coat, pulled out his pistol and plopped it on top of the table. Bettie brought the plate of food over to Floyd. She looked at Sidna and then swept her eyes over to the gun sitting on the table. Sidna reached across the table and grabbed the pistol.

"We don't keep these out around here. I'll put it away until morning," Sidna said.

"Did you take that into the courtroom with you today?" Bettie asked.

"Of course. I don't leave home without it," Floyd said.

"Did you take yours too?" Bettie asked, looking at Sidna.

"Yes."

"I didn't think they would allow weapons in the courthouse," Bettie said.

"Oh yeah. They don't check," Floyd said.

Bettie rolled her eyes. "How did the trial go today?"

"The judge adjourned until tomorrow morning. Both sides got through their closing arguments, but the jury hasn't reached a decision yet. The judge has them sequestered in a hotel and is giving them the evening to deliberate and come back in the morning," Sidna said.

Bettie got up from the kitchen table and started fixing Sidna a plate. He followed her to the cooking stove and warmed his hands over its hot surface. He pecked her on the cheek while she filled his plate with pinto beans, half a hock of ham, and a triangle of cornbread.

"Floyd is going to spend the night with us. The trial ended late today, and it would be hard for him to go down the mountain to his house and then travel all that way back to Hillsville, especially in this nasty weather."

"Okay, I'll get the guestroom ready."

They joined their daughters at the table. Bettie had already cleaned her plate and she nursed a hot cup of coffee. Sidna crumbled the cornbread into the beans and ate quickly.

"I'm done, Mama," Pauline said, pushing her plate to the

middle of the table. There was no peace at the table once his daughters decided supper was over.

"Just hold on a minute and let everybody else finish," Bettie said.

"I'm done too," Marguerite said.

"I'm a chicken!" Pauline screamed.

"I'm the fox!" Marguerite yelled.

Pauline jumped down from the chair and ran into the middle of the kitchen. Marguerite popped off her chair and they were off running through the dining room and through the foyer and around the parlor and back into the foyer and up the stairs to their bedroom. Sidna chuckled and kept eating. He would enforce manners another time.

Floyd crumbled the cornbread into the beans and mixed it all together. Sidna got up and poured two cups of coffee, one for Floyd. He carried them back to the table and cupped his hands around the hot coffee mug.

"Was there a big crowd?" Bettie asked. Sidna kept chewing and Bettie waited patiently for him to answer.

"Oh, good gracious. I've never seen that many people crammed into such a small space. It'll probably be worse in the morning."

"Do you think they will find him guilty?" Bettie asked.

"I am worried about foul play. They painted a black picture of Floyd today in court. You'd think Floyd was down there running his own little dictatorship after listening to William Foster, the Commonwealth's Attorney, talk about ridding the county of the mob violence that has been perpetuated by Floyd and his kin for the last twenty years." Sidna laughed at the ridiculousness of that statement.

"I ain't worried much. My attorney, old Judge Bolen, seems to think that I will get fined, or it will get dismissed altogether.

Says that's usually what happens in these cases, no jail time. There ain't no way in hell that I'm a-going to jail."

Sidna wasn't as confident as Floyd. Dexter Goad's visit and offer to drop the charges if he and Floyd backed him in the next election had convinced Sidna that Goad was corrupt. Even so, it was still up to the jury. Sidna stretched his hand across his forehead and rubbed his temple under his thumb.

"I probably should have told you this but…Dexter paid me a visit last week. Came to the store and offered to drop all the charges if you and I backed him in the next election. I told him no and I know that you would have said no too."

"You are right, brother. I would have told him to go to hell. They are crooked. Goad and Foster have been using their power to line their pockets, protect their allies, and resolve disputes in their favor. Just like those boys who started the fight with Wesley. Those boys didn't even get in trouble. Wesley served two months and here I am facing the possibility of a year in jail."

Sidna could sense Floyd's anger rising. Floyd had spent the whole day sitting in the courtroom listening to testimony without being able to respond and now the pressure in the valve was being released. Sidna drifted in and out of the one-sided conversation as Floyd's words ran together into a long diatribe. The more Floyd talked about their situation and county politics and his trial the more Sidna believed that maybe Floyd was going to be found guilty, maybe it was all rigged against them. Maybe he was next. He was trapped between Floyd and the law and wondered just how far Floyd would take things to stay out of prison. Floyd slapped his knee with his palm and leaned forward closer to Sidna and continued his seething diatribe.

"You 'member that time I reported Dexter Goad for selling

moonshine out of his office when he was the United States Commissioner? He wasn't Commissioner for much longer, was he? People say that he is still making that nasty shit of his and he can get away with it now that him and all his republican lackeys are in power. You know they would throw us in jail if they discovered our operation," Floyd said.

"Your operation. I haven't done that in almost twenty years. I don't need to anymore," Sidna said.

Floyd continued like Sidna hadn't said anything. "I've opposed Goad and his cronies every time they ran for another office. These Progressive Republicans are changing this county for the worse. They don't care about loyalty to place or traditions or independence. They want to hand over power to the government, stamp down our independence, and then use that power to protect themselves. They are a bunch of damn hypocrites and by God if I'm going to stand by and let them get away with it. And William Foster don't stand for nothing, the way he vacillated from Democrat to Republican, just to win. Going all the way back to 1905 when they got away with ballot tampering. That tampering brought Goad to power. Goad stole that election and the corrupt Republicans have been in charge ever since."

Floyd trailed off his rant and leaned back in the kitchen chair and stared up at the ceiling like he was thinking on something.

"You just can't trust any of them damn politicians."

"Except for when you held office," Sidna chuckled.

"Nah, you couldn't trust me neither," Floyd said.

"I need to get the girls ready for bed," Bettie said.

"Let's retire to the parlor and get a drink," Sidna said.

"I was hoping you'd say that. Lord knows I need one or two."

Floyd followed him through the dining room and across

the foyer and into the parlor. Sidna opened his liquor cabinet and grabbed a bottle of Jack Daniel's No. 7. He had been saving it for a special occasion and he figured now was as good as anytime. He poured the brown liquid in two whisky glasses and handed one to Floyd and raised his up and chinked with Floyd. Sidna held the bottle at arm's length, squinted, and read the bottle.

"Jack Daniel's No. 7, Bottled in Bond, and Gold Medal winner at the 1904 World's Fair in St. Louis. Here's to old Jack Daniel," Sidna said.

Floyd raised his glass again. "Here's to not being in jail tomorrow night."

"I'll drink to that one too," Sidna said.

"You hear that Jack died from blood poisoning. He injured his toe when he forgot the combination to his safe and kicked it in frustration," Sidna said. "The infection in his toe spread and he died from blood poisoning."

"Hellfire, I ain't heard that one. That's a shitty way to go. I didn't know he had passed. When did it happen?"

"It was sometime last fall."

Floyd turned up his glass and drank the remaining finger of whiskey in one gulp. Sidna pulled the two dark leather chairs from the corner closer to the fireplace and motioned for Floyd to sit. Then he lifted the lid on the brass fire-building box and pulled out a handful of kindling. He placed the kindling in a teepee and stuffed some old newspaper inside of the teepee and lit a match. He slowly moved the tiny flame toward the fireplace, sheltering the flame from the updraft of the chimney with his cupped left hand. The bedrooms, kitchen and living room all had fireplaces, but the one in the parlor was his favorite. The tiles around the fireplace were imprinted with raised vines that stretched up from flowerpots and across the top underneath the Italian marble mantel. The intricate vinework was covered with gold leaf that gleamed above the yellow flames. Sidna waited for the kindling to catch and then he added some smaller, well-seasoned logs and sat down in the soft leather chair and admired the fire as it came to life. Floyd refilled their glasses with generous pours. They talked about this and that and nothing important for a while, like two old brothers. They talked about farming and running general stores and the sawmill business and their long-dead daddy. They stared at the flames when they had said all that they could say, and Floyd started drifting off in the silence of night. Sidna decided to call it a night when Floyd started snoring by the dying fire. Sidna stood and reached his arms up to the ceiling in a tired stretch. He walked over and shook Floyd's shoulder.

"Let me know if you need anything else before bed. I'll show you up to your room."

Sidna stopped at the bottom of the stairs and waited for Floyd to go up with the lights on. He stood under the crystal Tiffany light fixture in the foyer with his hand on the switch and admired his beautiful entryway, the staircase and the curved handrails leading up to the second floor and the way the soft light from the gaslit fixtures gave the room a rich orange glow. Once Floyd reached the landing, he flipped the light switch and felt his way up the curved staircase and took Floyd down the hall to the guest room and said, "I'll see you in the morning."

"Bright and early," Floyd said.

Sidna was surprised to find Bettie still awake, in bed reading. He opened the wardrobe to the left of the bedroom door and changed into his sleeping clothes. He shuffled over to his side of the bed. Bettie didn't look up from her book.

"Floyd is probably already passed out," Sidna said.

"What time is it?" Bettie asked.

"It's a little past midnight."

Bettie closed her book and turned off the lamp. Sidna scooted across the bed and pressed himself up against her warm body. He leaned up on his side over her and kissed her. He started rubbing over her soft curves, over her hip and then down her leg. Sharing her bed still turned him on.

"It's too late for that. We've got to get up early. Goodnight, honey."

He relented and kissed her goodnight.

"Please don't go in the morning. You are a good man and husband and father. Me and the girls need you here with us. You should just stay home tomorrow. They don't need you there since they have already had their closing arguments and the jury is deliberating."

"I have to go, Bettie. I'm a witness. I think they can still make a motion to add new testimony and I could still be called. I'm supposed to be there until the end and if I'm not then I might get in trouble."

"I'd rather you be in trouble for not showing up than being caught up in something worse if Floyd's temper takes hold. I'm afraid of what Floyd might do if they find him guilty."

"Floyd is not stupid enough to defy the law."

"It's not about being smart. It's about control. He loses it."

"Floyd is my brother. He has been good to us. He let me work on his farm after I quit teaching and he taught me how to run a profitable farm and general store. Without his help, we wouldn't have this beautiful home. Think about that before you say that I should abandon him when he needs me the most. If he is planning anything sinister tomorrow, then he didn't let on about it. I think everything will be fine. The worst that could happen is that we wake up in the morning and Floyd is gone, fled to Carolina or hiding out in the woods."

"He's too prideful for that. I am not saying that you should abandon him. I just want you to be careful and use your judgment. You have your own family now."

"I'll stay out of trouble in the morning. I will never do anything to hurt you and the girls or the life we've built," Sidna said.

Bettie said goodnight and Sidna lay there awake in the black silence. He knew he hadn't done enough to stop Floyd from releasing Wesley. He wondered if he should have taken Dexter Goad's offer of dropping the charges in exchange for political support. Trapped in the dark, his mind raced over the events that had led up to the next morning and tried to think of how it could have been avoided.

EIGHTEEN

SIDNA

The smell of buckwheat cakes and bacon filled the house early the next morning. Sidna washed his face and shaved and got dressed in his typical work attire, a cotton sack suit with a single-breasted vest. He hurried downstairs. Buckwheat cakes were piled high in the middle of the table with bacon and jars of sourwood honey, molasses, and butter. All the ingredients were produced on his land. The food on his table always tasted better when it was grown on his farm. His wit, sweat, and blood were mixed with the soil to produce the bounty on the table. He cut his stack of pancakes into small triangles, and he added butter and poured his farm's honey over the pancakes and mixed it all together ensuring that each triangle was coated liberally in the melted butter and honey.

"Good morning," Bettie said.

"Mornin'," Sidna replied.

Bettie brought a cup of coffee and then she sat down to eat. Sidna watched as Bettie lifted her cup from its saucer and took one cautious sip of the hot coffee. She deemed it too hot and then poured a small amount onto the flat saucer, gently blew on the thin layer of liquid, and sipped from the edge.

"Is Floyd up yet?" Sidna asked.

"I haven't seen him, but I think I heard him pacing around up there."

Sidna finished his breakfast and went upstairs to check on Floyd. The door was closed. Sidna knocked gently and Floyd grunted.

"We need to get going if we don't want to be late," Sidna said.

"I'll be down in a few minutes."

Sidna went back down to the kitchen and got another cup of coffee. He waited for ten minutes and started getting anxious. He filled his coffee cup again and started getting fidgety. Floyd's nervous postponement was only making him more uneasy. Sidna checked his watch and panicked. The trial was supposed to resume at nine and it was already eight-thirty. They were going to be late. Floyd strode into the kitchen a few minutes later with a queasy look on his face.

"We need to get going," Floyd said.

"Grab you some bacon and pancakes for the road," Sidna said.

"Love you," Sidna said, pecking Bettie on the cheek. "I don't know when I'll be home."

"Love you too."

They headed out the back door to the stable and saddled their horses. A dense fog had settled over the cold plateau. Floyd set a quick pace over the rolling tableland. The low-hanging fog and the cold drizzle kept Sidna's hands tight on the reigns and his thoughts tight in his head. The fog burnt off by the time they reached town and smudges of blue sky poked through the blanket of gray clouds. They were fifteen minutes late when they hitched their horses in the muddy lot behind Blankenship's Stable. The stable was across the street from the courthouse down a tight alley that skirted the jailhouse.

Floyd's sons, Claude and Victor, were already there waiting in the hitching lot with Wesley and Friel. Wesley walked over and grabbed the reins on Sidna's horse and tied it to the open post. Claude intercepted his father at the corner of the stable.

"Morning, Uncle Sid," Wesley said.

Sidna said good morning and watched Floyd and Claude whisper with their heads together. Floyd's right hand was clasped over Claude's shoulder. Claude was focused on his father's eyes and listened and then Floyd patted his breast pocket. Floyd and Claude started walking up the alley between the jail and Nuckols Drug Store. Sidna, Wesley, Friel and Victor followed. They all crossed the main street together. A court official stuck his head out of the door on the second floor and called out, "Mr. Allen, your presence in the Courtroom is needed immediately!" They marched past the massive Greek columns and climbed the stairs to the courtroom.

The small courtroom was packed with people. The court officials were already behind the bar. The bar formed a square in the middle of the courtroom with railing between the court participants and the public seating. Ornate wooden railing further separated the judge's platform from the attorneys and other court participants. Sidna stood in the entrance. He scanned the room for open spaces. It was impossible to find seats together. They scrambled for openings scattered around amongst the standing-room-only crowd. Claude ended up to Sidna's left in a corner of the courtroom. Wesley and Friel were further down past Claude in the back against another wall near the jury. Sidna spotted Betty Ayers on a bench down below him. The young woman was in Sidna's store shopping the consignment clothing section on the afternoon when Floyd had released Wesley. She hadn't seen anything that day, but they called her as a witness anyway. Floyd's son Victor was seated just outside of the bar behind Floyd and his attorney.

Inside the bar William Foster, the Commonwealth's Attorney, was seated at one of the tables facing the judge. Floyd was already seated at another table with his attorney. Floyd was dressed in the same black suit with a red-and-gray-striped sweater underneath that he had worn the day before. Floyd was probably the most well-groomed man in the entire building. Sidna watch Floyd nervously stroke and twist his mustache. Floyd's attorney, old Judge Bolen, hunched beside of Floyd with his gray, unkept beard covering the front of his collar. Dexter Goad sat to the left of the judge's platform on a lower platform that was still within the bar. Sheriff Webb stood to the left of Dexter. Sidna watched as Dexter Goad, William Foster and Sheriff Webb talked cheerfully amongst themselves like men who were about to vanquish a sworn enemy.

Judge Massie entered the courtroom and took his seat on the platform above the bar facing the attorneys. The crowd quieted and a few unseated people jockeyed for position. Dexter Goad rose and brought order to the court.

"Please rise. The Circuit Court is now in session. The Honorable Judge Massie presiding."

"Please swear in the jury," Judge Massie said, eyeing Dexter Goad.

Dexter stood and walked from his desk that was behind the bar and opened the door to the jury room and motioned for them to enter the courtroom. The jury, all men dressed the same in white shirts under black or brown suits with black ties, entered the courtroom and occupied the jury box in front of the judge's platform.

"Members of the jury, please raise your right hand. Do you solemnly swear that you have listened to the facts and that you will render a true and fair verdict to this defendant?" Dexter asked.

All the jurors proclaimed at once, "I do."

"Gentlemen, have you reached a verdict?" Judge Massie asked.

The foreman stood and declared, "We have."

The foreman brought a folded piece of paper up to Dexter Goad and he delivered their verdict to Judge Massie. Judge Massie read the verdict, frowned, and asked William Foster to approach the platform. Sidna wondered why the judge was questioning the verdict. Foster whispered with the judge and wrote something down on a piece of paper as the judge dictated. Then after a minute of discussion, William Foster left the judge's platform and handed the note to the Clerk of Court, Dexter Goad. Sidna watched Dexter unfold the small note and a slight grin crossed his face before he read the verdict.

"We, the jury, find the defendant Floyd Allen guilty as charged in the indictment and fix his punishment at confinement in the penitentiary of this state for one year."

Some in the crowd gasped. Whispers filled the room for a few seconds before Judge Massie popped his gavel. Sidna held his breath and felt his pulse quicken.

"Thank you," Judge Massie said.

Sidna kept his eyes on Dexter and saw him wink at Floyd. The wink said *we've got you.* Floyd and his attorney remained standing. Sidna couldn't see Floyd's face, but he knew that Floyd's blood was boiling. Floyd's attorney leaned in and said something to Floyd. Floyd said something back. Floyd's attorney cleared his throat and addressed Judge Massie.

"Your honor, I would like to make a motion for a new trial. We have discovered some new evidence that should be included in the record."

"Both counsels, please approach the bench to discuss this newly discovered evidence," Judge Massie said.

Sidna had no clue what the newly discovered evidence could be. Way he reckoned, this was Floyd's way of scratching and clawing until the bitter end. The Commonwealth's attorney and Floyd's attorney stepped up onto the judge's platform. Claude walked out of the crowd and into the bar and started talking to his father. Floyd stuck his mouth against Claude's ear and then Claude responded whispering into his father's ear with his hand cupped over his mouth to conceal their conversation. Sidna swallowed hard against the lump that had formed in his throat. His own trial would be set soon. What would they do to him if he didn't play their game? Would they try to ruin him too?

"Request granted. The hearing for the new evidence will be tomorrow morning, March 15th," Judge Massie said.

"Your honor, I'd like to make another motion for my client to be released on bail, with the possibility of a new trial pending new evidence," Floyd's attorney said.

"Motion denied. Mr. Allen has already been convicted and sentenced. Sheriff Webb, take charge of the prisoner immediately," Judge Massie said.

The Sheriff approached Floyd with gleaming handcuffs.

"Gentlemen, I just ain't a-goin'," Floyd announced.

Sidna watched Floyd fiddle with the button on his breast pocket. Then, a gunshot shattered the thin layer of justice. Sidna stiffened against the back wall. More shots echoed around the room. The courtroom descended into chaos. People rushed for the exits and screams penetrated the short intervals between gunshots. The room suddenly felt small, and the shots merged into one continuous boom of gunfire. Floyd and Dexter and the sheriff and the Commonwealth's attorney were all shooting at each other inside of the bar, not twenty feet from each other. Floyd fell under the defendant's desk. Shots echoed from Sidna's left. He turned and witnessed Claude, Wesley, and Friel shooting toward the court officials. Sheriff Webb was still inside of the bar fiddling with the jammed slide on his semiautomatic pistol. Bullets buzzed by Sidna's head and the wallboards behind him splintered. He ducked behind the bench in front of him. He kept his head down and looked up when the bullets stopped hitting the wall behind him. He peeked over the bench and saw Dexter reloading his pistol. Sidna ducked behind the bench again, drew his revolver, and then raised back up and fired at Dexter. Gun barrels flashed through the gun smoke on the opposite side of the courtroom. He emptied the cylinder and took cover again behind the bench. He reloaded and then closed his eyes. He tried to calm his breathing and tamp down the surge of adrenalin. The gunfire continued. He sat there on his knees for half a minute afraid to move, but afraid to stay put, while the spectators and witnesses and court officials dashed for the exits. Bullets pierced the wall above him once again in a flurry and he started crawling toward the door. Then the shooting stopped.

Sidna raised his head and peeked over the top of the bench that had shielded him. He squinted through the stinging black smoke. Goad had vanished. The room smelled bitter, and smoke choked the air. Sidna struggled to breathe. The room was quiet except for moans of the wounded men, writhing and dying on the courtroom floor. His ears were ringing from the deafening sound of half a dozen guns firing simultaneously for over a minute. He cautiously moved toward the exit, keeping low under the smoke. Shots rang out again and the barrel of a gun flashed at him from the judge's chamber. He returned fire with one shot and the shooter retreated into the judge's chamber. He stood in the doorway and swept his gun across the room. The judge's high-back chair was blown apart. The chair's fluffy white stuffing wafted through the smoke above where Judge Massie lay motionless. Sheriff Webb and the Commonwealth's attorney were lying on the floor, their dead bodies still behind the bar. Then a head popped up from inside of the bar. Floyd suddenly sprung up and jumped over the railing that separated the bar from the rest of the courtroom. Floyd fell when he landed and winced with pain.

"Over here, Floyd!" Sidna shouted.

Floyd managed to pull himself up. He hobbled toward the exit. Sidna covered the room for Floyd while he limped down the stairs. Sidna followed Floyd down the stairs and the shooting started again just as he hit the ground floor. He felt a searing pain push through his upper left arm and into his back just below his shoulder blade that felt like a hot iron had punched through his flesh, forever branding him. He sought cover with Floyd behind one of the large Greek columns. He inspected the wound. The bullet had gone clear through his arm and then lodged in his back. He glanced up from behind the thick Greek column and saw Dexter aiming at him from the top of the open-air stairs. Dexter let loose another volley of bullets. Sidna waited behind the column and then fired three shots back up at Dexter from around the left side of the column. Dexter slumped and fell to his knees. Dexter stayed on his knees and crawled back into the courtroom. Sidna dashed across the courthouse yard and into the muddy street where Wesley, Friel, Floyd, and his sons Claude and Victor were hiding behind the Confederate Statue. The monument was circled by a four-foot perimeter of wrought-iron fence and the space behind the fence was adorned with manicured grass. The zinc-alloy soldier was twenty-one feet tall, and its base was wide enough to shield them from the courthouse. Floyd was sitting with his back propped against the fence and his injured right leg stretched out in front of him with his left leg bent up at the knee. Sidna squatted down next to Floyd.

"What the hell happened in there, Floyd?"

Floyd didn't answer.

"Are you alright?" Sidna asked.

Floyd winced and pointed to his leg. His britches were soaked in dark blood that had turned his black suit pants two shades darker. Floyd sat up and tore his britches out from the bullet hole. Blood was smeared on his thigh. It gushed out from the bullet hole.

"Go bring the horses 'round," Sidna said looking at his nephews. Wesley and Victor nodded. They both peeked around the base of the statue to see if it was clear. Claude stared at his father with glazed eyes.

"Claude, Claude. Listen. We need to focus if we are going to get out of town alive. Go with Wesley and Victor."

Sidna waved his hand over Claude's face to get his attention.

"Go. Now. Bring the horses and see if you can commandeer a wagon for Floyd," Sidna said pointing to the alley that led to Blankenship's Stable.

Sidna watched Claude, Victor, and Wesley as they moved like soldiers flanking their enemy. He kept his eyes on the courthouse as his nephews ran down the alley with their heads low.

"Did you start this?" Sidna asked. "I saw you reach into your coat."

"I didn't fire the first shot."

"Who did?"

"Don't know. I couldn't hear where it come from. Goad winked at me, but he didn't fire the first shot." Floyd spoke slowly with labored breath. "I don't know. They are going to blame us no matter what. We won't never find justice here."

Wesley and Claude returned with the horses and a commandeered wagon. They grabbed Floyd under the arms and tried to help him up. Floyd pointed toward his horse and stubbornly tried to mount. He winced in pain and fell when he tried to throw his wounded right leg over the saddle. Claude caught him before he hit the ground. Floyd let out a guttural groan and appeared to pass out.

"He isn't going to make it out of town. We need to get him somewhere close, make him comfortable and get a doctor to check him," Sidna said. "Take him down to the hotel."

"I agree," said Victor. "I'll take daddy down to the hotel. Y'all get the hell out of here."

Victor climbed up onto the commandeered wagon. Sidna mounted his horse and watched the front of the courthouse while Wesley and Claude bid farewell to Floyd. Sidna doubted that Floyd would survive the day with all the blood seeping out of his leg. Wesley and Claude took their time conversing with Floyd, embracing their father and uncle for what might be the last time. The last thing Sidna heard Floyd say to his boys was to fight till the last Allen's alive. Claude jumped down from the wagon with tears in his eyes and climbed onto his horse.

"We need to get going," Sidna said.

Sidna and his nephews Wesley, Claude, and Friel rode out of town past small groups of curious onlookers gathered on the sides of the muddy road. Sidna felt their eyes upon him as they rode down the main street. No one dared stop them. They galloped out of town as the outlaws that their enemies had always wanted them to be.

PART II

A PECULIAR ATROCITY

NINETEEN

EDWIN PAYNE

Edwin Payne led a small group of Baldwin-Felts guards up a narrow road through the large block of identical company-owned houses. He trudged through the deep snow that covered half of his tall boots. He despised working security in the coal mines. He had been stationed at the Winding Gulf Coalfield for two months to infiltrate and expose the miners trying to form a union. As much as Payne hated living near the filthy mine, he loved breaking the unions more. One of his undercover agents had infiltrated a group intent on unionizing and fomenting a strike and his detectives finally had a lead that might break the labor organizers. He smiled at the thought of busting another attempt before it got to full-blown strike. Payne stopped in front of one of the fifty small company houses that were all uniformly built from the same cheap materials and economical design.

"This is the one. House 52," Payne said.

He turned around to the five men behind him and motioned toward the front door. They quickly moved past him and one kicked in the flimsy front door. A woman screamed from inside of the house and a young child shrieked through the open front door. His men dragged the miner's wife out of the house and down the warped and grey wooden stairs of the front porch and shoved her into a deep snowdrift. Her little boy, no older than three, stood in the doorway screaming. Payne walked up the steps and picked up the little boy. The boy wiggled against Payne's grip. The boy was stronger than Payne expected, and he had to use both hands to restrain the little one. He planted the boy down into his mother's arms. Payne hovered over the woman while she sobbed as the guards tossed her family's possessions out of the house and into the snow. He stood, unmoved by the scene and blew into his cold hands, rubbed them together and put on his black wool gloves.

"Payne, we found something," one of his men shouted from inside of the house.

"You stay put and shut him up," Payne said, pointing at the woman.

Payne walked up onto the deformed porch and ducked his tall body under the short door.

"What did you find?" Payne asked.

"Found a document behind the kitchen drawer," one of his men said.

All the company-owned homes were built from the same simple plan and the detectives had long ago figured out the few hiding places tucked away in the tiny rooms. This miner had chosen the space behind the kitchen cabinet drawer to hide his correspondence with union leaders.

"What does it say?" Payne asked.

"They are planning a strike and this letter looks like a list of their demands. They are going to strike and demand that the mine operator recognizes their union. They are demanding an increase in pay per ton, cribbing be discontinued, minors be allowed to bring in their own weighmen as a check against the company checkweighmen, and they want to end compulsory trading at the company store. There is also a list of other miners who are willing to strike," the detective said.

"Sounds like we are going to be busy," Payne said.

Payne took the letter and read it for himself. He read over the list of demands and laughed. His father was a steelworker in Cleveland, Ohio, and belonged to the steelworkers union his whole career. Payne had seen firsthand how workers and unions took advantage of companies. His father spoke of workers sitting around all day while others worked and some who were only allowed to do one specific job because of their union contracts. If that one specific job was discontinued during the contract period, then they sat around and collected a check for not working, costing the company thousands of dollars in lost productivity. Unions fostered mediocrity and complacency. It was a free country and if someone felt that a company was not paying high enough wages or taking advantage of its employees then those employees have a right to quit and get a different job. Payne despised unions and worked against them with zeal. That zeal made him a favorite of the coal-mine operators who contracted with his employer, the Baldwin-Felts Detective Agency, to provide mine security and strike-breaking services. Payne walked back outside and saw that the miner had returned home from his shift. The minor was consoling his wife surrounded by their few belongings that were now scattered haphazardly around them in the snow.

"You have until the end of the day to get off company property. Union organizers like you are not welcome in this mine," Payne said.

The miner stood and walked with a purpose towards Payne, raised his fist and threw a long, loopy punch at Payne's left jaw. Payne sidestepped the punch. The miner slipped and fell face-first into the snow. The miner pushed himself back up leaving black smudges in the snow from the coal dust that covered his face and hands. The miner lunged at Payne again and Payne jabbed at the miner's head with his left hand, striking him in the nose and then threw a hook with his right hand that hurt his knuckles as it landed on the miner's large jaw. The miner continued towards him, charged, and wrapped his arms around Payne's waist and tackled him into the snow. One of the other Baldwin-Felts guards intervened and pulled the miner off Payne. Then two more guards jumped on the miner and started kicking him in the torso. The miner's wife was screaming and pleading for them to stop as her husband curled up, looking like a filthy snowball.

Payne shook the annoying pain out of his right hand and pulled the notebook out of his breast pocket. He kept a list of all the men he had fought in his career. Sometimes he would write short descriptions of the men or the details of the fight alongside the name of the men in his book. It was not an exhaustive list of the men he had bested. Some men didn't make it into his book. If they were weak or didn't put up a fight, then he didn't bother to include them. He walked over to the miner who was curled in pain on the ground.

"What's your name, boy?" Payne asked.

"Harold Johnston," the miner said.

Payne wrote down the number ninety-four and then the miner's name after it. He had deemed Harold Johnston worthy of inclusion on his list, but just wrote his name. Harold Johnston was not worthy of the additional descriptors that he sometimes included. He slid the book to his back pocket and put the pencil back in his breast pocket pouch.

"Get your shit off company property," Payne said.

Payne left his men to supervise the miner's exit and returned to the Baldwin-Felts headquarters. The small office building was nothing more than a converted company house with a hastily built addition out the back. He entered the building and, after removing his coat and hat and gloves, immediately made his way to the warmest corner near the stove. The secretary interrupted and he didn't make it to the stove.

"Sir, you have an urgent phone call. Mr. Felts called and is expecting to hear from you as soon as possible. Should I call him back for you?"

"Yes, please."

The secretary spoke to the operator and waited for half a minute and then held out the receiver for Payne. Payne nodded and hurried over to the phone and picked up the receiver with his cold hand. His nerves flared up as he thought of all the bad reasons why the co-owner and president of the agency would be calling him directly. In his experience, phone calls from the top of the chain were never just for pats on the back.

"Hello, sir, this is Detective Payne. How can I help you?"

"There has been a shooting at the courthouse in Hillsville, Virginia. The sheriff, the prosecutor, and the judge were killed. The governor of Virginia has put the agency in charge of the county. The governor wants us to get things under control and hunt down the fugitives. I need you to meet me there tomorrow and help lead the manhunt for these outlaws," Felts said.

"Tomorrow? How far is it to Hillsville?" Payne asked.

"Just go to Mabscott and catch the train east. Tell the depot that you need a ticket to Pulaski, Virginia. Then proceed to Hillsville by way of Betty Baker Station. You'll have to go on foot from there to Hillsville. I've chartered a special train from Pulaski on to Betty Baker through the night."

Payne paused for longer than he should have.

"Payne. Are you still there?"

"Yes."

"You're one of my best detectives. I need you now."

"The only way I can reach the railway station in Mabscott today is to walk. I don't have access to a horse right now. I'll have to carry my baggage through nine inches of snow."

"Well," Felts said.

Payne paused and let those words linger. His boss was not giving him any options. He would have to endure the long journey through the snow or Felts would be dissatisfied. If he declined to leave now or waited for the storm to break, Felts may never give him another opportunity like this again.

"Yes, I'll slide if necessary."

"You're a good man, Payne. I'll see you tomorrow in Hillsville."

Payne hung up the phone and picked the receiver back up. He almost called his wife, but hesitated and put the receiver back down. He hadn't seen her in the two months since he had been stationed at the Winding Gulf Coalfield, but he decided he didn't have time. He'd do it when he arrived in Hillsville. It was a nine-mile walk from the Winding Gulf to Mabscott and the deep valleys and high ridges of West Virginia were unforgiving. He had to pack and leave within the hour if he wanted to catch the next train.

TWENTY

SIDNA

Sidna walked into the house and called for Bettie from the foyer. She didn't answer and he walked down the short hallway and shouted her name up the stairs.

"I'm upstairs. I'm sewing. I'll be down in a few minutes."

He couldn't wait and he hobbled upstairs while holding his injured back where the bullet was lodged. His white shirt was soaked with blood. The pain pulsing from the wounds in his arm and side steadily increased the farther away he got from town as the shock and adrenalin wore off. By the time he got to the house, the wound in his arm where the bullet had torn through and the wound in his back where the bullet had lodged were both on fire.

He found her in their bedroom. She stopped sewing.

"Hi, honey. What do you need?" she asked.

She turned and gasped when she saw the blood on his shirt.

"Oh, my God, Sid. What happened?"

"There was a shootout after they found Floyd guilty. I'll tell you about it after you tend to my wound."

Bettie led him into the bathroom and Sidna sat on the toilet next to the claw-foot bathtub. The wooden water tank hung high on the wall and the dull brass pipe stretched down to the commode. Little drops of blood fell from his saturated shirt and dotted the white tiles on the floor. Bettie gently removed his white dress shirt and his undershirt. She wiped the blood from his wound and then cleaned it with soap and water. The water bit into the wound and he clenched his fist and let out a low moan that started in his diaphragm and moved through his chest and out of his clamped lips.

"I don't think it hit anything important. You would be in worse shape if it had hit something important. It will do more damage if we take it out. You need to see a doctor about it though," Bettie said.

"I can't see a doctor. Any good doctor would turn me in," Sidna said.

The sting of the soap and water subsided, and he started to tell her what happened as she wrapped his wounds in gauze. They sat there for a while in stunned silence after he finished re-living the horrible scene.

"What about Wesley and Claude?" she asked.

"Wesley is here. I've got him watching the road out front. I sent him out to the barn with the horses and then told him to watch the road from Hillsville. Claude and Friel went to Jack's house. We are all meeting back up with Claude and Friel at Jack's house later tonight. They were all unharmed."

"How many people you think are dead?" she asked.

"I don't know, at least three. I saw Judge Massie and William Foster fall after being shot and I think that Sheriff Webb was also killed. Floyd was seriously injured, and I don't think he will survive the day. He was bleeding out from his upper thigh when I left town. Victor was taking him to the Elliot Hotel. There may be others. It was a constant barrage of gunfire for a minute or two."

A tear slid down Bettie's cheek. Sidna wrapped his arms around her. Sidna's hand trembled and Bettie squeezed it to settle his nerves. He tried to hold back the tears, but the pressure built up until he exploded with rage, loss, and helplessness. They sat on the cold floor with their heads resting together and their tears ran slick between their coupled cheeks. They held each other for a while and then, when he regained his composure, Sidna told her his miserable plan.

"I have to run until the truth of it comes out. I didn't plan this and didn't participate until I was forced to defend my life."

"If you are innocent then why do you have to go on the run?" Bettie asked.

"Floyd was right. We won't get a fair trial in this county. We have to run. Maybe public opinion will be on our side once the facts come out, but right now I have no other choice."

"If we go get the girls out of school now then we can be gone by dark. We can take a train out West and start a new life. I don't want to stay here without you. I would be worried sick about you not knowing where you are," Bettie said.

"You and the girls can't go with me. I have to leave tonight. I need to be able to disappear for a while until the initial surge of searching ceases. We would be easily caught if we all went together. We would have to stay in more conspicuous places, and we would stand out more as a family on the run." Sidna paused and took a deep breath and stared into her eyes. "Bettie, we can't hide out with our little girls. We can't put them through that. I am going to hide out around here with Wesley and Claude so we can draw on the help and resources of our friends and family," Sidna said.

He didn't know when he would be alone with Bettie again, if ever. The consequences that his family was about to endure for the acts of others crushed his will to move. The life that he had struggled and worked hard to build was being ripped away in a two-minute flurry of powder and smoke, animus, and revenge that the bonds of family had wrought around him.

Bettie walked down the road to pull the girls out of school. Sidna walked out of the house and stood in the front yard holding a rifle in each hand. He gripped a lever action rifle in his right hand and a bolt action in his left hand. He was ready to bring hell if that's what it took. He handed Wesley the lever action and looked down the muddy dirt road towards town and stood there expecting a large posse of townsmen on horseback to descend on his property at any moment. The late-winter sun hovered at the horizon. Sidna took in the view, maybe for the last time.

"I left the saddles on the horses. When are we leaving?" Wesley asked.

"We aren't taking the horses. We have to go on foot if we want to get away. We need to stay hidden in the bush and only move at night. These horses can't take us where I'm planning on going," Sidna said.

"I was thinking we'd just make a break for the state line," Wesley said.

"I don't know that land like I know here. We need to hide-out where we have friends and family to help us until this all calms down."

"Are you sure, Uncle Sid?"

"Listen, Wesley, you need to trust me, or we aren't going to make it very long. How long did you last the last time you ran from the law?"

Wesley nodded in acceptance.

"Stay in the front yard and watch the road. Yell if you see anyone suspicious come up the road. I am going up to the store to pilfer some supplies. Bettie is going to get the girls out of school." Sidna paused and choked on the words that would be too real when he verbalized the pain that came along with them. "So I can say goodbye."

Sidna walked the hundred yards to his general store. He grabbed extra pairs of britches and shirts and socks. He got bigger sizes for him and Wesley so they could layer up. He knew from his time in the Klondike that layering was the key to staying warm. He grabbed two long raincoats, extra blankets, a flint and a box of matches, a pair of binoculars, and a new canteen and stuffed a large canvas bag with cans of beans and potted meat and crackers. Then he wiped out the small shelf of ammunition for his rifles. The floor behind the glass counter had a hidden compartment where he kept a few bottles of untaxed liquor or anything else that needed to be hidden. He moved the floorboards behind the counter and grabbed the two jars of Floyd's homemade whiskey and the stash of money hidden in a small envelope. He counted out a thousand dollars in twenties and tens and stuffed the bills into his front pocket, locked up and hurried back down to the house.

Back inside of the house, he found his old canvas backpack that he had carried to the Klondike in the upstairs hallway closet. He filled it with the items taken from the store and hoped the supplies would see them through the next couple of weeks. He heard Bettie and the girls come in through the front door. He rushed downstairs and met them in the foyer. He knelt in front of them, grabbed them both at the same time, and squeezed. He felt their tiny bones against his chest and hugged them tight. He gathered their long hair between his fingers and stuffed his nose into their little heads and held them close until they started to squirm.

"Daddy is going away for a while and I don't know when I will see you again," Sidna said.

"When will you be back, Daddy?" Marguerite asked.

"I don't know, sweetie. You girls be good for your mother."

He finally let go. The girls were confused and looked at each other with big eyes. Sidna turned to Bettie and pulled the wad of money out of his front pocket. He counted out two hundred dollars, put it back in his pocket and handed the rest to Bettie.

"Sid, you are going to need more than that. How much is this?"

"Eight hundred. I'll make do. You need to take care of our girls. Hide it in a safe place."

"I'll do whatever it takes to see you again."

He wrapped his arms around his wife. He didn't want to let go. The life he had built was wound tight like a round bale of hay on the top of a ridge. The twines were being cut one by one. The bale could unfurl and tumble down the ridge, scatter loose and unwind at the seams at any moment. The only thing keeping the twine taut was family. He said one last goodbye and he and Wesley disappeared into the darkness. They walked up the road a little ways and Sidna told Wesley to stay put in the weeds for a few minutes. He walked the hundred yards up the road to the little building that housed the telephone switchboard for the phone line that ran through Fancy Gap. He found the point where the cable entered the building and pulled his knife out of his backpack and started sawing across the thick cable with the thin blade of his pocketknife until the wire was completely severed.

TWENTY-ONE

WESLEY

Wesley followed Sidna as they felt their way across the pasture to his Uncle Jack's house. The low clouds blacked out the night sky. He could barely make out the dark outline of the farmhouse up on the highpoint of the pasture. Sidna stopped and pushed the bottom string of a barbwire fence down with his foot and pulled the middle string up to the top string and Wesley bent through the gap. Then he held the gap open for Sidna. They walked the remaining two-hundred yards in silence. The only noise was their legs sweeping through the dormant grass. Sidna knocked on the door and called out, "It's Sidna and Wesley."

Garland opened the door.

"Didn't expect to see you here," Sidna said.

"Friel fetched me. Figured y'all need all the help you can get."

"Y'all come on in. Jack and Friel are sitting at the table."

Wesley and Sidna followed Garland across the front room into the dining room and sat down at the table. Jack was sitting at the head of the table and Sidna took the seat on his left. Friel was sitting to the right of his father. Wesley sat down beside of Sidna with Garland across from him. Claude, so far, had failed to appear. An oil lamp bloomed orange on the wall behind the table. The light flickered and cast their turbulent shadows across the floor.

"How did this happen?" Jack asked. "That stupid son of a bitch just doesn't know when to give up."

"Now, Jack, don't bring our mother into this. You know she did the best that she could. We all turned out different and she couldn't help that Floyd was born to be a son of a bitch," Garland said.

Sidna started telling them what happened that morning. He told them his side of the story all the way up to when he said goodbye to Bettie and his daughters. Wesley let him talk and his mind drifted as Sidna's lips moved and hands waved and his words wafted off into other ears. Wesley was still trying to make sense of what happened in the courtroom earlier that day. He didn't know what to do. Way he figured, he would follow along with Sidna's plan for a while until he made up his own mind. He didn't like the idea of staying around the area any longer than they had to, and he knew that eventually they were going to have to leave the state. They might as well leave now before the county organized some grand posse to come after them. The hard truth about what had happened and what he had participated in was starting to hit him like a heavy axe head splitting a thick log. Wesley could feel the impact coming down on all of them.

"I should have killed him when I had the chance. I've still got the scar, here from where he grazed that bullet off my forehead. We never intended on killing each other, but now I wished I would have taken him out and saved our family." Jack rubbed his forehead in the spot where Floyd had shot him in the dispute over the inheritance of Wesley's grandfather's whiskey stash.

"Who fired the first shot?" Garland asked.

"I don't know. I saw Floyd fumbling with his coat after he said he wasn't going to jail and then the shooting started. I think that Floyd's unbuttoning of his coat set off the whole thing. Dexter Goad, Bill Foster and Sheriff Webb were ready for Floyd to resist," Sidna said.

"It happened fast. The clerk and Floyd were looking at each other after the verdict was read. It was like they had a whole conversation across the courtroom without talking. I'm pretty sure I saw Goad wink at Floyd and the next thing I knew all hell broke loose," Wesley said.

"Did you fire your weapons?" Garland asked.

"I had to. I had to protect myself and my family," Wesley explained. "There was no choice."

Garland frowned and shook his head.

"It's true," Sidna responded. "We had no choice once the shooting started. Bullets started splintering the wall behind me. Goad took direct aim at me."

"You won't get no justice around here," Jack said. "Y'all are going to hang for this if they catch you, for sure."

"I know," Sidna said. "Our only hope is for the truth to come out. That may get the community on our side."

"Brother, we are going to do everything we can to help you get through this tragedy. We will check on Bettie and the girls as much as we can and help them out as much as we can. How else can we help?" Garland asked.

"I need some extra bandages for the bullet lodged in my back," Sidna said.

"We've got some extra bandages," Jack said.

"I appreciate it. We are going to need more supplies. I gathered up enough supplies to last us for the next few days, maybe a week. Could you help resupply us every week or two?" Sidna asked.

"No problem. I'll help you any way I can. I just don't know how I am going to get them to you."

"You know that little rock outcropping over behind our office at the sawmill?" Sidna asked. Garland nodded and Sidna continued. "Let's set up a drop point there. That would be a good place for you to leave some supplies. Leave a white cloth hanging on the office building after you make a drop."

"Done. I can't tell you how frequently I can make the drops, but I hope a couple of times a week."

"Where will you go?" Friel asked. It was the first thing he had said since they all sat down at the table.

"We may go hide up on Buzzard's Roost for a while. I don't know where from there," Sidna said. "Are you coming with us?"

Friel looked at his father. Jack shook his head.

"No," Friel said.

"Friel is staying here with us. We've got a big farm and some nooks and crannies here and there. You two are welcome to stay here too."

"I think we'd be better off hiding up in the nooks and crannies in the mountains and ridges and hollows," Sidna said. "What about you, Wesley?"

"I'm coming with you," Wesley said.

"We better get going. I want to be up on Buzzard's Roost before daylight," Sidna said.

"What about Claude?" Wesley asked.

"We can't wait for him any longer. If he shows up, tell him we are on Buzzard's Roost," Sidna said.

"Hold on a minute," Garland said.

Garland pulled a Bible from the bag beside of his chair. The black Bible was worn and flimsy from considerable use. The sides drooped over Garland's left hand as he flipped through the pages. Garland went directly to the verse he had in mind without hesitation like a workman familiar with his favorite tool. Garland grabbed Friel's hand and Friel took his father's hand and Sidna held Wesley's hand and they completed a semicircle.

"Your situation reminds me of Jeremiah. I've preached the lessons of his story many times. I've always been fond of his story and its lesson. Partly because that was our daddy's name," Garland said.

Garland began to pray out loud. The cadence and tone of his voice changed from Uncle Garland to the preacher that Wesley had listened to since he was a child.

"Dear Heavenly Father. Please watch over my brother and nephews. Please guide them through these tempestuous times." Wesley closed his eyes tight and tried to feel the presence of the Lord. It was something. Something to comfort him and ground him and it calmed his nerves to hear his uncle's rhythmic voice. Garland continued and Wesley felt eyes upon him. He opened his eyes and Sidna was staring at him, eyes wide open, head up. Wesley had always thought that opening your eyes during a prayer was a subtle defiance of God. Wesley closed his eyes and bowed his head again, but it distracted him from Garland's words. He caught fragments of the words that Garland emphasized, *exile*, *redemption*, and *God's plan*, but then he drifted off again worrying about where they would go next. Where would they hide? Would he ever see Maude again? How many people would be coming after them? His mind went through a thousand calculations during that minute-long prayer.

"Amen," Garland said.

The utterance brought Wesley out of his own thoughts, and he instinctively repeated the word. Sidna stayed silent.

TWENTY-TWO

PAYNE

The train rumbled down the track in the dark hour before sunrise. He was the only passenger on the one-car train that the Baldwin-Felts Agency had chartered from Roanoke to some small depot called Betty Baker Station. Payne could never sleep on trains. He stared out the window into the darkness wondering what the next few days would bring. He had started his career with Baldwin-Felts as a train guard and traveled widely on those slow haulers protecting them from outlaws and robbers until the train robberies decreased in the early aughts and by 1910 the agency shifted from guarding trains to guarding coal mines. By then he had worked his way up to full detective and was assigned to the coal mines in West Virginia leading a team of security guards and undercover detectives. Their mission was to protect the mining companies from their own rebellious workers. He missed the days of traveling over the rails across Virginia, West Virginia, Ohio, and Pennsylvania investigating train crashes and robberies.

It was just before daybreak and the deserted train depot was dark except for the two kerosene lamps burning on either side of the closed ticket booth and one man lying on a bench with a hat covering his face. He immediately recognized the man, Detective Hugh Lucas. Hugh Lucas used to work for him busting unions until he was promoted out of the mines and up to full detective. They all called him Luke. Luke had been one of Payne's best spies in the mines. His good looks and easygoing attitude always endeared him to people. They trusted him, sometimes to their detriment. Luke had shown up at the mine Payne oversaw one night under the cover of darkness and they inserted him into the mine as a new employee. His job had been to infiltrate a group of suspected unionizers. He did his job and exposed a massive plot amongst the miners to unionize and strike against the company. He also brought down the management of the mine by having an affair with the colliery manager's wife. Luke was promoted to the Baldwin-Felts headquarters in Bluefield after he wrecked both the miners' hopes of unionizing and the home of the colliery manager. Payne hadn't seen him since. After the long journey through blizzard conditions on the special night train, Luke was not the first person he wanted to greet. Payne had kept track of Luke's career since he had moved to headquarters. Luke was ten years younger than Payne and he had climbed the ranks fast with his clever political strategy, charming personality, extremely competent work ethic, handsome looks, and the confidence that came built into that package. Payne thought that this was his opportunity to show his worth to the agency. If he did whatever it took to capture these fugitives, then maybe he would be promoted out of the isolated mines and away from those filthy miners. Now he would have to deal with Luke's suggestions and opinions and damn it, Luke was usually correct. He walked over to the bench and tapped Luke on the leg with his boot. Luke didn't flinch and slowly pushed his hat up and peeked out from under the brim.

"Good morning, Ed," Luke said.

Payne nodded.

"How have you been?" Luke asked.

"Great."

"You still working the mines?" Luke asked.

"Coming from there," Payne said.

He didn't care to ask how Luke was doing. He knew Luke was doing better than himself and Payne didn't want his dissatisfaction with the mine-security work to show. Payne inspected the empty platform and wondered how they were going to get to Hillsville. He checked the time on his wristwatch. He didn't know how long they'd have to wait for their ride into town. The light from the platform stretched out over the tracks and scattered into the dense growth of weeds and trees on the other side. He sat down on the bench beside of Luke and they both pulled their hats down over their eyes.

TWENTY-THREE

PAYNE

They arrived in Hillsville by mid-morning. The road leading into town was scattered with unorganized houses of various sizes, some large and well-built, and others no more than simple shacks. Smoke curled up from a bonfire in the middle of the main street and Payne spotted several armed men huddled around. One of the armed men walked out to greet them. Payne recognized the man as Detective Elmer Brimm. He had worked with Elmer guarding trains a decade prior. Elmer was a small man, tough and wiry. Just the kind of man you would need to wade through the bush on a manhunt.

"We've got one of the fugitives holed up in that hotel. Just waiting for the word to go in and get him," Elmer said.

"What the hell are you waiting for, Elmer?" Luke asked.

"Nobody here has the authority to arrest him. All the county officials with the authority were killed yesterday. We have to wait for another judge to come in and deputize us all 'fore we can round 'em up."

"That ought to be easy. Just walk in and drag his ass out. Take some photos and on to the next one," Luke said.

"We are worried that some of his gang may come and try to rescue him. That's why we've got this place guarded so well. Floyd ain't going nowhere. He was shot several times and is bedridden. Going to be like catching fish in a puddle," Elmer said.

Payne smiled thinking it might not be that easy. "Is Mr. Felts here yet?"

"Uh huh. All the big wigs are already up yonder in the courthouse," Elmer said.

Payne walked out into the main street. Within the two blocks of dense buildings that made up the bulk of the town, he could see two hotels, one bank, one pharmacy, and a post office. The courthouse stood out among the other buildings with its strong brick construction and large white columns. The courthouse loomed over the small town and the surrounding area like a fort in the middle of the wilderness. Payne heard the heavy clops of a team of horses trotting up the street. A fancy covered buggy being pulled by a team of black horses was hauling ass up the hill. It sped past them throwing mud from the large wagon wheels and pulled right up in front of the courthouse. A tall man in a black suit with a full mustache got out of the wagon holding a leather briefcase. The man walked up the courthouse lawn with the stride of a soldier and disappeared under the veranda behind the large white columns. Luke said come on and they walked up the muddy road to the courthouse. Payne stopped to look at the statue in the middle of the street. The statue was about twenty feet tall with a Civil War soldier on top holding the barrel of a gun, the stock resting on the ground at his feet. Payne got the impression that the soldier was tired and ready to lay down his arms. He studied the statue and read the inscription:

> CONFEDERATE DEAD 1861-1865. FATE DENIED THEM VICTORY BUT CROWNED THEM WITH GLORIOUS IMMORTALITY. THOUGH MEN DESERVE, THEY MAY

NOT WIN SUCCESS; THE BRAVE WILL HONOR THE BRAVE, VANQUISHED NONE THE LESS.

Payne wondered what kind of people would erect a statue in honor of traitors who betrayed their country and its founding ideals. His father had fought on the right side, and he liked the locals a little less for propping false heroes who were on the wrong side of history. He hurried to catch up to Luke who was already walking into the courthouse.

The brain trust was reviewing a map of the area in a small office on the first floor off the veranda. William Baldwin and Thomas Felts and Felts' brother Lee were joined by three other men that Payne didn't know. William Baldwin was smaller than Felts and had a friendly face and Payne could tell that he was excited by the imminent manhunt. Baldwin was dressed in a gray three-piece suit with a blue bow tie. A gold chain looped from his vest into his pocket, no doubt leading to an expensive watch. Baldwin didn't stand out from the other men in appearance except his fine suit and his command of the meeting. Baldwin was the founder of the agency. He had rambled about in his youth and before starting the agency had tried running his own general store and dabbled in dentistry before turning his love of detective novels into a business. Baldwin was a free spirit and lacked organization and Thomas Felts countered that with an attention to detail and focus that Baldwin lacked. Thomas Felts was of medium build and slack-jawed with lips that curled downward into a permanent frown. Felts was a lawyer who became a partner with Baldwin in 1900 and by 1910 had added his name to the agency. Felts helped grow the agency from a small train-guarding operation that investigated train robberies and wrecks and occasionally provided private detective work to one of the largest private detective agencies in the country guarding all the Norfolk and Western Railway. The agency had been dubbed the Pinkerton of the South and neither Felts nor Baldwin minded the comparison. Felts diversified the agency into providing security for the coal mines in West Virginia and Southwest Virginia and occasionally provided investigative assistance to federal and state agencies. They acknowledged Payne and Luke as they entered the room and continued their conversation.

"The governor knows how your agency operates and that kind of operation is needed here, but don't cross the line. The whole country is watching right now," said the unknown man who had arrived in the fancy buggy.

"We are going to do whatever it takes to hunt down these fugitives. Thank you for trusting us with the responsibility," Baldwin said.

Felts spoke up. "We don't need the militia. We aren't going to war. We'll take the guns that they brought and then they can leave. Baldwin and I are both from these parts. We understand how to deal with the people around here. You can't bring in the militia for something like this."

"Let's continue this conversation later," Baldwin said

Baldwin smiled and greeted Luke as if they were good friends and then walked over and shook hands with Payne.

"Gentlemen. This is Hugh Lucas and Edwin Payne. Lucas is one of our brightest young detectives and Payne is one of our best veterans," Baldwin said, looking back at Payne and Luke. "Of course, you two know Mr. Felts."

Baldwin started going around the room introducing the men to each other. He started with the Attorney General of Virginia, Samuel Williams, the man with the mustache who had ridden up just after they arrived in town and hastily entered the courthouse. Next, Baldwin introduce Judge

Staples, the Circuit Court Judge out of Roanoke. The judge was short and pudgy and barely acknowledged the introduction with one quick head raise before returning to the large law book he was flipping through. Baldwin explained that the judge for Carroll County had been killed the day before and that Judge Staples was there to perform the duties of the circuit court judge. Next, Baldwin introduced Captain H.W. Davant of the Virginia State Militia. The Captain was powerfully built and stood like he had a stiff board strapped on his back.

Baldwin moved back over to the map spread across the large desk and motioned for Payne and Luke to join them around the desk.

"Ed, we are putting you in charge of one of the two search parties. Thomas' brother Lee is overseein' the other party. Each team will have from six to eight men, and we will have couriers constantly running between each team and the town to relay important information. Luke, you will stay here at headquarters and help coordinate the information and the couriers," Baldwin explained.

Payne flashed a Luke crooked smile. Luke would be dry and warm inside, sipping coffee and smoking his little hand-rolled cigarettes while Payne would be cold, wet, and miserable out in the bush.

"We are having a briefing after everyone is sworn in. We have a local deputy, who was there, scheduled to update everyone on what happened and give some history on the Allen Clan," Felts said.

"The Allen Clan. Are they the ones who did this?" Luke asked.

"It's a whole mess of old political disputes and family quarrels. The perpetrators of the shootout were Floyd Allen, his brother Sidna, Floyd's son Claude, and his nephews Wesley

Edwards and Friel Allen. Floyd was on trial for interfering with a deputy transporting Wesley to the jailhouse. They found Floyd guilty yesterday and sentenced him to a year in jail. He refused to go and started shooting up the place. The judge, Commonwealth attorney, sheriff, and a juror are dead," Felts said.

"Yes," Baldwin interjected. "These men are violent and fiercely independent. They have their own law and moral code out there in the south end of the county and no respect for the law unless it benefits their interests. Floyd Allen and his brother Sidna are two of the wealthiest men in the county. We've got Floyd cornered in the hotel across the street, just have to go in and take him, so he is not really a threat at this point. Sidna and his nephews, however, should be considered extremely dangerous and handled with caution. Sidna runs a general store and owns over a thousand acres of land in Fancy Gap. The rumor is that Sidna and Floyd built their wealth through the illegal manufacture and distribution of untaxed liquor and counterfeit coins. Sidna, in fact, was put on trial for counterfeiting last year in North Carolina. He was found not guilty but one of his business partners was found guilty. It will not be easy to track him down. He has employed many people through his various businesses. His people will help him. He knows that area like a husband knows his wife's body. He knows every holler and rock outcrop, every farm, and every ditch. He has also traveled widely and knows his way through the outside world. They tell me that Sidna went to the Klondike during the gold rush and may have earned his start there before speculating on real estate in Hawaii. Sidna is rich enough to burn a wet mule. I don't know much about Wesley, Friel, or Claude. Someone just told me that Claude is a college graduate, some business school in Greensboro, North

Carolina. What I'm trying to say is that they are smarter than what us outsiders might think."

Felts pointed to the topographic map and traced his finger along the mountain range that cut southwest across Virginia and down into North Carolina. "Fancy Gap is about six miles south on the crest of the Blue Ridge. The mountains drop off sharply into Carolina. It's wild country and it is where I would hide if I was them, little hidey holes scattered all over those ridges. We must go on horseback and foot. The roads are unsuitable for automobiles. Don't expect much help from the locals. From what I hear they are loyal to the Allens out there and will most likely work as a hindrance to us. I'll fill you and the rest of the detectives in on the plan after everyone has been sworn in."

"Can we have a look at the courtroom?" Luke asked.

"Sure, go on up to the courtroom and have a look around," Felts said. His tone turned somber, and his voice cracked like he might shed a tear. Felts cleared his throat and continued, "I already had one of our men count the bullet holes in the walls and the floors and the one's inside of the bodies. Nearly sixty bullets, give or take, fired within ninety seconds, is how we figure. Unbelievable. The undertaker is in there now dealing with the bodies."

Payne followed Luke up the stairs to the courtroom stepping over bullet holes in the risers and drops of dried blood on the treads. They entered the courtroom on the second floor. The gruesome aftermath of the previous day's violence had been lined up in neat rows by the undertaker. The smell of gunpowder lingered, and the smell of bodily fluids hung underneath the acrid layer of spent powder. Four bodies were covered with blood-stained sheets by the door. The undertaker and his assistant were just starting to move the bodies out, one at a time, on a wheelless gurney. Payne meandered around the room examining the aftermath and Luke reached in his inside coat pocket for his cigarette kit and started rolling a cigarette.

"Good morning," Payne said.

The undertaker gave an upswinging nod and continued prepping the bodies for relocation. Payne walked around the outside perimeter of the courtroom. He weaved around overturned chairs and looked at the bullet-peppered walls. He stuck his figure inside of a splintered hole in the wall where a bullet had penetrated the wood paneling. The hole had been enlarged and Payne could see the marks where someone had used a pocketknife to pry the bullet loose. Several of these larger holes were scattered amongst the smaller bullet holes and he figured that people had taken home souvenirs from the shootout. He turned back to the undertaker.

"Which one is which?" Payne asked.

"Well, that'n there is Judge Massie," the undertaker said. He continued pointing down the line of four bodies as he said their names. "That'n is Sheriff Lewis Webb and that'ns the Commonwealth Attorney William Foster, and the last one is Augustus Fowler, one of the jurors. God bless 'em."

Payne knelt over the judge's body. He didn't think the bodies had been searched yet. He pinched his nose closed and grabbed a top corner of the blood-stained cloth and pulled it from the body. The cloth cover stuck to the dried and congealed blood that had seeped out of the judge's body. He kept pulling until the judge's head and torso were revealed. On a hunch, Payne started going through the judge's pockets.

"What are you doing?" Luke asked.

"Checking for clues. I don't think these bodies have been investigated. Why don't you check that one?"

"What for? Sounds like they already know who's responsible.

All we have to do is hunt down these outlaws," Luke said, his words laced with sarcasm.

Luke left the rolled cigarette in his mouth and haphazardly checked one of the other bodies. Payne reached into the inside pocket of the judge's black robe. He pulled out a piece of paper and unfolded it. It was a handwritten note that said, "If you find Floyd Allen guilty you will die."

"Are you done?" asked the undertaker. "We need to get these bodies moved out now."

Payne pursed his lips and nodded, satisfied with the evidence he had discovered.

TWENTY-FOUR

WESLEY

Buzzard's Roost was a partial cave covered by a rock shelf hidden behind a large grove of pine trees and thick mountain laurels. The evergreens provided the perfect late-winter cover. Three boulders were strewn across the shelf providing additional coverage between the small gaps in the thick pine limbs. Wesley and Sidna had felt their way there through the night after they left Garland's house. Buzzard's Roost was well-known by the locals, both on top of the mountain and at the foot of the mountain. Wesley had been climbing up to Buzzard's Roost since he was a kid. He would follow a game trail about halfway up the mountain until the trail ended abruptly and then push his way straight up the side of the mountain. It had been his haven before. He had gone there to get away from the world after his father died. From up on Buzzard's Roost, he could see lights burning across the Carolina Piedmont. He recalled one Fourth of July when he had climbed up by himself and could see fireworks in Mount Airy and further away in Dobson and even further out in Winston-Salem. During the day he could see Pilot Mountain protruding up from the piedmont, looking like a giant had scooped out a chunk of rock from the top and flipped it over to one side leaving a dip where the chunk had been. He could see for hundreds of miles and on the clearest of days thought he could see the curve of the earth. It made him feel like he was watching over the entire Southeastern United States. Closer below, he could see his mother's house and a little farther out he could pick out what he thought was Maude's farm. He felt large and small at the same time: large because his fingernail could cover his house below and small because he could never know all the vast area that stretched out beneath him. A man could disappear out there like a copperhead in a carpet of dead leaves.

TWENTY-FIVE

PAYNE

People trickled in and by noon all parties summoned by the governor had assembled on the front lawn of the courthouse. The gray clouds hovered above looking like they would burst with rain at any moment. About thirty Baldwin-Felts employees filled the front lawn of the courthouse including detectives, couriers, and administrative assistants. The attorney general and Judge Staples stood above them on the veranda along with Thomas Felts and William Baldwin. The attorney general spoke first.

"The governor asked me to personally thank all of you who traveled here on such short notice. The current weather conditions are awful, and I thank all of you for enduring the snow, rain, and cold to get here. The governor wanted me to tell all of you that he has the utmost confidence in your agency's ability to bring law and order to this county and capture the instigators of this heinous crime. He is familiar with the Baldwin-Felts Agency from his investments in the coal mines and he has always been impressed with your organization's effectiveness and diligence. We have no doubt that you will bring this matter to an end quickly. We can't let this tragedy go unpunished. This was an attack on innocent lives, but it was also an egregious attack on the very authority of our state government and our justice system. Four innocent men were killed in this house of justice yesterday. Judge Massie, the County Commonwealth Attorney William Foster, County Sherriff Lewis Webb, and juror Augustus Fowler were all gunned down in cold blood for no other reason than trying to protect and defend the laws of this great Commonwealth. A witness, nineteen-year-old Betty Ayers, was also shot and is in serious condition. She may not survive the day. Let's honor their lives by swiftly apprehending the men who cut their lives short. Our first order of business is to get all of you deputized by Judge Staples. You all will be the bullets in the Commonwealth's gun, aiming towards justice."

The attorney general stepped aside and motioned for Judge Staples to step forward. The judge was considerably shorter than the attorney general and Payne could only see the top of his head from the back of the crowded lawn.

"Good morning, gentlemen. I am Judge Staples, appointed by the state to the Roanoke District Circuit Court. The attorney general called me here today to swear you all in as deputies of Carroll County. Judge Massie was murdered in cold blood yesterday in an egregious attack on law and order in the Commonwealth. All the elected court officers who were empowered to swear in deputies were murdered yesterday. For the past twenty-four hours, no one has overseen law enforcement in Carroll County. I was summoned to deputize a *posse comitatus* to hunt down and arrest the perpetrators of this outrageous defiance of our state judicial system. Please stand and raise your right hand. By the authority vested in me as a judge and by the authority given by the Attorney General of the Commonwealth of Virginia, all of you are hereby deputized until such a date as the attorney general declares that your services are no longer warranted."

"What's our title now?" Luke whispered in Payne's direction.

"Deputy Detective, Detective Deputy or posse commodores?" Payne asked.

"I think that's *posse comitatus*. Do we get a pay raise with these new titles?"

"I think I'm also going to need hazard pay. I'm likely to get shot at," Payne said.

William Baldwin started to speak, and Payne turned his attention to his boss. Baldwin took the cue and stepped forward.

"Detectives and staff. I am going to do whatever it takes to support you during the hunt for these fugitives. I will be there with you along every step of the way. Our first order of business is to go arrest Floyd Allen who is just down the street licking his wounds in the Elliot Hotel. It is well guarded, and he is not going anywhere. Then we are going to ride out together, as one, later in the afternoon to Fancy Gap to raid Sidna Allen's house. I will not rest until we have hunted down every damn member of the Allen Clan. Alright, line up and get a rifle and a pistol from the militia if you don't have one," Baldwin said.

The officers from Virginia Militia had set up a tent on the courthouse lawn to distribute arms and ammunition. The detectives and couriers who needed a weapon lined up for their government-issued rifles, pistols, and extra ammunition. Payne held back and walked up to Thomas Felts and William Baldwin who were talking amongst themselves. Payne waited for them to finish their conversation, but Felts quickly walked off with purpose leaving Baldwin there with Payne. Payne pulled out the note he found on the judge and showed it to Baldwin.

"I found this on the judge, in one of his pockets."

"Interesting," Baldwin said. "Thanks for sharing this with me."

Baldwin folded up the note and put it in his right front pants pocket.

"One more thing, Payne. You heard what the attorney general said back in the office. The governor knows how we operate. That means you can live up to your last name and bring it down on them if needed. Whatever it takes, I'll back you up. You hear me?"

Payne nodded.

"Good man," Baldwin said as he was walking away.

Luke walked over towards him with two rifles and two pistols and said here you go and handed Payne one of each of the guns. Payne inspected the handgun and admired its cold, blued steel.

"Thanks, fellow. What you got those for? You aren't going to need a gun holed up here by the stove with a cup of coffee in your hand. They might as well give yours to the secretary."

"You never know when those Allens might decide to take our headquarters."

"I guarantee you that those hillbillies will be far away from here," Payne said.

"Watch who you are calling a hillbilly," Luke said.

TWENTY-SIX

PAYNE

A handmade wooden sign hung over the hotel door identifying it as the Elliot Hotel. One block down and across the road from the courthouse. The three-story hotel's brick façade made it look nicer than it was. Two detectives were stationed on top of the roof as snipers. Four detectives were stationed at the back of the hotel in case Floyd or whomever was in there with him decided to slither out the back door. The muddy street in front of the hotel was crowded with half of the Baldwin-Felts staff, couriers and detectives, and a dozen reporters and photographers there to document the tragedy and the manhunt. Baldwin was as giddy as a pig at a trough full of slop. Baldwin looked at Felts with a big smile and they walked through the front door. Thomas Felts and his brother Lee followed Baldwin inside. Payne went next. He ducked under the short front door and entered the hotel with Elmer Brimm and a handful of detectives behind him all dressed in gray or black wool suits and fedoras on their heads. The front-desk clerk led them up the stairs to the second floor and down a short hallway to Floyd Allen's room. Baldwin and Felts stood on each side of the room's door and motioned for the detectives with their guns drawn to proceed. Both detectives clicked off their safeties and burst through the hotel door with their rifles leveled.

Payne stood across from the door with both hands wrapped around his pistol, ready to advance if needed.

Floyd Allen didn't flinch, and it was over the instant they entered the small hotel room. Floyd was lying on the bed looking feeble and unable to fight. A younger man, presumably his son, was sitting in a small wooden chair next to Floyd's bed. Baldwin and Felts entered the room and Payne followed.

"What'd you say there, Floyd?" Baldwin asked.

Elmer Brimm kept his rifle pointed at the younger man in the corner. The young man held up his hands above his head.

"I'm unarmed," the man in the corner said.

"Identify yourself!" Felts shouted.

"I'm Victor, Floyd's son."

"I expected you before now," Floyd said.

The photographer pushed his way past Payne and through the door. William Baldwin and Thomas Felts knelt beside the bed and posed for a photograph beside of Floyd. After the first photograph with just Baldwin and Felts, they asked Payne and the other detectives to join them in the frame. Floyd didn't say a word and just continued lying there, immobilized by his injuries. Floyd posed for the photographs. Payne thought it odd. Floyd stared at each flash with confidence. Payne thought he even saw the tinge of a smile behind Floyd's thick mustache. When the photo shoot was complete, Detectives Elmer and Virgil carried Floyd out of the hotel on a stretcher. Floyd asked for a sheet to cover up and they obliged. Payne walked to the side and watched Floyd pull the sheet all the way up over his head. Payne assumed this was to avoid being seen by the gawkers and the newspaper photographers lined up outside of the hotel. Floyd was fumbling around underneath the sheet, a back-and-forth movement that appeared to be Floyd's knuckles moving underneath the sheet near his head. Payne grabbed the sheet and pulled it off Floyd's head and was shocked when he saw Floyd sawing away at his throat with a knife. Payne drew his pistol and pointed it at Floyd.

"Put down the knife or I'll shoot you. Put it down!" Payne shouted.

"Just grab it from him," Baldwin said from behind him. "He isn't going to put it down. Take it."

Another detective pounced on Floyd and restrained his arms at the elbows. Payne reached down and grabbed the knife from Floyd's hand before he could finish the deed. The dull knife had barely broken the delicate skin around Floyd's neck.

"We won't let you go out like that, Floyd. Your ass is going to fry in the 'lectric chair and the state will decide when, not you," Baldwin said.

Floyd didn't succeed in taking his own life, but Payne watched the will to live drain from Floyd's blue eyes and Payne realized he was going up against desperate men with nothing to lose.

TWENTY-SEVEN

PAYNE

Payne and his men hunkered down behind a mess of dead weeds and bare tree limbs down the hill from Sidna Allen's house. The house lorded over the rolling plateau like a castle with its two conical roofs perched on short turrets. The rain clouds had moved out and a stiff wind penetrated Payne's black wool coat. He oversaw a team of six detectives and the inbred-looking deputy. Payne squatted down and waddled with his knees bent, keeping his head below the brush over to a little gap in the dormant vegetation. He peered up at the house on the hill through thick binoculars. There were reports that Sidna Allen and his nephews were holed up in the house, ready to fight to the death. He didn't see any sign of them as he swept the binoculars across the property surrounding the house. He slithered back behind the brush to his men.

"Start getting your gear ready and make sure you have extra ammunition. There are rumors that they are all holed up in that big house or in the basement of Sidna Allen's general store. We are going to raid his house and his general store simultaneously. Our team is going to raid Sidna Allen's house and Lee Felts' team will take the store. We expect that they are heavily armed and stocked with ammunition and prepared to battle till the end. This hillbilly farmer couldn't have afforded to build a house like this without selling untaxed whiskey and counterfeiting. The entire property will be searched for illegal liquor stills and counterfeiting equipment. We have reason to believe that he gained his wealth through various nefarious activities. Please watch each other's backs, gentlemen. We have permission to take them dead or alive."

Payne double-checked the extra magazines for his pistol attached to the side of his belt. He wore an ammunition vest that formed an X around his chest with extra rounds for his rifle slotted into the straps. The weight of the ammunition vest made him feel secure against the chaos that was sure to erupt. He had confidence in most of the men on his posse. Payne requested that Elmer Brimm be on his team. He liked Elmer's attitude and although he was of small stature his wiry muscles appeared more capable of traversing the rough terrain than the other detectives. Then there was Virgil Gray. A tall man, almost as tall as Payne. Virgil had only been with the agency for six months and was originally from the coalfields of Southwest Virginia. Virgil rode with the Rough Riders in the Spanish War and worked for various detective agencies, including Pinkerton, before joining Baldwin-Felts. Virgil was the son and grandson of coal miners and his knowledge of the mines in far Southwest Virginia made him a good fit for Baldwin-Felts' security work in the mines. Payne had no clue if Virgil could handle the manhunt, but he looked the part with his square jaw and steel eyes. Payne wasn't very familiar with the other detectives in his posse. John Faddis was originally from Knoxville and had worked out of the Roanoke office for several years. Phil Phaup had been with Baldwin-Felts for a long time, but Payne had never had the chance to work with him. He liked Phaup based on the few times he had interacted with him, despite Phaup always smelling like liquor.

Two other detectives named Harrison and Burwell had been assigned to his posse.

Payne turned his head to the right, across the road, where Thomas Felts and William Baldwin were sitting on their horses, well out of harm's way. The simultaneous raid of Sidna Allen's home and general store had to be coordinated at precisely the same time and Baldwin and Felts were situated in a place where they were visible to both teams. Baldwin removed his cap and raised it to the sky to signal the start of the raids. Then Payne understood the danger that he and his men would face as they ran up that hill, exposed in the middle of a cow pasture while their bosses watched on horseback as they charged across an open field. They approached the house from the north and quickly closed the gap across the field. Payne listened for gunfire over the huffing of his men's hard breathing and the rustling sound of their legs running through the tall grass. The gunfire never came. Payne and his men rushed up the well-built stairs that didn't budge as they pounded up the treads. The house was immediately overrun by Baldwin-Felts agents.

Payne was the first to bust through the door with his rifle shouldered. His men streamed into the house behind him and scattered into different rooms. He turned left and entered what looked like the parlor. The room was empty.

"Front left room clear!" Payne shouted.

"Dining room is good," Elmer Brimm called out as he met Payne by the front door. Payne motioned toward the staircase. Elmer nodded and jogged down the hall. Payne followed. They moved with caution, their rifles pointed up the S-shaped stairs that snaked in a half-spiral to the second floor.

"Kitchen clear!" Phil Phaup shouted.

"Living room clear," Virgil Gray yelled from the back of the house.

Elmer paused on the top step. Payne sensed Elmer's fear. If anyone was in the house, then they were hiding on the second floor. He slid past Elmer and pointed across the landing to the room on the right. Payne turned left and entered a bedroom. He figured it was the master because of the large bed frame and the bulky wardrobe to the left of the entrance. The ceiling was angled on both sides like the room was built in an attic and Payne had to duck his head as he walked down the left side. The bed was in the middle of the room with a fireplace on the far end. A rectangular mirror hung over the mantle, and he saw their reflections between the far side of the bed and the fireplace. They were huddled together on the floor, two women, two little girls, and one man.

"Don't move!" Payne bellowed.

He pointed his rifle at the unknown man.

"Who are you?" Payne asked, his finger on the trigger.

"I'm Garland Allen. Floyd and Sidna's youngest brother."

Payne kept his gun on the man. He wasn't sure who the man was, but he didn't trust that he was telling the truth. This man could have been Sidna for all he knew.

"Go get the local we brought with us. We need confirmation on this man's identity."

He pointed his rifle at the two women, not taking for granted that they didn't have guns hidden somewhere. Payne had evicted too many miners whose wives mysteriously produced a pistol from under their dresses.

"Which one of you is Sidna's wife?"

A plump-looking woman with a round face spoke up. The two little girls huddled closer to the woman as she spoke.

"I am Bettie Allen. These are our two daughters. Please don't hurt anyone. Sidna is not here."

"Where is he? Has he been here?" Payne asked.

They stared at him and then at each other. No one answered. He looked at the woman beside of the man who had called himself Garland. She was younger and attractive. She was the most attractive woman Payne had seen since he stepped off the train the day before. He was surprised by her beauty and expected most of the women in this area to be worn and weathered from the toil of the hard mountain life or genetically inferior from the inbreeding that no doubt happened frequently in this isolated place.

"Search them all for weapons," Payne said.

The agents kept their guns drawn while Payne separated Garland from the women.

Elmer brought the local deputy upstairs to confirm the identity of the man.

"This ain't him," Deputy Spence said.

"Alright, search these upstairs rooms for any sign of Sidna," Payne said.

Payne kept his rifle pointed at them and didn't speak. A minute later, Elmer returned holding a white, blood-stained sweater. Elmer handed the sweater to Payne. The sweater had a deep red stain where the blood had soaked through, and thin tentacles of blood reached out in all directions around the hole where the bullet had entered Sidna's body. Sidna had been there.

Payne handcuffed Garland. He shoved the barrel of his rifle into Garland's back and forced him down the stairs. The first floor was now filled with Baldwin-Felts agents. Thomas Felts and William Baldwin were walking through the door as Payne brought his prisoners downstairs.

"Nice work, Payne," Felts said.

"Any sign of Sidna?" Baldwin asked.

"I think this belongs to Sidna," Payne said.

Payne handed the bloody sweater to Baldwin, and he nodded in agreement.

"Set him up in the dining room. We'll give him the third degree," Felts said.

Payne dragged Garland into the dining room. He tied him to an ornately carved wooden chair. Elmer and two other detectives escorted Sidna's wife and Garland's wife down into the dining room and forced them to sit down like they were waiting for the start of a meal. The pretty woman started crying when she saw her husband bound to the chair. Baldwin started circling around the dining room.

"Where is Sidna? Where are Wesley Edwards and Claude Allen? We know they have been here," Baldwin said as he held up the bloody sweater and then pointed at Payne. "You see that big man there. He is prepared to beat the answers out of you. We are the law around here now. Why don't you make it easier on everyone and cooperate?"

Payne made sure that Garland watched him prep his knuckles for the resistance by flexing his fingers back and forth. He bent his right four fingers backwards and then his left four. Garland glanced over at his wife who tried to mouth a few words back to him. Payne wasn't sure what she tried to say but that made him think that Garland was holding something back.

"We know who you are. The locals briefed us on your whole despicable family. What kind of preacher lies right to a man's face? A preacher with the last name of Allen, I assume. Go ahead and keep looking at your pretty wife. In just a few minutes we will make sure that your eyes are swollen shut so you can't," Baldwin explained.

Garland remained silent and Baldwin pointed at Payne and said to get on with it. Payne didn't waste any time. He walked over from the doorway, cocked his right arm, and caught Garland on the side of his left eye. The first punch was not Payne's full strength. The goal was to hurt the man and not knock him out. Unconscious men didn't talk. Garland absorbed the punch a little too easy and Payne threw two more punches into his left side of his face. Payne stepped back and gave Garland a breather to think about the length of his punishment. Baldwin turned his attention to Sidna's wife. Sidna's wife kept her composure and comforted the other woman. Payne walked over to the women and stood behind them.

"We know Sidna came here after he killed those men in cold blood. When was he here? Where did he go?" Baldwin asked.

She didn't answer.

"I told my men to be gentle with your property. Not because I value your property. It is hard for me to value property that was purchased by illicit means. No. The reason I told them to be gentle is because all your land and personal property is going to be sold off and the proceeds given to the victims of this terrible tragedy. You and your daughters will be left with nothing. The longer this search goes on the more it is going to cost, and you will have to work off the debt till the day you die," Baldwin said.

Baldwin looked at Payne and motioned his head at Garland. Payne walked back around to the head of the table and cocked his right elbow, ready to strike. Garland spoke up before Payne could strike again.

"I'm a preacher. I'm a man of God. I'd tell you if I'd seen 'em."

"I don't care if you're the fucking Pope," Payne said.

He punched him in the left eye again and then in the mouth and moved up to his temple. Again, in the mouth. Garland's lip busted and blood started dripping from his clean-shaven chin. Payne didn't enjoy this part of the job. Wrecking a defenseless man's face was not a fair fight. He could gage the strength and will of a man by how he took the punishment and when he broke down. It wasn't long for this one.

"Are you ready to talk?" Baldwin asked. "Or we can keep this up all evening."

Payne stepped back around the table behind the women again and the room stayed silent as the blood dripped from Garland's face onto his white button-down shirt. Susie wiped the tears from her cheek and started to speak between the huffs and gasps of her sobs. The floodgates opened. It was confession time.

"Garland met with Sidna and Wesley the night of the shootout," she confessed.

"Where were they going?" Payne asked.

"He didn't tell me where he was going. He left here just after sunset. I'll cooperate with anything you need. My husband is a good man, and he didn't plan this. He just got caught up in Floyd's mess. I despise Floyd after what he has done to our family. Floyd is the one who instigated this tragedy. My husband's name will be cleared once all the facts come to light," Bettie said.

Baldwin motioned for Payne to start again. He didn't want to. It was clear that the man had had enough. Any further punishment would incapacitate him. But he had to keep it up and be loyal to the agency and their mission. Garland's head slumped to the right with his chin resting on his chest, blood trickling down his chin and down his cheek from his busted eyes. He again stepped toward the battered man who finally spoke up.

"What my wife said is true. I met with Sidna, Wesley, and Friel at my brother Jack's house the night after the shooting."

"Where were they going?" Baldwin asked.

"Said they were heading to Carolina."

"We are done with them," Thomas Felts said in disgust. "Keep them under guard here while you search the property. I want every nook and cranny turned over before we leave here."

Payne turned his attention to the family pictures on the sideboard behind him. He picked up a portrait of a man.

"Is this Sidna?" Payne asked.

"Yes, that is my husband," Bettie said.

Payne picked up the picture. Sidna had a broad nose, long face, and a large mouth. Intelligent eyes stared back at Payne from the black-and-white photo.

"Is this the most recent photo of.... Sidna?" Payne asked.

"Yes," Bettie said.

Payne put the photo in his pocket to keep until he could pass it along to a courier to be given to a secretary to include in the wanted posters. He pulled out his notebook from the inside pocket of his wool coat and wrote down the name Garland Allen. Garland had held his own and Payne wrote *tough* out beside of his name. He put the worn notebook back in his breast pocket and walked around the impressive house while the other agents turned over every corner and every closet. He marveled at the fine architecture and the intricate design of the wood trim. The house was cozier than he thought it would be. From the road, it looked like a mansion on a hill, but it was smaller than it looked once you walked inside. He felt the solid oak floors underneath his feet as he walked through the foyer and into the parlor. The fireplace was topped with a large mirror and the mantel was framed by two small Greek columns and surrounded by off-white tiles inlaid with intricate vines that started in flowerpots at the base and climbed up and over the firebox. He walked back down the hall to the living room where the floors changed to what looked like high-grade maple. He circled through the kitchen and back through the dining room where Sidna's wife and Garland Allen and his wife were still under guard. He thought of his own wife.

"You don't happen to have a phone, do you?" Payne asked.

Elmer spoke up, "It ain't working. The line's been cut."

Payne nodded and continued inspecting the house. He hated Sidna Allen. Hated him for having to travel through the miserable weather to this backwards place. Hated him for being forced to beat the preacher into a pulpy mess. Sidna and Floyd and their kin, they schemed and cheated and got ahead. He felt anger welling up inside his chest. They were lazy moonshiners and counterfeiters who lived the high life while good, honest people, their own neighbors, lived a life of tedious toil to survive. Payne thought of the innocent victims whose lives were taken in the courthouse. He felt the fire again like being back guarding the trains from bandits and hobos and tramps. He had lost that fire the last few years working in the coal mines. In the mines, the lines between black and white were blurred into gray like the thick, black coal dust that coated men's insides and dulled their spirits. In the mines, he didn't know if he was in the right or in the middle or on the wrong side. Hunting down the Allen Clan reminded him why he joined the agency in the first place, to bring justice to those who had turned their backs on the law.

TWENTY-EIGHT

WESLEY

It was Wesley's turn to watch. He glassed the land below. Sidna was asleep under four blankets with his back against the flat face of a large rock. The clouds had vanished during the night and the low morning sun didn't provide the warmth that its yellow glow promised. His bones were numb from the cold. They had a fire the night before, but the smoke would give them away during the day. He scanned the road below that led to his family's farm in a little indentation between two small hills. He squinted through the binoculars. A group of men were approaching the house on horseback.

"Uncle Sid. Come here and look," Wesley whispered.

Sidna didn't respond. Wesley picked up a pebble and tossed it in his uncle's direction. The rock bounced off the ground and up into the blankets around Sidna's hip.

"What is it?" Sidna asked.

"There are some men on horseback going down the road to Mama's house."

Sidna scooted over and grabbed the binoculars out of Wesley's hands. Wesley squinted against the bright sky and watched another four men ride down the road toward the house. They turned off the road and went over the little hill between the orchard and up through the pasture. Wesley walked away from the edge of the rock face and went over to get his rifle. He peered through the scope. It wasn't as powerful as the binoculars but better than the naked eye. Wesley watched as a tall man dismounted about twenty-five yards from the house and started giving orders to the other men. They separated. Wesley counted eight men total. One group walked slowly and deliberately around the back of the house with rifles against their shoulders and the other group approached the front door. Wesley put the crosshairs on the head of the tall one who appeared to be the leader. He put his finger on the trigger. It was at least two-thirds of a mile down to the target and Wesley knew that it was too far for him to be accurate. He'd have to account for the wind, the distance, and the elevation change by aiming off somewhere away from the man and he didn't have the skill to make the shot. The leader and another man walked up onto the porch and knocked on the door. Wesley's heart raced and he thought of his mother being questioned, or worse, by the men who just went inside. Wesley watched the rest of the posse search around the outside of the house and around the barn. Then, five of the men walked behind the house and started up the mountainside down the worn path that led to his still. A half hour passed, and the men finally emerged from the woods carrying the still pot, thumpkeg, and condenser that once composed Wesley's still.

"It looks like they found your still," Sidna said.

"Yep," Wesley said. It didn't bother him. He had much bigger things to worry about now than the law finding his still site. He figured being executed for participating in murder was as bad as it could get and being charged with illegal liquor production would have no impact on his punishment.

"We've got to escape, Uncle Sid. Let's head on down to

Carolina after dark and disappear into the lowlands," Wesley said.

"I know that running feels like the right thing to do, but we need to stay around here for a while longer. We have friends and family that we can rely on for food and shelter," Sidna said. "I've got a goddamned fresh bullet in my side. I need to stay close to where I can get worked on if need be. If we go off on our own where we don't know anyone, then people will be suspicious of us when we ask for help. We will leave the area when I say it's time or you can go off on your own. How long did you hide out last time before you got caught?"

Wesley sensed anger and frustration in Sidna's words, but he kept at it.

"This is different," Wesley said. "Our lives depend on us not getting caught now. I was running from a few months in jail back in the fall. Now I'm running from the electric chair. The quicker we get out of Carroll County the better off we will be."

"I've already coordinated with Garland. He is going to make some supply drops for us out near our sawmill. We have plenty of friends and family to rely upon and there are plenty of places to hide," Sidna said.

Sidna shook his head and sat down behind the rocks. Wesley turned back toward his house and looked through the binoculars. All the men were lined up together with a photographer in front of them. Some sat atop their horses. Others knelt in front of the mounted men. They posed with their rifle butts resting on their thighs, barrels pointed toward the sky. After their photoshoot, they formed a semicircle around the tall man and he spoke to them. They stood around listening to their leader talk for a few minutes and then they mounted their horses and headed south.

"There they go towards the state line. You reckon they think we went down into Carolina?" Wesley asked.

"They aren't going to Carolina," Sidna said. "I figure they are going to Floyd's house."

TWENTY-NINE

PAYNE

Payne dismounted his horse in front of Floyd Allen's home. He rode up by himself. His men had left their horses a half mile up the road and formed a half circle spaced out fifty yards from each other and moved slowly toward Floyd's house. They eventually encircled the house and waited. Payne hoped to flush them out of hiding and his men would be there, waiting, if they decided to run. Floyd's wife was sitting on the porch in a weathered rocking chair. Payne shouldered his rifle and approached the porch cautiously. He raised his arm and wiggled his index finger. His men moved forward from their positions and surrounded the house. Elmer Brimm and Virgil Gray walked slowly across the front yard with rifles pointed towards the front door. They climbed the stairs two at a time onto the front porch past Payne and Mrs. Allen and burst into the house.

"Mrs. Allen, I'm Detective Edwin Payne of the Baldwin-Felts Detective Agency. We have jurisdiction here now since the sheriff was killed."

He pinched the badge between his thumb and index finger and gently wiggled the badge. The bronze badge flashed in the sunlight.

"Do you know that we captured your husband yesterday?" Payne asked.

She solemnly nodded her head. He took note of how tired she looked. Obviously broken down by the turmoil her family had put upon her. He removed his hat and stood below the front porch of the handsome two-story house. He sat down on the top step and placed his rifle on the edge of the porch.

"Have you had any contact with your son, Sidna Allen or Wesley Edwards since the shooting?" Payne asked.

She didn't say anything but shook her head to indicate that she had not and continued to rock like she might rock right off the porch. Payne sensed a lie.

"Can you tell me about your family, Mrs. Allen?" Payne asked. "I'd like to know more about the men I'm hunting down."

"Would you and your men like something to eat?" she asked. "It's about suppertime and I'm hungry. The neighbors and family have been bringing food for me and I've got too much and not enough mouths to feed. I'd be happy to fix y'all up something."

"Yes, Mrs. Allen. That would be nice. I'll tell my men."

"You can call me, Frances."

"We can bring this nightmare to an end. Just tell me where Claude and the others are hiding. I will make sure that they take it easy on your poor boy."

She kept rocking and stared off over his head. He stayed quiet and let her think. A loud crash came from inside of the house and Frances closed her eyes and winced. A door slammed and Elmer Brimm shouted, "All clear!" on the first floor from somewhere deep inside of the house.

"He was here yesterday. He says he wasn't responsible for it, and he was just defending himself and his daddy. I believe him and if he gets to tell his side of the story his name will be cleared. My boy is innocent. If you want to blame anybody then blame my husband and blame the courthouse republicans."

"You may be right, Frances. The quicker we find him then the sooner he gets to tell his side of the story and maybe get himself out of this mess and come back home to you. Did he tell you anything else about where he might go?" Payne asked.

"He told me he was planning on getting out of Virginia and heading across the state line. That's all I know," Frances said.

"Thank you, Frances. Please contact the Baldwin-Felts Detective Agency if you get any information on his whereabouts."

"Let me tell you one more thing. Those republicans up in Hillsville are just as responsible for this as my husband. Do you know about what happened before the shootout?" she asked.

"Not really."

"My husband and son were not...are not outlaws. Floyd has a temper and I've seen his wrath firsthand, but he is also a good and kind man. Floyd is a respected member of the community. He has been a public servant, both as an elected official and as a sworn special deputy for the sheriff on numerous occasions. He was pushed too far by those republicans, Goad and Foster and Webb. It all started with Wesley Edwards getting charged for that fight but them other boys weren't charged at all and they's the ones that lured him out of church that morning. Didn't you say that you were the law here now? Ain't it your job as the law to figure out what led up to the shootout and hold all parties responsible?" Frances asked.

Payne paused and pondered her question. Frances glared at him with conviction. She was correct, but she didn't know that Baldwin-Felts had never been concerned with justice.

"I have one job and that is to hunt down the men who

perpetrated the shootout and killed five people. It was four, but yesterday we learned that a young woman named Betty Ayers passed away from the bullets that your men put in her," Payne said.

"God bless her soul, but you don't know it was their bullets. That is why you need to get to the truth of what happened. If you ever want to know what really happened then go talk to Dexter Goad, he ain't as innocent as he looks. Sidna's wife Bettie told me that Dexter Goad offered Sidna and Floyd a deal the week before the shootout. The offer was to back Goad in the next election, and he would drop all the charges. If you care about the truth, then you need to start looking for it."

Payne looked up across the road. Phil Phaup was trotting toward them.

"You need to come over to the store and see what we found," Phaup said.

Phaup turned around and was back across the road as quickly as he came. Payne stood and tipped his hat to Frances, and he walked across the yard and across the dirt road towards Floyd's small general store. Frances said Mr. Payne and he stopped in the road and turned his head back toward the house.

"This ain't no one-sided affair."

He thought about what Frances had said. He didn't really know much about the events leading up to the shootout and he would have to remedy that. Obviously, Floyd's wife's perspective was biased, but he could tell from her tone and sincerity that there was some truth in her statements. He knew that there was probably more to the story than just crazed outlaws shooting up the courthouse. What if it was true and there was more to it and this whole abysmal situation was one big shade of gray like the coal-covered faces of all those miners he had beaten and evicted in defense of the coal company's profit line?

Floyd's store was about half the size of Sidna's and the white paint on the wood siding was peeling and cracked. He went through the busted front door and found them at the back near the entrance to a small stockroom.

"We found a still in the back of the store. Just in the back through a small door that we thought led to the stockroom. We found three barrels of home brew in the feed house out back behind the store," Detective Phaup said.

"Let's not get distracted by this. We need to focus on our task of finding these outlaws. Have our courier tell headquarters what we found and to contact the federal marshal," Payne ordered.

"When are we going to get to sample some of this mountain honey?" Detective Phaup asked.

"Raiders never sample the whiskey that they confiscate. Do you want to get poisoned?" Payne said. "These hillbillies probably don't care if it poisons their customers or not, as long as they are making a profit off of this nasty home brew."

"If they want repeat customers then they care," Detective Phaup said.

"Don't touch it."

Elmer Brimm walked into the store and yelled, "Detective Payne!"

Payne answered, "Back in here!"

He waited for Elmer to find them in the back room.

"We found some tracks around the back of the house. They come from the house and go across that field and then back out onto the road going back towards the mountain. Probably made early this morning," Elmer said.

"Have a courier send a message to headquarters that we

need to stake out Floyd's house. I'm willing to bet that Claude will be back here. And go tell Mrs. Allen to hurry up with our dinner. We can't stay long."

THIRTY

WESLEY

It was well after dark when they left their sanctuary on Buzzard's Roost. They dodged branches and rocks and little bare limbs on their way down the mountain to Wesley's house. Sidna stopped them at the tree line fifty yards from the house and they watched and listened for any signs of activity. They waited there for about fifteen minutes and did not see anything unusual. The dim lights from inside of the house illuminated the front windows and they could see the shadowy figure of his mother pacing in the front room.

"It looks safe," Sidna whispered. "You've got twenty minutes, alright. We can't stay here too long."

Wesley crouched down and walked across the open space between the woods and his mother's house and onto the porch. He knocked on the door. His mother cracked the door open and stuck the barrel of a shotgun through the crack.

"It's Wesley."

"Get in here, son."

She opened the door and let him in. She peeked her head out of the door and scanned the front field for movement, shut the door, and propped the shotgun up against the wall and hugged Wesley for a good long while. He rested his chin on the top of her gray head and started to cry. The emotions of being in his home hit him hard. He wanted to be back in his own bedroom. He wanted to wake up in the morning to the smell of smoke from the stove and bacon, eggs, and coffee.

"Me and Sidna were hiding up on Buzzard's Roost. We watched the search party raid the house this evening. I just had to come down and see you one more time. Being so close. Are you alright?"

"I'm fine, just a little shaken from everything."

"Who were they?"

"Baldwin-Felts detectives. Said they was the law around here now. Said they broke down Garland and he said you was headed this way. I was honest and told 'em I hadn't seen you. I think they believed me."

"They found my still."

"Yes. They tore the still apart and poured out the barrels you had down in there. Said you would be charged with producing untaxed liquor when they got you."

"I figure that is the least of my worries."

"I'm sorry, son."

"For what?"

"I should've steered you toward Sidna after your father died instead of letting Floyd be the father figure."

"It's not your fault, Mama. Sidna still got caught up in this mess, I still would be too. Don't blame yourself."

"What are y'all going to do?" she asked.

"Sidna wants to stay around here where we have friends and family to help hide us and give us supplies. But I'm not sure. I think we need to head into Carolina. The more distance we can get away from here, the better."

"You listen to your Uncle Sid. He's got good judgement. You might just have a chance if you follow Sid."

"Yes, Ma. I'll listen to him."

They sat there for a while in silence. His mother grunted the occasional *hmm*, which indicated she was thinking on saying something. He took a deep breath and savored the slightly musty smell of the house. It was the smell of his childhood. Most of the time he didn't notice the smell, but he did when he had been away for a while. It wasn't bad. It just smelled like home. His mother had never liked cleaning and after his father died, she preferred to sit on the front porch and rock away the evenings late into the night. As a result, the house was always a little dusty and musty. A gentle knock on the front door broke the silence. Wesley opened the door.

"It's time to go," Sidna said.

"You take care of my boy."

"I will, if he'll allow it."

"Take care of yourself, too, brother."

Wesley and his mother shared one long hug and he and Sidna eased back across the dark pasture.

"We need to start moving if we are going to be up on the ridge by sunrise," Sidna said. "Did she say who the men in the search party were? They didn't look like locals."

"Baldwin-Felts detectives."

"Huh." Sidna grunted, looking surprised. "The Pinkerton of the South are after us. They got up here fast."

"She said they told her that they are the law around here now."

"All the more reason to stay around here for a while longer. I don't think the local people are going to like seeing outsiders tearing across the county looking for us," Sidna said.

"Where do you think we should go next?"

"The opposite direction from that posse, back up on top

of the mountain. I've got a few people in mind. I know somewhere they won't expect us to hide. Someone who owes me a favor."

THIRTY-ONE

SIDNA

He hadn't seen Jack Akers since that day in the store when he offered him store credit. He didn't know how much help Jack could provide, but he knew that Jack was kind and that they shared a loose connection that could not be easily traced.

"Have you been here before?" Wesley asked.

"No."

The sun rose and the morning sky turned from black to pale pink and blue. A dim glow bloomed through the front window of the small cabin.

"Looks like they are awake," Wesley said.

"Let's go up there and find out," Sidna said.

It was a primitive log cabin that had probably been built as temporary shelter but had turned permanent. The old cabin had clay chinked between the horizontal logs and a small lean-to structure had been added on the left side. They eased up to the small cabin. A dog started barking. Its gravelly bark sounded big. Sidna figured it was chained up to the barn or it would have already been on them either licking them or biting them. He knocked on the door and waited. He knocked again and waited longer. Sidna knocked again and yelled, "Jack!"

He knew they were in there and he wasn't leaving. His peripheral vision caught a glimpse of a head peeking through the small window to the left of the front door. Jack opened the door.

"What are you doing here?" Jack asked.

"I need some help, Jack. Can I come in?" Sidna asked.

Jack turned toward his wife for approval. She shrugged.

"Yes, yes. Sorry. Come on in. We just ain't used to having visitor's this time of day."

He opened the door and Sidna stepped into the dank cabin. The main room was not much bigger than the kitchen in Sidna's new house. There was a single bed that sat low on the floor in the front left of the house. A stone fireplace was on the right side of the cabin and inside of the fireplace was an old three-legged crane and skillet hanging down over a fire. Jack offered Sidna a seat in a little wooden chair that wobbled when he sat down.

"I'm Sidna Allen. This is my nephew, Wesley Edwards."

"I'm Ella Mae."

Jack was skinnier than when Sidna had last seen him. Ella Mae looked just as weak as her husband. She moved slowly and deliberately about the hearth. Her face was sunken in and gaunt, all hanging skin and cheekbones. Her tattered night-gown hung off her shoulders like she was a wire coat hanger. Ella Mae pulled out her snuff can and used the small wooden dipper and scooped a tiny amount of the fine tobacco into the little spoon. She held it up to her left nostril and pushed her right nostril closed with her finger. She quickly inhaled the snuff and pinched both sides of her nostrils together for a moment and then released her nose and sniffed hard and wiggled the tip of her snout.

"Can I have a pinch of that?" Wesley asked.

Ella Mae walked back over and handed the small cylin-drical can to Wesley. Sidna watched Wesley reach in and get a little pinch between his index finger and thumb. Wesley formed a fist with his left hand and put the fine brown powder in the natural bowl formed between the crook of his thumb and index finger and inhaled the tobacco through one side of his nose.

"Y'all want some coffee?" Ella Mae asked.

"Yes, please," Sidna said.

"You want some breakfast?" Ella Mae asked.

"Sure," Wesley said.

"I can't pay you back that store credit yet. I'm working on puttin' it together though," Jack said.

"Don't worry about that. Just go ahead and consider it written off. Did you hear about what happened?" Sidna asked.

"Yeah. Hell, we pretty much live under a rock, and we still know. Y'all are in some shit."

Ella Mae already had a kettle of hot water on the edge of the hearth and brought three tin mugs filled with coffee. Jack wrapped both of his skeletal hands around the hot cup and sipped.

"I've got something for you," Sidna said.

Sidna reached in his bag and pulled out the two jars of corn liquor. The clear liquid sloshed in the jars as Sidna handed them over to Jack. Jack shook the jar of clear liquid vigorously and turned it horizontal and watched as the large bubbles vanished quickly. Jack's face brightened and then he opened the jar and held it away from his nose before he took a sip.

"Ewwwwh, boy! That's some good stuff. Thanks, fellow."

"I didn't know you had that on you. You been holding out on me, Uncle Sid," Wesley said.

"Where did you get this stuff?" Jack asked.

"That's the Allen family recipe," Sidna said, looking over at Wesley.

"That's better than the shit we've been drinking lately," Jack said.

"Who you been gettin' it from?" Wesley asked.

"Been buying it from the Nester boys over in Laurel Fork," Jack said.

"Well, if anyone asks, tell them you got it from your neighbor, Dexter Goad," Sidna said.

Sidna and Wesley laughed like neither of them had in a long while.

"Hell, that bastard is probably dead anyway. He won't mind," Wesley said.

Ella Mae returned and handed them some leftover corn pone. The corn pone was dense and dry and crumbled when Sidna bit out a chunk of the golden-brown bread. He had become used to the fluffy corn bread that Bettie prepared with eggs and buttermilk. He washed the dry bread down with the stale coffee that had obviously been cut with chicory. Sidna grabbed a second piece of corn pone from the humble serving plate that Ella Mae had placed on the table.

"Jack, can we stay in your shed for a few days?" Sidna asked.

"Yes, you can stay as long as you want to. As long as you don't get me in trouble. I'll help you any way I can. I just have one question. Why do you trust me? You don't even know me," Jack asked.

"I helped you and I reckon you'd return the favor. Not knowing you helps me in this case because they won't think to look for me here," Sidna explained.

"Come on, let me show you the shed," Jack said.

THIRTY-TWO

SIDNA

The ferocious-sounding dog turned out to be good-natured. It was chained up outside the shed and Sidna was thankful for its vigilant ears and loud bark. He would know if they had visitors. Jack gave them the run of his tiny building. The shanty shed was drafty. The walls tilted to the right and the roof bent to the left in natural compensation. Old farming implements hung on the back wall, a rusty mattock, a dull scythe, and a dirt-encrusted hoe. It looked like it had been several seasons since the tools were used for cultivating. They settled into the small space and turned stacks of hay and blankets into beds.

Sidna kept watch on the second morning while Wesley slept. He occasionally peeked out of a hole in one of the vertical wallboards that gave him a view of the road that ran past Jack's house. He'd already whittled a spoon out of an old piece of maple and fired it over the small campfire they kept behind the building at night. He had just started whittling on the second spoon when the dog started barking. He heard the long chain unfurl over the bare dirt, worn from years of the dog walking and lying around his little piece of land. The chain jerked when the dog reached the end of the chain's length. Sidna peeked through the little hole. He stuck his face so close to the little hole that he thought his eye was going to pop through the other side. He reached over and shook Wesley on the back and whispered.

"Wake up. We've got company."

A tall, thin man in baggy britches that made his legs look like twigs tied his horse to a fencepost and walked up onto Jack's crooked front porch. The man wore a large, brimmed hat and Sidna could not get a good look at the man's face. Sidna watched as the man opened the door and entered holding a basket covered with an embroidered cloth. A few minutes later Jack and the unknown man emerged from the cabin and walked directly toward the small shed where Sidna and Wesley were hiding. Sidna started gathering things and stuffing them in his pack in a panic. Wesley moved to the spot that Sidna had just vacated and stuck his left eye up against the hole.

"It's too late. There's no time to run. We're caught," Wesley said.

Sidna stopped gathering his things and sat there with his pack between his legs. They waited for the door to open. Wesley made a move for the rifles, but Sidna waved his hand and whispered, "No." The door opened and Jack walked inside the shed with a big smile on his face. The unknown man removed his hat and Sidna immediately recognized him as Jacob Boyer, a former sawmill employee.

"Mr. Allen," Jacob said. "It's been a while. I'd ask how you are doing but I know the answer."

"It has been a while," Sidna said. "This is my nephew, Wesley Edwards. How do you know Jack?"

"This is my brother-in-law. Ella Mae is his sister. He came over to check on us and brought us some breakfast," Jack said.

Jacob handed over the basket. Sidna grabbed the corner of the embroidered cloth and his mouth watered when he saw a big jar of pickles, two loafs of bread and four dark-brown pieces of fried chicken.

"It's the least I can do. As good as you were to me all those years at your sawmill. You helped me and my family through some hard times. All that overtime you gave me helped me pay off our farm and go out on my own. I appreciate you always paying a little more than the going rate. Them Baldwin-Felts detectives are riding around tearing up the county looking for y'all. They ain't been over this way yet but I figure it's just a matter of time. People don't much appreciate their tactics. I heard of one account where they raided a farmhouse and beat the farmer. They tore that place apart looking for you and beat the farmer senseless because he wouldn't cooperate." Jacob shook his head in anger. "I've got a plan to fix 'em up good."

"What's your plan?" Sidna asked.

"I'm going to ride into town like my ass is on fire and tell them I saw y'all hiding over on Dick Gwyn's property."

"I remember him. That miserable bastard was one of the meanest I've ever employed. He'd come get his pay from me on payday and not thank me or even look at me in the eye. He'd just spit that nasty tobacco juice on the ground beside of me and snatch his pay."

"Yeah, he died last year but not before he married that second wife of his. She was thirty years younger and quite a looker. I don't know how he pulled that one off. Anyway, I had to work tandem with that miserable bastard for two years and he barely spoke a word to me the whole time," Jacob said as he removed his hat and laughed. "His wife is a piece of work too. Had to be to be married to a son of a bitch like that. I'm going to tell them that I saw y'all over on their property and that I think you are hiding in their barn. Y'all head the opposite way. That ought to throw 'em off your trail for a while.

We'll send them detectives on a wild goose chase around these mountains."

"I don't know. I appreciate the help but I'm not sure it is wise to engage with them that way," Sidna said.

"This could be our chance to get out of the state, Uncle Sid," Wesley said with wide eyes. "Throw them off and make a run for the state line."

"I don't think it is time for us to leave yet. The weather is still too cold, and these wounds need more time to heal before I can go walking twenty miles a day," Sidna said.

The three other men stared silently back at Sidna. His eyes darted back and forth between each of the men as they waited for him to decide.

"Whatever you can do to help is appreciated. When are you planning on executing this plan of yours?" Sidna asked.

"I'm on my way into town right now. Might as well set it in motion. Are y'all ready to move?"

"Sure. We can head the other way from Willis Gap and set up camp back on a mountain somewhere," Sidna said. "You just watch yourself. These aren't men that you want to mess around with."

"I'll watch. Y'all watch out too," Jacob said.

Jacob Boyer left, confident in his plan. Sidna and Wesley dug into the basket of food. Sidna pulled off chunks of the crispy fried chicken and put it between two large slices of bread with a sliced pickle. They ate one whole loaf of bread and saved the rest for dinner. They packed up their gear and headed out just after dark. He didn't know exactly where they would end up, but it would be west, back toward Fancy Gap and away from Willis Gap where the detectives were undoubtedly headed.

THIRTY-THREE

MAUDE

Everything was black and shades of gray. Black veils, long black dresses, and black suits covered in long black coats. The sky and the headstones and the dormant grass all blurred into one shade of gray. A crow flew up into a large oak tree on the edge of the cemetery. Maude stood in the crowded cemetery with her right arm hinged in the crook of her mother's elbow. Her mother sobbed. Her mother had never even met Betty Ayers and was a loose acquaintance with Betty's mother, but she sobbed. Was it selfishness? Was her mother thinking about how she could lose her own daughter, of the same age, who had been so close to one of the men accused of killing Elizabeth Ayers?

They waited in line to pay their respects to the family. The line moved slow, and her mother wept the entire time they waited. As they got closer, she could hear the quiet condolences people expressed to Betty's family: sorry for your loss, let us know if you need anything, she was a fantastic young woman, rejoice because now she is with God. Maude felt awkward when she and her mother stepped to the front of the line. Betty's large family was lined up with solemn looks. She could pick out the mother and father, older, grayer, and shorter than the brothers and sisters and in-laws. A gauntlet of people who had just lost one of their own. And they knew. She could see it in their eyes as she went down the line delicately shaking their hands and offering sorrow for their loss. They knew the man she had been courting participated in the shootout that killed their daughter, their sister. It was then that she grasped why her mother had forced her to go to the funeral. She understood what her mother hadn't said out loud. Look at what the man you love did to that poor girl and her family.

THIRTY-FOUR

PAYNE

Payne headed east at half past two in the morning. Both posses of Baldwin-Felts detectives followed a local guide blindly into the night. Luke joined Payne's team at the request of Thomas Felts. They had received a tip the afternoon before from a local man saying that he'd seen Sidna and Wesley and Claude hiding together on the Gwyn property in a place called Willis Gap. The low rain clouds made the night completely black, and they had to feel their way through the dense mountain forest. The darkness felt like a heavy blanket weighing down on his shoulders. They dismounted after nine miles of hard riding on a small mountain road that was not much wider than a foot trail. They hitched their horses at the end of the road and walked the final mile through the thick underbrush. Payne was glad it was early spring. The forest would have been almost impenetrable in the summer.

They reached the clearing at the edge of the Gwyn property around five in the morning and halted there until half past five. It was still over an hour before sunrise. Payne huddled with his men under the long limbs of a large white pine that provided some shelter from the light drizzle of rain. They huddled together in two inches of standing water under their slickers on the edge of the woods until the eastern sky turned dull gray.

Payne pulled his pocket watch out of his inside coat pocket. He shook it and tiny drops of water sloshed around under the dial. The hands were seized up and the roman numerals were distorted under the fogged-up glass face. Baldwin came up from behind, smiled, and smacked Luke on the back.

"Luke, just a reminder, you and Payne are responsible for covering the north side of the property and clearing the two barns in the middle there. We figure that they will be hiding in one of the barns and not in the main house." Baldwin addressed Luke directly. "You watch for Lee's men. Rush the barns when they start to move. We want one guard stationed at each compass point on the property to stop any escape. Leave one of your men here to watch this side of the pasture."

"We got it," Payne said.

"Payne, I'm counting on your men. This is our best chance yet to get them," Baldwin said.

Payne found himself, once again, preparing to risk his life leading his men across an open field, anticipating violence. This was their chance to bring justice down on these outlaws and get back to their lives away from these miserable mountains. He wanted it to be over and felt giddy with excitement when he thought about how close they finally were to capturing Sidna and his clan. He thought about cornering Sidna by himself in the rickety barn on the other edge of the clearing and bashing in his face, taking out all the frustration and misery that he had felt over the past two weeks. Then he thought about winning a transfer out of the coal mines and into the headquarters in Bluefield with Luke where he would be warm and comfortable and finish out the next decade of his career pushing paper and directing the younger guys out in the field.

Lee Felts' team emerged from the woods on the west side of the pasture. They fanned out and formed a semi-circle around the sturdy-looking two-story farmhouse. Payne jumped out of the dead brush and led his men across the open pasture. He stopped in the middle of the field and gave his men the signal to split. They fanned out around the other side of the house and encircled the compound of buildings trying to close any possible escape routes. Payne and Luke reached the two barns. The barns were surrounded by life. Chickens pecked at the patchy grass. An old milk cow stood still behind a fence with her engorged utter almost touching the ground. Goats and little calves ran up to the corner of the fence as Payne ran by and the guinea fowl started making an awful racket.

Luke and Virgil Gray and Phil Phaup went into the smaller barn and Payne took Elmer Brimm and two other detectives into the larger one. He undid the metal latch on the door, kicked it open, and crept in with his rifle pointed toward the dark back corner. Elmer Brimm and the two others followed and searched the inside of the barn while Payne stayed near the entrance to provide cover. There was no sign of the fugitives. The building looked sparsely used. Payne felt cobwebs stick to his face as he moved inside. Satisfied that the barn was empty, Payne led his men out of the barn. Luke was already out of the smaller barn and started shaking his head indicating that it was all clear. Shouts came from the house followed by the boom of a shotgun. Payne and his men took off running around the back of the barn to the house. Luke sprinted ahead and when Payne rounded the corner of the barn, he saw a woman on the front porch frantically waving a shotgun around at the Baldwin-Felts detectives who were standing in a semicircle around the front yard with their rifles aimed at her.

Payne called out orders to his men, "Brimm, Virgil! Go around the back of the house. Make sure nobody escapes out the back door."

As Payne got closer, he started picking up the conversation between Baldwin and the woman with the shotgun. Baldwin was holding up his hands and he had thrown his rifle down on the ground in front of him while the other men continued to point their guns at the woman. Payne kept the firearm aimed at her torso but there was no way in hell he was pulling the trigger. He had expected an old woman because the property had been described as owned by a widow. To his surprise, she turned out younger.

"Unless you want fifty bullet holes, you better put down that shotgun. Now!" Baldwin shouted.

She complied. The agents were on her as soon as the shotgun fell onto the weathered floorboards of the front porch. One agent straddled her back and pulled her arms around and started tying her wrists together while another agent pressed her face, left cheek down, onto the porch floor.

"Stay on her," Baldwin said. Baldwin crouched down close to her face. "We are here to search for the fugitives of the Hillsville Courthouse shootout. We were given a tip that you may be harboring some of them here. Specifically, Sidna Allen and Wesley Edwards and Claude Allen. You will let us search this farm or there will be consequences," Baldwin explained.

"I don't know what you are talking about. I don't know anything about a shootout in Hillsville," she said.

"What's your name? Are you the daughter? Where is Gwyn's widow?" Baldwin asked. The agent let up on her face and she raised her head to speak.

"I'm Dick Gwyn's wife. My name is Evelyn Gwyn. There ain't nobody here but me and my mother. Y'all just go ahead and get on."

"My name is William Baldwin of the Baldwin-Felts Detective Agency and I'm the law around here now. We have a warrant to search your property for the fugitives of the shootout. We are going to finish searching your property whether you like it or not. We can do this easy, or we can do it hard. I'd prefer the easy way and I bet you do too."

"Go ahead and search the place. All you'll find is a rundown farm that I don't have the money nor help to keep up with," Mrs. Gwyn said.

Baldwin said get her up and two agents escorted Mrs. Gwyn into the house. The detectives had their run of the place and turned over every alcove while the widow and her mother sat around the kitchen table watched over by a ridiculous number of armed men. Payne's instincts told him that she was telling the truth. He left the house and went out onto the quiet front porch. Payne stood on the porch and listened to the robins as they flew around the pasture, picking worms out of the wet ground. The sky had cleared, and Payne moved down to the sunny end of the porch to warm his damp body. He had a bad feeling about this raid and the fact that Mrs. Gwyn didn't know about the search for the Allen Clan. They had been given bad information and purposefully led off course. He wondered how long this search would go on and if his body could withstand the abuse. He closed his eyes, leaned back against the house, stretched his legs out across the porch, and welcomed the impending spring. He sat there for five minutes without interruption and until William Baldwin walked out of the front door, followed by Luke.

"Detective Payne, I think we've been thrown off on purpose. You and Luke take your men and go find the man who gave us this erroneous tip. We can't let the locals lie to us like this," Baldwin said.

"What was his name?" Payne asked.

"Jacob Boyer," Luke said.

Baldwin went back inside. Luke sat down on the edge of the porch, legs dangling off the edge and started rolling a cigarette. Long rays of sunlight beamed through the clouds, illuminating a distant hillside. Payne wanted to stay on the porch and let the sun thaw his weary body.

"This one was a dead end. You ready to move on this next one?" Luke asked.

There was only one answer.

THIRTY-FIVE

PAYNE

"Whoooo, ieeee!"

A long shout carried down from the hillside and echoed through the valley. The calls of warning disturbed the otherwise peaceful valley. Payne's posse cut down the center of the shallow valley that followed along a narrow creek that the locals called Snake Creek. There were no mechanized sounds to drown out the warning calls. No Model T's, no trains, and no engine-powered farm equipment. There was no hiding as they snaked their way through the quiet valley. A lone farmer stood in his open pasture on the gradual incline up the mountain and watched with his rifle barrel propped up on his shoulder, slumped, but strong like a weary soldier. They continued and a single gunshot pierced the air from behind them. They rode deeper into the valley. The local deputy acting as their guide halted the posse before they rounded a curve.

"It's just up there where the creek turns back to the left at the fork in the road," the deputy said.

"Elmer, you go up on the hill above the house and see if you can see anyone being flushed out as we approach the house. You can also give us some cover with your rifle, if necessary. Go now," Payne commanded.

A large-sounding dog started barking from behind the

house as they approached and ruined any chance of sneaking up on the fugitives. Payne dismounted in the tall grass in front of the shack. He snapped open the holster on his hip that held his pistol and shouldered his rifle. The little cabin looked derelict. The steps leading up to the small front porch were warped and the roof over the front porch was held up by two small tree trunks about four or five inches in diameter with rotten bark peeling off.

"You stay here and watch our backs, watch the road," Payne said to the deputy. "You two, Gray, Phaup, go inspect that little barn out back. Luke and I will take the main structure."

Gray and Phaup went around to investigate the little building where the dog was barking in an almost continuous drone. Payne and Luke slowly approached the house and climbed the two rotten steps up onto the warped porch. Payne knocked once and no one answered. He knocked again, louder, and more forcefully. The inside of the house remained silent. Payne knocked again. This time the flimsy door rattled on its hinges when he rapped hard against the edge. Payne acted as if no one was home and kicked in the door. The door flung open and bounced off the interior wall and ricocheted back to its original shut position, almost striking him in the nose as he entered. He continued into the house and Luke followed.

The one-room shack was dark and musty. Payne's eyes adjusted to the dark room. The furniture was rough-cut and homemade. The small wooden chairs still resembled the branches of the trees from which they were sawed off. Luke chuckled from the left side of the room and motioned over to the two lumps in the bed covered up under several layers of frayed patchwork quilts. Luke walked over and poked one of the lumps with his rifle. The man rolled over, snorted, and settled back down into slumber.

"I think we found them," Luke said.

"Drag his ass up," Payne barked.

Payne watched as Luke grabbed the corner of the stained quilt and jerked it off the bed. Dust flew up from the quilt, illuminated by the thin strip of sunlight coming through the small window. The man was wearing a pair of full-body long johns that were tinged yellow with soiled marks where he'd wet himself and then it had dried. The woman was naked.

Payne walked closer to the bed and shouted, "Mr. Akers!"

The man popped up and jumped out of the bed. Payne leveled his pistol and the man tripped on a shoe and fell face down on the dirty floor. The woman stayed in the bed and started rubbing her eyes. She flipped her long stringy hair out of her face and exclaimed, "What the fuck are you?"

She laid her head back on the pillow and went back to sleep as if nothing had happened. Payne and Luke jerked the man up off the floor and dragged him over to the rickety wooden chair. The chair legs wobbled when they sat him down.

Virgil poked his head through the front door. "Ed, Ed! Somebody has been sleeping in the shed. There are two large depressions in the hay inside the shed. There are some dirty plates and cups scattered around with some little wood chips."

"Wood chips?" Payne asked.

"Yes. Little wood shavings. Like somebody's been whittlin' wood."

"Hmm. Alright, head out back and start searching the property for more signs. We will take care of this'n here."

Payne walked over to the scrawny hillbilly slouched in the chair. He covered his nose, trying to diminish the foul smell of the filthy little shack invading his nostrils. Payne could tell that they were both still drunk from the previous night's round.

"We'd a let y'all in if you just knocked," Jack said.

"Tell me where Sidna Allen is, Mr. Akers," Payne said.

"Y'all can call me Jack."

Payne walked over to the bed and covered up the woman. She was back asleep, and he was tired of having to see her boney, wrinkled body. He picked up a jar of clear liquid that was sitting on the floor by the bed. The jar was three quarters empty and Payne lifted the jar and smelled it. The high proof stung his nose, and he poured the contents of the jar onto the floor. He threw the jar across the room, and it shattered into a hundred shards. He leveled his gun at the drunk and cocked the hammer down. Jack laughed. He shoved the barrel under Jack's chin and took the smile off the skinny bastard's face.

"Listen you scrawny, inbred, piece of shit. We know you've been harboring the Allens. We found where they have been sleeping in your filthy barn. How long have they been hiding here?"

Jack didn't answer and Payne put the palm of his large hand on Jack's face, shoved his head back, and removed the pistol from under his chin. Payne walked back over to the woman who was back asleep. He brushed the greasy strings of hair from over her eyes and studied her face. Then he looked back over at Jack and then back at the woman.

"Are you related to her?" Payne asked.

"She's my wife."

"No, I mean blood related. Is she your sister? Aunt? Cousin? All of the aforementioned?"

Jack shook his head to indicate no.

"Just my wife."

"Who's been staying on your property?"

"Just those two old nanny goats that roam around. They like to sleep in there when it gets cold."

"That's bullshit. There are dirty plates and cups and wood

shavings laying around in the outbuilding. You better stop lying to me, or you can get in serious trouble. I'm the law around here right now. The Baldwin-Felts detectives have been deputized to hunt down the Allen Clan. I'll arrest you right now for harboring and aiding fugitives and for possession of illegal liquor."

"Hell, I don't know if anybody's been here. My wife and I are half lit most of the time."

Payne figured that was the first honest thing to come out of the filthy hillbilly's mouth. Physical punishment was not going to get answers and probably would send him back into his deep, drunken slumber.

"I'm going to ask one more time and if you don't tell me the truth then we are going to arrest you and your woman and drag you up to Hillsville to sober up. Who has been staying here with you and where are they?"

No response.

"Alright, we are taking your ass to jail so you can sober up. Then we're putting you through the third degree. Jacob Boyer bellowed like a donkey when we put him through the third degree. He told us you helped Sidna and Wesley. Told us they were here and told us about his dumbass plan to throw us off track. Tell me where they are now, or we'll do the same thing to you."

"What's the third degree?" Jack asked.

"It's a euphemism for torture. We beat you until you start talking," Luke said.

Payne grabbed a rickety ladderback chair, swiveled it around directly in front of Jack, and sat down in it backwards with his chest facing the slats. He perceived a change in Jack's eyes. Fear of being hurt and fear of being thrown in jail had finally settled into his intoxicated brain.

"Why didn't you turn them in? There is a huge reward out for them. You could have changed your life if you had that reward money."

"This is a small community that looks out for their own and they are good people. It didn't even cross my mind to turn 'em in," Jack said.

"Where did they go?" Payne asked.

"Don't know. I didn't talk to them much. They was trying to hide and wanted to keep to themselves."

"Where did you get the moonshine?" Luke asked.

"Dexter Goad."

"Really, Dexter Goad, huh. You expect me to believe that?" Payne said.

"Dexter Goad is where I got it. Been getting' it from him and his people for years," Jack said.

Luke walked out of the shack. Payne stood up and the chair he was sitting in toppled over onto the rotten floorboards. He walked out past the woman who was still passed out on the filthy bed. The deputy was sitting on the porch steps.

"Go in there and arrest both of them for aiding a fugitive and possession of illegal liquor," Luke said.

"You get anything out of him?" the deputy asked.

"He needs to sober up before we interrogate him," Payne said. "Do you know where Dexter Goad's house is?"

"Yes, sir. Just down the creek a piece. He owns over a thousand acres that starts just down the road at the end of this property. His house is the big white one with the black stained fence around it on top of the hill about half a mile down the creek."

Payne looked at Luke. "We might pay him a visit. I'm thinking there might be more to this courthouse dispute than we thought."

Payne and Luke left the deputy and walked around to the back to the shed. The medium-sized brown dog that was strung up between the shack and the shed started barking again. It lunged toward them. The rusty chain stiffened against the pull of the dog and held it back. Payne skirted out of the dogs reach and went into the shed. The shed was maybe five by five and very cramped. The perfect place to hide for a few days. Two nests made of straw were in the corner. One of the nests was full of wood shavings. It looked like someone had been whittling. He stepped back out and the dog growled and lunged at him again. He and Luke walked up the pasture towards Elmer Brimm and the other detectives.

"It looks like we missed them by a day. We found some old tracks leading into the woods up here," Elmer said. "We searched up and down the woods and found two sets of tracks leading up the back pasture and then back down again into the bottom of the valley and disappeared in the creek. Hard to say who made them. Could've been Sidna or Wesley or Claude or just a local who took a meandering walk around the valley the day before."

"Elmer, you take some men downstream to see if they exited anywhere down there. Phaup, you go upstream and check. I'm going to check for tracks that way," Payne said as he looked down the small valley towards Goad's property. "Luke, you're coming with me. This is the second time that Dexter Goad's name has come up. The first was when I was interviewing Floyd Allen's wife. She said that Dexter Goad offered Sidna and Floyd a quid pro quo before the trial."

"A quid pro quo. Really?"

"Well, she didn't say that. I doubt she knows what quid pro quo means. She said that Dexter Goad offered to drop the charges against Floyd and Sidna if they backed him in the next election. She said that Sidna refused. She was earnest about it, and I believed her. That poor woman has been through hell."

"You better be careful going after anyone else other than the ones we're after. Thomas Felts is from around here and he is a republican. While you were out in the field for these past few weeks I was in the headquarters. He knew two of the victims personally, the Commonwealth attorney and the sheriff. Felts is a political supporter of Dexter Goad. He visited Dexter in town right after the shootout."

"Something just feels off. It's a peculiar atrocity. Don't you think?" Payne asked.

Luke shrugged and pulled his cigarette box out of his inside pocket. Payne watched Luke palm a tiny square of tobacco paper in his left hand and sprinkle bits of tobacco inside the paper. Luke rolled it up and licked the seam, lit the end, and stood staring at Payne with the high ridge of barren trees behind him looking intrigued. Payne knew that this was a golden opportunity. This was his chance to prove his worth to the agency and get out of the coal mines for good. There had been an uptick in union activities and the coal companies had increased their efforts to root out the unionizing miners. He could feel a conflict brewing between the coal companies and the miners and he would rather be in the Baldwin-Felts headquarters in Bluefield when the tensions boiled over than in the mines. He was going to try to hunt down these fugitives to the best of his ability and maybe figure out who fired the first shots in the process.

"I'll go with you, but we better tiptoe around Goad," Luke said with the little cigarette hanging out of the left corner of his mouth.

THIRTY-SIX

DEXTER

Every swallow felt like he was consuming fire. Saliva felt like molten lava going down his shredded throat and sometimes, when he couldn't bare the pain, he would let the drool accumulate in his mouth until it dribbled out onto the pillow instead of forcing his mangled neck to swallow. He wasn't quite sure what time of the day it was. The sunlight cast soft shadows through the curtains, and it could have been early morning or late evening. They'd found eleven bullet holes in his clothing and said he was lucky that only four of them entered his flesh. He didn't feel lucky. The worst of the four bullet wounds was the one that went through his left cheek and out the side of his neck, ripping the back button from his collared shirt. His head was wrapped in white bandages that went around his chin and across his neck and up around the top of his head restricting the movement of his jaw. The pain was unbearable without the steady flow of morphine, and it was excruciating when he was caught in the horrible gap between when the last dose wore off and when the next dose kicked in. It hurt to talk. He was forced to communicate using a notepad and wrote down his requests and complaints in almost illegible broken sentences that only his daughter Jezebel could translate. The last dose of pain medicine finally blocked his scorching nerves and he drifted off to sleep again.

Sometime later, there was a knock on the bedroom door. His wife led two men into their bedroom and woke him from the nonsensical morphine dream that his mind was trapped inside. Jezebel got up from one of the chairs in the corner and asked who the two men were. From his position in bed, one of the men appeared abnormally tall and had to duck his head when he walked through the door. The tall man wore baggy dress slacks and a black wool coat with a black fedora on his head. The other man was shorter and had a handsome and welcoming face and wore better-fitting clothes in the same style as the tall man.

"Good afternoon, Mr. Goad. I'm Detective Edwin Payne and this is Detective Hugh Lucas. We work for Baldwin-Felts Detective Agency. We are investigating the courthouse shootout. Do you feel like answering a few questions?"

The tall one spoke in a Yankee accent. The shorter one extended his hand to Jezebel and smiled. Jezebel looked at the floor when she took his hand.

"You can call me Luke. You can call him Payne."

"I'm Jezebel, Mr. Goad's daughter. I don't think he will feel like answering any questions. He is having trouble talking because of the wounds in his cheek and neck."

Dexter tried to talk, but no one in the room understood what he'd said. His butchered neck and the tight bandage made it difficult for him to speak. Jezebel leaned in close, and he spoke again.

"Can they read?" Dexter whispered.

She took the notepad and pen from the nightstand beside the bed and turned back towards the detectives.

"He wants to know if you can read," Jezebel said.

"What?" the tall detective asked.

"Can you read? He can give a written statement."

"Of course, we can read. Can you write?"

Dexter put his weight on his elbows and pushed himself up the headboard to prop up in a reclined position. Jezebel handed him the notepad and pencil. He sat there with pencil in hand, notebook on his lap ready to start the interview. He started writing on the notepad and tore off the top piece of paper and handed it to his daughter.

"It says, 'I will be happy to assist. What are your questions?'" Jezebel said.

One of the detectives walked over and grabbed both sturdy chairs from the corner of the room and pulled them down at the foot of the bed facing Dexter. Jezebel sat on the side of the bed next to Dexter.

"Mr. Goad, I know you have been through hell. I want to commend you for your bravery in the gun battle. You were a hero and never backed down," the handsome detective said.

Dexter smiled and mouthed, "Thank you." He had already forgotten the detective's names.

"Miss Goad, I'm also aware of your heroics. The bravery you displayed by never leaving your father's side and assisting him by reloading his weapon should be commended as well."

Dexter turned to his Jezebel with a look that said, "Accept it as the truth."

They both knew the truth. She hadn't rushed through the gunfire to his aide. She was in the courthouse when the shootout started because she was one of his deputy clerks. She had been inside of his office on the second floor of the courthouse just down the hall from the courtroom. Dexter had made sure that his beloved daughter was not inside of the courtroom when Floyd's guilty verdict was read. He didn't know who started the rumor, maybe someone who witnessed the shootout thought that she helped and told the newspaper reporter or maybe an ambitious newspaper reporter made up the story to make the dramatic news even more sensational for the benefit of his own career. It was a lie, but Dexter was not going to refute the story. The governor's wife had already written Jezebel a letter commending her bravery and had proposed presenting Jezebel with a medal. The recognition could help him politically when he ran for one of the higher state offices. Dexter started writing and handed the notepad to her. Jezebel squinted and struggled to read his response.

"She hasn't left my side since the shootout started. I am proud of her bravery and her love for her father."

"Why did you have a gun in the courtroom?" the tall detective asked.

Dexter started writing and handed the notepad to his daughter. Jezebel hesitated as she tried to decipher his handwriting.

"The judge and William Foster, the Commonwealth's Attorney, received a threat, a note regarding the Floyd Allen case. I didn't write the note. Floyd or one of his kin did, I'm sure. But I did not write the note."

Jezebel stopped reading and looked at Dexter. She leaned closer and whispered in his ear that he wasn't making sense. He shook his head and motioned with his hand to continue. He was making perfect sense.

His daughter continued, "The judge refused to search the occupants of the courtroom before the trial. I wanted to be prepared for the worst. I knew that Floyd was not going to accept the jury's verdict. He is too proud and independent to accept any fate but the one he chooses for himself."

"I know about the note. I found the note on the judge. It was still in his pocket. I never accused you of writing the note," the tall detective said. "Why did you let your daughter go inside the courtroom that morning if you thought there would be violence?"

Dexter started writing again. He handed her another sheet and she crumpled up the previous sheet and placed it on the bed. Dexter watched the tall detective reach over the footboard and grab the crumpled paper. The detective read the discarded note and then stuffed it into his pocket. Dexter thought it was odd that the tall one, he couldn't remember the detective's names, took the note but his daughter started reading and he let it go.

"Jezebel is also one of my deputy clerks. She was in my office down the hall from the courtroom and I told her to stay away but she rushed to my aide when the shooting started," Jezebel read aloud.

The tall detective raised his eyebrows at Jezebel. "You ran towards the sound of gunfire?" he asked.

Dexter felt the morphine dulling his wits, but he had to defend his daughter and keep up the false narrative. He took up the pencil again and began to write. He handed the note to his daughter, and she hesitated before speaking.

"As I said before, my daughter has been by my side since the shootout and her love for me compelled her to come to my aide."

Dexter knew it was a lie, but it had already been printed in several national newspapers. That made it the truth no matter how many witnesses disputed it.

"I have another question for you, Mr. Goad. Did you offer Sidna and Floyd a deal, under the table, to drop all charges against them if they backed you in the next election? Is that true?"

Dexter spoke despite the pain in his neck. "That is a damn

lie. You can't trust any of them. Haven't you figured that out yet? It doesn't matter now."

"What doesn't matter now?" the tall detective asked.

"They are all dead now," Dexter said, through gritted teeth. "She was there. She never left my side. I swear to it."

"He is still on a lot of pain medicine. Sometimes he don't make any sense," Jezebel said.

"Pardon me. I am just trying to put the puzzle together. What deal? What doesn't matter?"

Dexter narrowed his eyes at his daughter. He was making perfect sense, but she just didn't understand. He picked up the pencil again, unable to bear the pain of speaking. He wrote one sentence and handed it back to his daughter, she squinted her eyes and pulled the paper closer and shook her head. He grabbed the paper back from her and flipped it over and tried to write more legibly. He handed it back and she read.

"I thought your job was to hunt down the Allens, not interrogate innocent victims," Jezebel read.

"That is what we are doing right now. We tracked them to one of your neighbor's property, Jack Akers. It looks like they stayed in his shed for a few days. They may still be around here somewhere," the handsome detective said.

"Jack Akers said he bought his blockade whiskey from you," the tall detective said.

Dexter tried to talk but he couldn't bare it and he winced from the pain and placed his hand on his neck. He started writing. Faster this time. He filled up an entire page with rage and passed it to Jezebel. Jezebel read silently and looked back at him. Dexter waved his hand at her to go on, and she read.

"Are you implying that I am involved in illegal whiskey production? That is not true. It is no wonder that you haven't found them yet. Wasting your time on questioning innocent victims. I've never fooled with that despicable enterprise. Jack Akers is a notorious drunkard and loafer who can't pay his debts. I don't associate with his kind."

The detectives whispered something to each other and the handsome one shook his head forcefully, indicating no. The tall detective stood and walked out of the room.

"Thank you for speaking with us. I wish you a speedy recovery."

The handsome one smiled at Jezebel as he walked out of the room. Jezebel stayed seated on the edge of the bed beside of her father.

"Why don't we just tell the truth about where I was?" Jezebel asked.

Dexter picked up the notepad and pencil again. He wrote and his letters ran together in an almost illegible swarm of words.

"I don't know why they think you helped me that day, but we should go with it until they have evidence otherwise, it's been printed now so it is the truth, tale is more powerful than truth, it will not hurt to stretch the truth a little and maybe you can use the story to run for office yourself one day, maybe even be the clerk of the court and follow in my footsteps, telling a little lie to get ahead is worth it in the end, I know it feels wrong at first but trust me, you will forget when you enjoy the rewards."

Dexter finished writing and handed Jezebel the paper. She shook her head and said she couldn't make all of it out. He whispered one last sentence while he scooted back down the headboard into a more comfortable position.

He uttered through the pain, "Call Thomas Felts and tell him what happened here."

THIRTY-SEVEN

SIDNA

They had been hiding on top of Devil's Den for five days. Devil's Den was high up on the spine of the Blue Ridge with spectacular views all around the surrounding countryside. Perfect for waiting and watching. It was the coldest March he could remember, and the cold wind blowing across the mountain set a chill deep in his bones that wouldn't thaw. Wesley was curled up under thick blankets. He shook Wesley on the shoulder and Wesley unfurled out from under the blankets. Their supplies were running low, and Sidna was growing skittish about staying in one place for too long. They packed up and waited for the gray day to fade into grayer night. Before they left the top of the mountain, Sidna climbed through the dark to the pinnacle and looked out to the east toward Willis Gap and then west toward Fancy Gap and farther out to Pipers Gap. It was late evening, and he could see their fires burning. He thought how careless they were, giving away their positions. Every night he could look out across the valleys and hollows below, over towards Pipers Gap to the west and Wards Gap to the east and could pick out five different campfires in five different locations. It gave him hope that he and Wesley and maybe Claude and Friel, wherever they were, could outwit the Baldwin-Felts Detective Agency and escape with their freedom.

They walked off Devil's Den between large rocks and past slanted and stunted trees, permanently taking a stand against the strong winds that blew across the mountaintop. Movement eased his mind and helped him think about their next hiding spot.

"This weather remind you of the Klondike?" Wesley asked.

"This is balmy compared to that icebox. I made it to the Klondike in early spring of 1898, let me tell you, it didn't feel like spring. Felt like the worst winter I've ever lived through, times a hundred. I set out from Skagway towards Lake Bennett in April. There were several occasions when I thought my face would freeze off and my skin would break into icy shards. A lot of men and more horses didn't make it to Lake Bennett."

"Did you find any gold?" Wesley asked.

"None. I met up with Dr. Bolen in Lake Bennett, he was also from Carroll County, and we tried to make something of it, but for all the work that we put into building a cabin and then a boat we did not even get the chance to prospect for gold. We quit. We eventually sold our supplies for two-hundred dollars and took that money and got out of there as fast as we could. We went to the territory of Hawaii, tried to make money speculating real estate but we lost it all and I barely had enough to make it back home."

Sidna spared Wesley the gory details of his experience in the Klondike, like the dozens of frozen bodies and hundreds of dead horses that had lined the sides of the trail from Skagway to Lake Bennett and the frostbite and the horrible realization that there was far more misery there than gold. He made it back home in December of 1898 and swore that he would never leave the blue ridges of his homeland again.

They headed down the mountain in search of provisions. They reached the sawmill sometime after midnight. It was eerily quiet. Sidna was used to the lumberyard buzzing with activity. They stopped at the edge of the lumberyard and hid behind a large stack of red-oak logs and watched for a minute to ensure they were alone. A white piece of cloth hung over the front door of the little office building. Sidna pointed at the white rag and smiled.

"Garland left us a goodie bag."

They sneaked across the lumberyard through frozen mud that was mixed with sawdust. The land rose abruptly behind the office building and several large rocks jutted out of the hillside. Sidna saw an odd patch of disturbed soil that had been dug out and widened between two large rocks. He stuck his hand in between the rocks and felt around. He felt the rough texture of what he thought was a burlap sack and pulled.

"Got it," Sidna said.

"What's in it?" Wesley asked.

"Feels like some canned goods, extra clothes and a newspaper. We'll investigate further once we get back to camp."

They felt their way back up a dark mountainside to the top of a ridge and settled in for the next day or two. They climbed with their ears perked, listening for danger. They had turned nocturnal. Nighttime had always made Sidna uneasy, but he had gradually found comfort in the darkness over the past few weeks in hiding. He embraced the black nights. The things that used to make him nervous became his comfort. A dense thicket with a dark center where he could disappear became his refuge. The eerie silence of the night pierced by the crunching of leaves or the snap of a stick became his alarm bell. The only sounds were the occasional screech of an owl, a dog barking off in the distance, or a bellow from a cow on a farm in the valley below. The bugs and mosquitos and spring peepers were still dormant. The night air was silent, it was still and comforting. The nights were cold, but not unbearably so, and the temperature during the day was ideal for sleeping. They walked during the cold nights to stay warm and to avoid detection. On several occasions when the moon was bright, when they moved across the ridge in the middle of the night along the ridges, he could see his magnificent house on the edge of the rolling plateau. He would think of Bettie and his girls and send his thoughts their way.

THIRTY-EIGHT

PAYNE

Headquarters received a tip from a farmer out in Pipers Gap. The farmer said that he'd found a big bed made up of limbs and brush and pine straw up on the side of a mountain to the west of Pipers Gap. Said it looked like someone had been sleeping there for a while. Baldwin and Luke met Payne's posse in Fancy Gap with a wagon full of field supplies and they set out across the ridge to investigate. Baldwin had hired a local named McPeak with oxen to help ferry supplies across the county. The muddy road out to Pipers Gap was just wide enough for the oxen-driven wagon. The road stretched out over the top of a mountain for about thirty yards before it started bending back down over the other side. At the top, Payne craned his head out over the edge of a cliff. It dropped off sharply six feet from the side of the narrow road straight down over jagged rocks and pointed treetops about two hundred feet below.

"Some call this the jumping-off place. Others call it Lover's Leap," McPeak said. "More than a handful, that I know of, decided they couldn't take this world anymore and ended it right here."

Payne could never make the leap, but he could understand how some people in these hills and hollows could get to that point. The life of toil and misery that these mountain people trudged through day after day had to be more than some could take.

"Hoe!" McPeak shouted in a deep growl.

The two large oxen lumbered to a stop. The wagon was heavy with William Baldwin's camp supplies. The large wagon wheels cut down to the spokes into the rain-softened soil. The wagon driver jumped down from the bench and dug around for something in the back of the wagon underneath the thick canvass. He pulled out a large axe.

"I'm gonna fell this big pine here," McPeak said.

"Why?" Baldwin asked.

"The road down the mountain is too steep and muddy to take it without a stub," McPeak said.

Payne had no clue what the local was talking about. Luke shrugged like he didn't know either. The wagon driver started walking towards a good-sized pine. He took off his wool coat and rolled up his sleeves.

"I'll have to take this prickly pine log and stub it to the back axel. If we take that heavy wagon down this slick mountain it will end up dragging the oxen over the side. The log will dig in and weigh down the wagon and help hold 'em back," McPeak explained.

McPeak started chipping away at the trunk of the tree with long swings of the axe. Payne sat down on a large rock and watched him chop a little notch about one fifth the diameter of the tree. Payne looked up at the treetop. Its long limbs were tangled up with thick branches of the other large trees that grew on the mountaintop. A mix of evergreens and bare trees and weather-beaten dead trees with peeling bark. McPeak chopped for ten minutes. He finally looked satisfied with the notch and walked back to the wagon and pulled out a handsaw and a felling wedge. He started sawing a thin slot on the opposite side of the tree from the notch he had just cut.

"Y'all better watch yourselves. It is going to fall thataway," McPeak said. He pointed down the road toward where the notch was facing.

Payne eyed the notch and then looked up to gauge where it was likely to fall. Luke and William Baldwin moved deep into the woods about fifty yards away. Payne stayed put, satisfied that he was out of the way. McPeak started driving the felling wedge into the slot with the poll end of the axe-head. The tree started to creak and then it cracked loudly and broke right where the notch had been cut. It started to fall exactly where McPeak had intended. But the pine hung up on a large limb of another nearby tree. The large limb broke away from the nearby tree and hit the top of a dead tree and the dead tree started falling in Payne's direction. His eyes widened. Someone yelled and he started running. Limbs popped as they broke free and falling branches brushed against the tree trunks and crashed to the forest floor. Payne tried to run from the heavy noise of the large tree falling toward him. Then he felt a heavy limb crash into the back of his head and right shoulder. The limb tackled him down into the soft layer of decomposing leaves and everything went black.

Next thing he felt was blunt pain emanating from the back of his head. He opened his eyes, and he was on his back lying in the wagon bed on top of Baldwin's canvas tent looking up at the pale sky.

Someone said, "We are getting you some help."

He closed his eyes against the pain. Then, he was being carried by two of his men. One had him under the arms and the other had his ankles, dragging his ass on the ground. They carried him into a dark room and put him on a blanket that had been stretched out across the hard floor beside of a cold hearth.

"The granny yarb will be here soon," said a woman from somewhere in the dark room.

Payne closed his eyes again and thought he was dreaming. What is a granny yarb? His brain couldn't make sense. Was it the mountain accent that he couldn't make sense of or his brain garbling up the words? The woman said it again.

"The yarb doctor will be here soon."

Payne raised his head off the floor and looked around the room. Three shadowy figures stood in the corner.

"Ed. It's Luke. How are you doing, Ed?"

Payne lowered his aching head back onto the floor and closed his eyes.

Sometime later he felt warmth on his forehead. He opened his eyes and the wrinkled face of an old woman stared back.

"That were a lot of blood. It's no problem. Head injuries always bleed out like a water spicket," the old woman said. "Sit up for me and drink this."

She helped him lift his head off the floor and held a small wooden bowl to his lips. He took a small sip. The brown liquid was hot and bitter. Payne curled his lip up at the bitter taste and shook his head.

"Go on. Drink. It'll help you sleep off yer concussion," she said.

Payne raised his head and drank. He held his breath against the taste. The bitter broth coated all his taste buds and infiltrated his nostrils. It woke Payne's battered body and he tried to sit up. Luke stood in the corner with the old woman and two other unidentified people, a man and a woman. The old woman spoke softly with Luke and Luke nodded. Payne let his head turn to the side and rest on the floor. He gazed across the floor toward the people in the corner of the room. The wood floor planks were coated with a white sand. He stared in confusion across the sandy floor like he was stranded on a beach waiting for the tide to carry him away.

"Need to get a fire going," the old woman said.

"I'll go borry some fire," an unknown man said from across the room.

"I have some matches in my pack," Luke said.

"We don't need those. I'll go borry some fire from the neighbors."

The old woman returned, hovered over him, and brushed his forehead with the back of her hand. He wondered if the bizarre scene was real or if his head had been knocked loose. A granny yarb doctor, borrowed fire, and sandy floors. The last thing he heard before he fell back asleep was the cry of a baby and the soft shushes of its mother.

THIRTY-NINE

PAYNE

Payne woke to the shrieks of a crying baby, the smell of coffee and baking bread. He had slept on the floor all night and a sore back now accompanied the pain in his head and shoulder. His ears felt more sensitive than normal, and the screams of the baby pierced his eardrums like thin needles. He stood and tested his balance. He carried his weight surprisingly well and walked across the room making rippled footprints in the white sand that coated the floor. He bent down over the cradle and said *hush*. The baby screamed louder. He had to get out. The bright morning sun hurt his sensitive eyes and when they adjusted, he spotted a young woman pumping water from a well.

"Your baby's crying," Payne said.

"He'll just have to wait," she said.

"Where is your man?" Payne asked,

"He's already left for the day. He's a farmhand for Mister Combs. You hungry?"

Payne didn't answer. He watched her pump the handle of the spicket until the water bubbled up and splashed over the rim of the bucket. The young woman picked up the bucket and started walking back towards the cabin. She leaned to the right against the weight of the water bucket as she walked towards him.

"You need help?" Payne asked.

"I've got it. How are you feeling this morning?"

"Sore."

"Your partner is still asleep over there."

She pointed to a lump of blankets beside of a dead fire about twenty yards away from the cabin. Payne knew it was Luke by the back of his head sticking out from under the blankets.

"Let him sleep a while longer."

Payne followed the young woman back into the cabin. It felt different with her inside, like a gentle light had warmed the dark room. She motioned for him to sit down at the two-seater table. He knew he was sitting in her husband's usual seat and felt strangely comfortable as he watched her move about the room. The baby started crying again. She picked it up and walked towards Payne.

"Hold 'im for a minute."

She handed the bundle of blankets to him. Payne froze with fear. It had been years since he held a baby. The baby was heavier than he expected, and Payne figured it was no older than six months.

"Why do you have white sand covering your floors?"

"It polishes them up real good. Leave the sand on there for a while and the walking on it eventually shines them like you wouldn't believe."

"Hmm," Payne grunted.

She brought him a cup of coffee and a plate with two biscuits and a fat link of sausage. She took the baby and sat down across the little table from him. She unbuttoned the top of her dress and her breast fell out. She offered it to the baby and the little one latched on like a leach. Payne stared at her handsome face and her deep-green eyes. Some part of him felt like he had slipped into the skin of her husband. He should have felt uncomfortable there with the strange woman breastfeeding in front of him, but instead it felt like the home that he had never made. A knock on the door interrupted their queer domestic scene.

"I'll get it," Payne said.

He walked across the sandy floor and opened the door.

"You feeling better?" Luke asked.

Payne nodded.

"Baldwin said if you ever wake up then we are supposed to meet back at headquarters," Luke said.

Payne walked back over to the table. He chugged the warm coffee and stuck the sausage link inside one of the biscuits and gave her the kindest eyes he could make.

"Thank you," Payne said, reaching into his back pocket.

He pulled out a twenty-dollar bill and placed it onto the table.

"We don't need your money."

"I insist."

"Let's go. We have a long walk back over the ridge. You think you can make it?" Luke asked.

"I'm fine."

"That old granny yarb fixed you up, huh. What was that concoction she had you drinking?"

"I don't know. Most bitter thing I ever tasted."

"It knocked you out worse than that tree branch that hit you. I had dinner with that little family while you were unconscious on the floor. Nice people."

Payne didn't respond and they started walking out of the isolated hollow. He turned around when they reached the top of the hill just before the house was out of sight. The little log cabin didn't look like much, but the whole world was inside.

FORTY

SIDNA

They dug into Garland's bag of supplies at first light. Sidna opened two cans of beans and they scarfed them down cold with the two spoons that Sidna had whittled. Wesley went to fetch some water from the small stream that cut down the ridge beside of their camp. When his belly was full, Sidna turned his attention to the newspaper clippings that Garland had included in the sack. Sidna read the articles in disbelief. Wesley returned with the water and Sidna tossed the newspapers over to Wesley. Sidna sat patiently on the ground while Wesley read the articles. Wesley furrowed his brow and jerked his head back.

"The Allen Clan? A clan of ignorant hillbillies who ride shaggy mountain ponies and drink moonshine," Wesley said. "Well, at least they got the moonshine part right."

"I rode one of my finest horses into town on the day of the shootout. I own some of the finest in the county."

"This here says there was another shootout at your house the day after the courthouse."

"Lies and propaganda."

"Did you read the part about Goad's daughter Jezebel?" Sidna asked.

"Uh huh, I don't remember seeing her, but it was chaos."

"That is a load of horseshit. I never saw her with Dexter during the shootout and I would know since he and I were exchanging fire. They are the heroes and we're the villains. People will hesitate to help us with this news in circulation, especially if there are these huge rewards for our capture," Sidna said.

"Saw that too," Wesley said. "Three thousand dollars for us, dead or alive. Old Jack Akers could probably use an extra three thousand."

"Most people around here could."

"It's time, Uncle Sid. You said we were staying here until people knew the truth about what happened. Well, they ain't getting the truth. We can't hide out in drunkard's barns or on mountaintops anymore, people are going to turn on us."

"We are still getting help," Sidna said, pointing to the burlap sack. "I'm not ready to leave yet."

"I'm thinking of trying to visit Maude. I ain't seen her since before the shooting and I want to see her one more time. After that, I'm leaving. We can't stay here anymore."

"What are you going to do? Ask her to join us as fugitives?" Sidna asked. "That won't work either. We just need to keep on hiding and wait for things to shift our way. We have been out here for nigh on three weeks and they haven't even sniffed us yet."

Wesley scowled back and shook his head. Sidna wasn't ready to leave his homeland and he wasn't ready to leave his family.

"Let's get some rest. It's a good day for sleeping," Sidna said.

FORTY-ONE

PAYNE

A strong gust of wind whipped across the hillside where they had set up camp and provisional headquarters. The corners of the cream-colored canvas tent pulled in vain against the thick wooden stakes that fixed it to the dormant earth. The tent was the same kind that General Grant would have been standing beside of in an old Civil War photograph. Baldwin called it his war tent. Payne removed his hat pulled the flap door open and entered. Baldwin was seated behind his wooden folding field desk with Thomas Felts and Luke standing behind him, reviewing a map of the search area and drinking coffee. Thomas Felts walked over to the coffee pot and poured a cup and handed it to Payne. Payne caught a whiff of something rank and then was mortified when he realized it was emanating from him. He'd been living on the horse or in small camps and hadn't washed in several days. His damp, dirty clothes were starting to stick to his clammy body. He nodded in thanks and wrapped his cold hands around the mug and sipped. The hot coffee warmed his insides but didn't stimulate his tired body. He needed sleep.

"How's your head, Payne?" Baldwin asked.

"Fine, sir."

"We have Friel Allen in custody," Felts said. "His daddy Jack

Allen cut a deal with us and handed Friel over. We agreed to be lenient on him."

Felts chuckled like he had just pulled one over on Jack Allen and looked at Payne. "What's the word out there?" Felts asked.

"That's good news about Friel. We came up short again today. No signs and no tips."

"Well, I know you are working hard out there, Ed. They are bouncing around like lizards on a hot rock and we need to change our tactics. Why don't you tell me what happened the other day over in Snake Creek?" Felts asked.

"We found signs of two of the fugitives, probably Sidna and Wesley, in a small shed on Jack Akers property over in Snake Creek Valley. We must have just missed them. The locals in that valley were sounding alarms to each other and that must have spooked them out of their hiding place. We found tracks leading from the shed, across the back pasture that disappeared into the creek. We lost the tracks and couldn't pick 'em back up. We need to regroup and send extra men to search that area more thoroughly."

Thomas Felts looked at Payne but didn't say a word. Then Felts walked over to the window and stared out for a minute. Felts finally turned from the window. Felts carried a perpetual frown at the mouth, and his frown was droopier than usual.

"Is there anything else that you want to tell me?" Felts asked.

"No, sir. I don't think so."

"What about Dexter Goad?" Felts asked.

Payne looked at Luke. Luke shook his head ever so slightly, signaling to Payne that he had not told Felts about visiting Goad's property. Who had? One of the other men in his posse?

Payne saw disappointment in Felts' eyes. "Well. Tell me about what you found at Goad's."

"We didn't find anything on Goad's property. I had a hunch, but we didn't find any sign that the Allens had been there."

"Did you even look for them on Goad's property? And why the hell would they hide on the farm of their bitter enemy. You should know by now that Sidna and his nephews are smarter than that. Goad's daughter called me and told me how you treated him. Said that you were asking him inappropriate questions about a conspiracy that he had tried to buy off Floyd and drop the charges against him if he backed Goad in the next election. Said that you accused him of supporting the illicit liquor trade."

"I didn't inhibit the search for the Allens by taking a detour through Goad's property. I had my men searching around the Akers' house while Luke and I followed my hunch. Floyd Allen's wife said that Dexter offered to drop all the charges against Floyd if he and Sidna backed Dexter in the next election. Then Jack Akers had some moonshine in his little shack and he and his woman were laid up in the bed, still drunk from the night before. I asked him where he got the moonshine and he said he got it from Dexter Goad. I was just doing my due diligence," Payne said.

"Goddamn it, Payne. I'm of a mind to pull your ass right now. You were going off information provided by a drunkard and the wife of Floyd Allen. I thought you were a better detective than that. You need to let it go and focus your energy, and our resources, on tracking down these fugitives. It is not your job to investigate what happened before the shootout and it sure as hell ain't your job to accuse innocent victims of outlandish crimes. Hell, everyone in this whole damn county probably makes moonshine. We aren't here for that. I was shocked when Goad's daughter called me and told me about what happened. Goad is a good man. He is an honest public servant who has sacrificed better opportunities to be a leader in his community. From now on, the only thing I want to hear about your performance is your determination to capture these fugitives. The courts will decide what happened on that tragic day and act accordingly, not us and certainly not you. You understand."

Payne shifted his eyes down to the trampled grass under the tent in deference. He thought about the crumpled note in Dexter Goad's handwriting that he had swiped from Goad's bed. He thought he recognized the handwriting and wondered if it was the same hand that had written Floyd's threat before the trial. Why had Dexter said that he hadn't written the note? No one had suggested or accused Dexter of writing the note. Payne had no other evidence, just a hunch and he wished he had kept the note that he had pulled off the dead judge instead of handing it over to William Baldwin. He stayed silent about his hunch and Felts continued.

"We are desperate for a breakthrough. The longer this thing drags out the worse it makes us look. The national newspapers are portraying them as ignorant, inbred mountain men. If we don't capture them soon then we will look incompetent. People will turn to other agencies in the future. These men aren't stupid. We all know that. People are people no matter where they live. Hell, I grew up not twenty-miles from here and I'm a lawyer and a partner in one of the largest detective agencies in the country," Felts said.

Payne wasn't so sure about Felts' assessment of these mountain people, though his experience recovering in that small cabin had changed his perspective. It wasn't that the locals were stupid or lacked the physical constitution to live a good life. They were backward, uneducated, and accepting of their life of toil when better opportunities and easier ways of life existed outside of their dark mountain hollows.

"You need to change your tactics, Detective Payne. That ride through Snake Creek the other day is the perfect example of what you shouldn't do. We need to break up into smaller groups and move at dawn, dusk, and dark. The Allens have many allies in these mountains, and we need to watch them and avoid detection. They have been moving at night and staying in the dense woods off the main roads during the day. We need to start mirroring their movements and adapt to our quarry. You can't hunt deer in the middle of a hot summer day and right now we are searching at the wrong times and out in the open." Felts paused for a few seconds and looked Payne directly in the eye. "If you don't get this done then I'll remove you and put someone else in your place who will. I'm asking Luke here to ride along with your posse full-time now, as assistance."

Those words hit Payne like a hammer. He tried to keep the anger at bay and calmly walked over to the coffee pot and poured another cup. He wrapped his hands around the cup to warm them and took a long deep breath. The entire search had been hastily put together and they never discussed tactics after that first day when they raided Sidna's property. He was doing the best he could and making the decisions on the spot, in the moment. The thought of going back to the mines in West Virginia was devastating. Baldwin finally looked up from his map, satisfied with the scolding. Payne tempered his mind before he spoke and tried not to complain.

"Sir, you are right that we could have entered that valley more discretely and not raised the alarm of the whole community, but I'm working as hard as...."

Baldwin cut him off. "I'm not trying to send you home,

Payne. I've made mistakes during the past few weeks too. If we don't adapt and learn from our mistakes, then we'll never accomplish our goal here. I think that you and Luke will complement each other and make progress. You need some rest and a hot bath. You look like death and smell worse. I appreciate your dedication to apprehending these slippery bastards. We just received a credible tip on the whereabouts of Claude Allen. You and Luke are going to investigate. Your team will stay up here and spread out. You two will leave at dawn. Go get yourself cleaned up and get some rest. Luke and I are going to discuss some new strategies," Baldwin said.

"Yes, sir," Payne said.

Payne retreated to his small tent. He removed his damp, mud-encrusted clothes and washed his body with a dirty rag in the cold water from the wash bucket. He sunk down into his cot and fell asleep when his head hit the pillow.

FORTY-TWO

SIDNA

The valley below echoed with life. The sound of an axe felling a tree. Shouts from teamsters driving their horses and farmers plowing the land. Sidna wanted to join them and take a swing with the axe, plow the land, and drive the wagon home for supper. The idleness was starting to drive him mad. He was a doer and had always stayed busy working on his farm, in his general store, or managing his sawmill. Life on the run was hours of unbearable boredom mixed with fleeting moments of intense anxiety.

"I'm going to go check our trap," Sidna said. "It'd be nice to have something in our bellies tonight."

"Alright. I might not be here when you get back," Wesley said.

"What? Where are you going?" Sidna asked.

"I'm going down to visit Maude tonight. I have to see her. I'll be back before dawn. Maybe I can get some food from her while I'm down there."

"We can't go off and visit people right now. Don't you think I want to see my family? They probably have Maude's house under surveillance, you are risking getting caught if you go down there."

"I know but I have to go see her. I need to let her know that

I didn't plan this and I'm not a murderer. I want to go tell her that I love her and that I want to make her my wife."

"You go on then, do whatever the hell you want. I'm tired of it. I am going over to check the trap."

He was tired of convincing Wesley not to do stupid things and worrying about his reckless inclinations. Sidna walked down the ridge to where he set the trap the night before. His stomach felt hollow, he hadn't eaten all day. They had consumed all the food from Garland's supplies. He had spent part of the day foraging for ramps and morels and found enough for a nice pot of soup. He despised ramps, the overwhelming garlic-onion flavor had always upset his stomach, but his mouth watered thinking about hot soup. The soup would be even better with some meat. Wesley had wanted to fire off a few rifle rounds at the squirrels they had seen jumping from limb to limb and scrambling up the large oak and chestnut trees that grew on the ridge. He had to convince Wesley that shooting their rifles that close to dark was a bad idea and might attract unwanted attention.

Sidna had set the trap along a small game trail in the brush. It was a primitive fall trap with some nuts on the ground underneath a flat rock propped up by a small twig. Something had triggered the trap, but it was empty and the bait, a handful of peanuts he'd saved from Garland's rations, was gone. He inspected the trap and figured that his trigger wasn't sensitive enough. He reached into his bag and placed a few more nuts on the ground under the rock and used a flimsier stick to prop up the rock. He had to fiddle with it several times before the little twig finally held the rock in place. He walked slowly up the mountainside back to camp when he was satisfied with the reloaded trap.

FORTY-THREE

SIDNA

Sidna woke up hungry in the middle of the afternoon. He hadn't eaten anything besides ramp and mushroom soup in two days. It was enough to sustain him. He needed protein and fat to maintain his strength. He had saved some soup for Wesley, but decided to go ahead and eat it himself. He couldn't stand the thought of choking down the cold ramp soup, but it was too much of a risk to start a fire in the middle of the day. Someone could see the smoke in his random section of forest and decide to investigate. He heard a crack in the woods up on the ridge above the camp. His heart spiked and he reached for his rifle. Wesley emerged from the forest.

"You scared me."

"Sorry."

"You want some soup?" Sidna asked.

Wesley appeared haggard and there was a despair in his eyes that wasn't there before. Sidna offered him the soup.

"Thanks, I'm starving."

"Did you talk to Maude?" Sidna asked.

Wesley shook his head and finished the soup. Then he started talking.

"I got close, probably within a hundred yards of the house. I sat there for a few hours and waited for the right time. I saw two men loafing around in the field by themselves. At first, I thought they were just farmworkers, then I looked closer, through your binoculars, and noticed that they had rifles. I think they were Baldwin-Felts but they weren't dressed like 'em. They were dressed like local farmworkers. I waited on the edge of the farm until sometime after midnight. The two men stayed out in the field and their fire burned almost all night. I thought about going for it, throwing rocks at her window or something, thought about whispering her name beneath her window and thought about searching their barn for a ladder and climbing up to her window, but I couldn't get up the nerve. I stayed there all night and hoped that maybe she would go outside by herself to check on the chickens or start her chores early, but she never did and the two men in the field started stirring soon after daybreak, so I left. I had to cross back over Mount Airy Road to get back up here and damned if there weren't two more men riding down the road at about the same time. I almost ran into them. I hid up in some brush and watched them ride by. They were just joking and laughing and taking a leisurely ride, but I'm pretty sure they were with Baldwin-Felts. They didn't sound like locals. They ain't riding through like Sherman's army anymore. They are spreading out and covering more ground. It's time, Uncle Sid. If there ever was a time, it is now. We've overstayed our welcome here."

Sidna thought that was probably the most words Wesley had spoken at once since they had been in hiding. He was glad Wesley returned safe and he agreed with Wesley. He was starting to notice a change in the search party's tactics as well. During the first few weeks after the shootout the detectives were easy to avoid. They only traveled during the day and searched in large groups and stayed on the dirt roads and horse trails that Sidna and Wesley knew to avoid. At night, he could see their campfires burning in the distance, giving away their locations. On their marches through the low valleys the detectives would occasionally stop and pose for photographs to document their great search party, posing atop their horses with their rifles held up in the air, crouched on the ground, lined up, side by side like they were posing for a family photo or a class picture. He figured that Wesley was right, it was time to leave their homeland before it was too late.

FORTY-FOUR

PAYNE

The house was exactly as the courier had described in the notes. An old farmhouse that was once white but the horizontal wood planks had grayed over, and patches of green mildew grew on the siding near the ground. A limestone wall ran along the road beside of a creek with about twenty head of cattle grazing on the other side. The house was in the middle of the pasture surrounded by a stacked split-rail fence laid out in a zigzag pattern. Payne and Luke had been watching the house since before dawn, waiting at the edge of a small grove of pine trees. A courier had relayed an anonymous tip on the whereabouts of Claude Allen. The tip claimed that Claude Allen was getting help from a man named John Easter below the mountain in Tolbert Village.

"Let's move and check if anyone is home. We've waited long enough," Payne said.

They jumped both fences and approached from the right side of the house.

"You knock and I'll take a look around the other side," Payne said.

Payne walked to the other side of the house. Fresh boot tracks led from the back porch to the shed just over the fence. He shuffled back over the split-rail fence that separated the yard from the pasture and jogged over to the shed. He softly swung the door open. The door creaked and popped with age. He shoved his rifle in and wondered if Claude Allen was sitting there waiting with his own gun pointing back. The shed was empty. He followed the same tracks around the side of the barn and behind the fence around to the shed where the boot tracks turned to horse tracks. From there the horse tracks went over the back pasture and back into the road about a quarter of a mile from the house. Payne walked back to the house to check on Luke.

"You find anything?" Luke asked.

"Found some horse tracks leading back to the road. They look fresh from this morning. You?"

"Nobody's home. How did we miss them?" Luke asked.

"They must have gone out the back before daylight. Let's get on these tracks and see where they lead," Payne said.

They followed on foot for a quarter mile and then a man on horseback came around the curve about fifty yards ahead of them. He had a bushy gray beard that hung down past his collar. He was short and pudgy but stout-looking like an old bear. The man immediately pulled his horse to a stop and then slowly turned in the saddle to look back the way he'd came. Payne unholstered his pistol.

"Where you headed?" Luke asked.

The unknown man hesitated and fidgeted with both hands on the western saddle horn. His expression was one of guilt. He was hiding something. Luke nodded and flanked the unknown man.

"I'm headed back home."

"Where is your house?" Luke asked.

"Up yonder," he said pointing back to where Payne and Luke had just been.

"Are you John Easter?" Luke asked.

The man pursed his lips together, let out a huff through his nose.

"Yes."

"Why don't you come on down from there?" Payne asked as he pointed his pistol up at him.

"Where are you coming from?" Luke asked.

"I was just up at my daddy's place helping him with some chores."

"What kind of chores were you doing?" Payne asked. "You look too clean to have been doing farm chores."

Easter didn't answer.

"Can they corroborate your whereabouts?" Luke asked.

"Huh?"

"Would they tell us that you were there if we ask them?" Payne asked.

Easter hesitated and said, "Yes, sir."

"We know that you are harboring Claude Allen. Where is he?" Payne asked. "I'm going to ask you one more time. Where is Claude hiding? We are going to find him one way or another and if you refuse to cooperate then you will be prosecuted for aiding a fugitive."

Easter didn't answer. His silence indicated to Payne that they were getting close to Claude, maybe Sidna and Wesley too. They handcuffed Easter and tied him around the trunk of a tall tulip poplar that was off the road amongst taller pine trees. They tethered Easter's horse to Payne's and followed his clearly visible tracks back down the narrow mountain road for about a mile until the tracks turned off into an open meadow with another rock wall separating the road and the meadow. The rock wall appeared to stretch on forever as it climbed up a hill and back down out of sight. Each limestone perfectly placed amongst the others in varying shapes and sizes held together with dark-gray mortar. The tracks from Easter's horse stopped at the edge of the rock wall and his boot tracks started from there and appeared to trail straight across the meadow and up into dense woods on the other side.

Payne and Luke crawled about a hundred yards behind the long wall to conceal themselves from the dense forest on the other side of the meadow. At the halfway point, they came to a spot where a long perpendicular line of white pines intersected with the wall. They climbed over the wall and moved slowly through the line of pines until they had a good view of the meadow. They waited and watched, concealed in the limbs and soft needles of the white pines. Payne took the first watch. Luke napped.

An hour passed, and a tall young man emerged from the woods a hundred yards away on the other side of the field. Payne tapped Luke on the shoulder. Luke jumped awake and Payne placed his left index finger over his mouth and pointed toward the meadow with the other hand. The man had a small jug in his hand and walked down a hill towards a low spot and knelt at an old spring box and filled the jug and then walked back up the hill and vanished into the thick trees.

"That might be Claude," Luke whispered.

"I think it is. We need to move quickly. Let's pinch him in. You continue up this line of trees into the woods. I'll double back down to where we left our horses and go around into the other side of those woods," Payne said.

"Meet you in the middle," Luke said.

Payne walked back down through the pines to the road and crawled behind the wall to another strand of trees that led up to the woods where they had seen the young man. He slowly started making his way through the dense forest. About a hundred yards into the forest, Payne heard a branch snap twenty yards in front of him. He couldn't tell if it was Luke or the man they were tracking. The sound of crunching leaves carried down the hill and movement flashed in the corner of his vision. The dark silhouette of a man stalked through the thick laurel bushes down the hill. The man moved down toward the edge of the meadow, but Payne couldn't tell if it was Luke or their quarry. Payne leveled his gun at the man's shoulder and waited for him to clear past the thicket of limbs. He heard Luke shout, "Put them up quick," and Luke emerged from behind the bushes in the sights of Payne's rifle.

"I've got them up," someone shouted.

"Are you Claude Allen?" Luke asked.

"Yes."

Payne shouted through the bushes, "I'm coming down on your left side, Luke."

Luke kept his rifle pointed at Claude and Payne walked down and handcuffed him. Claude's face was smudged with dirt and his thin body hid under several layers of pants and shirts covered by a thick wool coat. Claude had two pistols on him, a .38 hammerless Smith & Wesson and a .38 Colt with enough cartridges to arm Payne's posse. Claude had a little hideout in a small depression amongst some laurel roots that he had covered with a brown rain slicker and lined with pine limbs and quilts. Payne searched the hole and found eighty-three dollars and a nice gold watch and enough bread and meat to sustain a man for several days.

"You get this food from John Easter?" Payne asked.

"Yes," Claude admitted.

"Where'd you get the money?" Luke asked.

"From my momma."

They escorted Claude back down to where they left their

horses. Claude's hands were cuffed behind his back and Payne helped Claude up onto John Easter's horse. Payne and Luke mounted their horses and put the confiscated horse with Claude atop between them and tied all three horses together.

"We can't forget about our friend tied up to the tree," Luke said.

"I'd forgotten about the fellow," Payne said with a chuckle. "I was thinking about that reward money."

"I don't think that applies to us," Luke said.

Payne and Luke exchanged satisfied smiles.

"Can we stop by my momma's house?" Claude asked. "It's on the way to Hillsville."

"Boy, I can't bear a scene like that. I'm weary enough as it is," Payne said.

FORTY-FIVE

SIDNA

Hunger drove them back to civilization. They walked down the mountain just after sunset and followed along the roadside back down the narrow valley and west towards Fancy Gap. The fog was starting to rise from the ground like the clouds had been turned upside down. They stayed off the road and pushed their way through the brush and thick woods that ran parallel with the road for two miles. They moved slow through the brush and over rotting tree trunks and uneven roots and rocks slick with moss. The narrow road ended perpendicular to a larger road that ran east to west towards Fancy Gap. The larger road was more exposed. It was surrounded by open grazing land that was flatter and dotted with patches of trees and the sawmill he owned with Garland was on the other side of the open pasture.

"We're getting close, ain't we?" Wesley asked.

"I think it's just across that pasture and behind that stand of pines," Sidna said.

"I hope Garland has left us some good stuff," Wesley said.

"Me too," Sidna said.

They ran across the lumberyard and behind the shed that he and Garland used as an office where the provisions had previously been hidden.

"Shit. I don't see anything," Sidna said. "It's empty."

"Maybe he put it somewhere else nearby," Wesley said.

"I don't think so. This is the spot we agreed upon and this is where he left the last bag of supplies."

"I'm going to go look around," Wesley said.

"Alright."

Wesley disappeared into the fog and Sidna sat down on the cold, damp ground and contemplated their next move. He had plenty of money in his pocket and he was prepared to pay for his food and supplies if he could find someone to help. He knew several people in the vicinity and was related to some of them. He had employed many of them in his sawmill and many more of them had been patrons at his store at one time or another. He ran those acquaintances through his mind and then he knew their next destination.

FORTY-SIX

SIDNA

They crept up on Sugar Smith's property just after midnight. Sugar Smith's house was just twenty feet off the road and his small general store was across the road from the house. It was a two-story house with fresh white-wood siding that shone in the fog-scattered moonlight. The roof had two small dormers over the stone wrapped front porch. The fog formed a dense overlay that thickened the night air. The visibility continued to decline as the fog gathered and he felt safe behind its pillowed walls so thick like he could reach out and grab a clump of it in his hand.

"Why don't we just break in? Nobody would catch us this time of night. We're already wanted for murder. Getting charged for robbery won't make no difference," Wesley said.

Sidna thought on that idea. They might be able to get away with stealing only a few items that Sugar would never notice were missing. Sugar didn't run a very tight ship. His shelves were perpetually half stocked. He'd often wondered if Sugar was lazy or stupid. Maybe both. Those qualities were often packaged together and complemented each other quite well in some people. Sugar had visited Sidna's store several times over the years asking for excess stock of this or that and Sidna had always obliged him, but not before asking a slightly higher price than wholesale. Sidna hoped that Sugar would reciprocate the favors and sell him some food and supplies.

"I don't want to be known as a criminal," Sidna whispered. "We need to keep the local people on our side if we want to have a chance to escape. If we break in, then when Sugar sees it in the morning you know who they will blame it on."

"Us," Wesley said.

"Yes. Then the detectives would know our whereabouts and the locals would turn against us," Sidna said. "We need to be smart."

"Do you trust him to not turn us in?"

"I think so."

"Alright. Let's go wake him up and see."

Sidna and Wesley crept across the road and up to the house and knocked. Sugar's wife answered the door. Sidna thought it odd. If someone knocked on his door this early in the morning, he would not send Bettie down to check on who it was. He would have also brought a gun with him that time of night, but Sugar's wife wasn't armed. She rubbed the sleep from her eyes. Sidna removed his hat.

"Hello, Mrs. Smith?" Sidna asked with a wide smile.

"Yes," she said while blinking slowly.

"Mrs. Smith, I am Sidna Allen. This is my nephew, Wesley Edwards."

Her eyes widened and she stood there speechless. Then she shut the door in their faces and Sidna could hear one lock close on the other side of the door, then another lock latched shut at the top of the door. Wesley started to walk down the steps, but Sidna stopped him.

"Wait. Maybe she will send her old man down next," Sidna said.

He knocked on the door again. Two rounds of knocking

later and Sidna could hear someone fiddling with the locks on the inside of the door. The door finally cracked opened and this time it was Sugar standing there with a shotgun pointed through the crack. Sugar pushed the double barrels farther up through the cracked door and almost touched Sidna's chest with the barrel.

"Sidna. What are you doing here?" Sugar asked.

Sidna hadn't seen Sugar in two years. Sugar's hair had gotten grayer and somehow Sugar had gotten shorter. Sugar had always made Sidna feel large and Sugar looked smaller than ever hunched over in the doorway. Sidna looked down the barrel of the shotgun that equalized the size difference between himself and Sugar.

"I need your help, Sugar. I'm looking to buy some food and supplies. Can you please open up your store and help me out?" Sidna asked.

"I don't have anything in stock right now," Sugar said with the shotgun still pointed at Sidna's chest. "You know, two of them detectives were just here this evening. You just missed them."

"No shit?" Wesley asked.

"No shit. They have been searching over this way for you. They cleaned out my stock too. I don't have anything left," Sugar said.

"You got anything in your house?" Sidna asked. "I'd pay you for any food that you have. I've helped you out several times when you were out of stock. I've never asked for anything in return from you and never intended too, until now."

"I'm sorry, Sidna. I can't help you. You get on now."

"After all of those times I helped you. You are just going to leave me out on my own?"

"I'm sorry. I can't."

Sugar cocked the twelve-gage double barrel and motioned it up toward Sidna's head. Sidna backed down the steps and heard Wesley running back across the road and into the high grass. Sugar shut the door before Sidna could get out another word. Sidna wanted to say *wait* but the word didn't come out. He walked back across the road and sat down on the edge of the dirt facing the ditch and the weeds where Wesley was hiding.

"We should have just broken in," Wesley said.

"I don't want to rob our neighbors. If we start doing things like that then we are nothing more than the criminals that they think we are. We aren't criminals," Sidna said.

Sidna sat there on the edge of the road thinking about where to go next. A noise behind them broke the silence. Sidna held his breath, fixed his eyes on one point on the ground and listened. Then the heavy huff of a horse cut through the fog and the sound of its hooves got closer. The horse emerged from the fog with Sugar Smith in the saddle. Sidna made eye contact with Sugar before the horse vanished back into the fog. Sidna knew where Sugar was headed.

FORTY-SEVEN

SIDNA

Bloodhounds bayed in the distance. It sounded like a whole team of bloodhounds fixed on a scent, his scent. The sound of the dogs terrified him. Their doleful howl and the knowledge that they were after him stiffened the hairs on the back of his neck and heightened all his senses. He stopped scrambling up the wooded slope, turned his head back and listened to gage how far away the dogs were. The fog rolled by and Sidna could make out the individual water particles as they floated past him. It scattered and softened the early-morning sunlight. He couldn't see more than twenty feet in any direction. He reached down and grabbed a few dead leaves from the forest floor, raised his hand high, and let go of the leaves. The leaves fell straight at first but then the wind caught them and blew the leaves away from his hand and into Wesley's face toward the direction of the howling hounds.

"We've got to get downwind from those dogs and we have to get as much distance between us and them as possible," Sidna whispered. "Let's quietly move across this hill on their right flank and get behind them. They won't see us in this fog unless we run straight into them. Don't make any loud noises while we are getting behind them. Try not to leave any tracks. Step on rocks and roots, anything but bare ground. Once we are downwind from them then we run and get as much distance between us and them as we can."

"Won't the dogs smell us if we get too close while we are going around?" Wesley asked.

"Maybe. But we've got to get downwind or they will smell us. The dogs are only as good as their handler. Just like hunting with a bird dog or a coon dog. The handler does most of the tracking and looking for signs to send the dogs after. Let's try to eliminate the dogs and hope the fog conceals us and our tracks from the handlers."

"How do you know about bloodhounds?" Wesley asked.

"I don't. I'm just guessing based on how I handle my hunting dogs. It's basically the same, right?"

Wesley bobbed his head in acknowledgement and took a long swig of water from his canteen.

"Take off your shoes and socks," Sidna whispered.

Wesley gave him a look of uncertainty.

"We can't outrun these dogs. Walk like me. Trust me. No snapping sticks, not tripping over rocks or crunching leaves. Let's move," Sidna whispered.

Sidna took off his boots and his thick wool socks. He started walking like a cat stalking prey. He bent his knees and gently put one foot down at a time. First, he placed the outer ball of one foot down and then rolled the rest of his foot onto the ground, placing his heel on the ground last. Then repeated this one foot at a time until they crept down around the side of the mountain above the barking dogs. They eased through the woods across the hillside. The dogs were getting closer. Sidna started to hear the shouts of the search party. As they closed the gap between the search party and themselves, Sidna began to second guess his decision to flank them. They were getting too close and risked the dogs picking up their scent.

He stopped and froze his body mid stride to listen. He could make out the voices. The voices were closer than he'd expected them to be. The detectives weren't trying to conceal their whereabouts. They were tearing a path through these woods just like they'd done for their entire search. He figured that the dogs were making them overconfident, and they had abandoned other, more discreet strategies.

Then a man shouted from somewhere up the hollow. "Payne. You take two men and go along our right and scout the hill. We'll meet you at the top where this hill meets the other hill. Shout if you see any signs and we'll send the dogs your way."

The voices were no more than fifty yards away. Sidna could see the fear churning in Wesley's eyes. Sidna pointed higher up the hill and they started to move slowly up the hill and away from the voices. This is where they were going to get captured and he silently cursed himself for trusting Sugar Smith. They moved a little, stopped and listened and moved again. The sound of the dogs got farther up the holler and the wind shifted. They moved a little farther up the hill and a large chestnut tree emerged from the fog. The tree was one of the biggest he'd ever seen and both he and Wesley could easily hide behind the trunk. They stopped and rested behind the girth of the chestnut tree and listened. He removed the rifle that he'd had slung around his back. Leaves and sticks crunched and snapped down the hill and the detectives got closer. He could hear them moving up the hill and around to their left. He and Wesley quietly shifted behind the tree to keep the trunk between themselves and the detectives.

Then someone spoke from down on their right side. "I don't see any sign of them."

Another voice pierced the fog to their left. "I don't either.

Let's keep on moving up this ridge and meet back up with Lee's team."

"Alright. I can't see for shit in this damn fog."

Sidna held his breath and tensed every muscle trying to keep still. He held the rifle tight to his chest with the barrel pointed up, pressed against his nose. He didn't want to use the gun, but he steeled his mind for the possibility. He heard shuffling of leaves and footsteps winding through the forest for another few minutes and then, gradually, the sounds moved farther away until the only sound was Wesley trying to slow his breath. They were alone again. Then they put their boots on and ran. They ran down through a creek and up another hill and over the top of that one and down through Levering's orchard. He called on the last reserves saved up from his former life of abundance. His lungs burned and the right side of his abdomen started hurting. The bullet wound in his back, which had almost healed, started pulsing with pain again. The lead still embedded in his left oblique, he figured it would be lodged there forever as a remnant of the terrible violence that he had participated in. They ran through the pasture, concealed by the fog. He pushed himself forward and fought through the pain. Wesley led the way. His younger legs pushed farther and faster than Sidna's. Wesley reached the edge of the pasture and stopped to wait for Sidna at the next patch of trees.

"Which way now?" Wesley asked.

Sidna tried to speak but his lungs stopped him as he fought to catch his breath. He pointed up through the woods and bent over with his hands on his knees. He caught his breath while Wesley scanned the pasture for signs of people. They had been running for twenty minutes and Sidna thought they had covered two miles since they lost the detectives. During those two miles, he decided that they had to leave Virginia.

"Give me some of that water now," Sidna said, gasping for air.

"We have a bit farther before we get to the gap. Let's keep going. You can make it, Uncle Sid. I'll carry you if I have to."

"No. I'm tired of this. Tired of hiding and running and living off other's charity. We have to leave Virginia," Sidna said.

"I've been thinking that for weeks. We can't keep this up," Wesley said. "I think Carolina is that way." He pointed to what Sidna also assumed was South. "If we leave now then we can be down the mountain by the afternoon. We need to move now before the fog burns off."

It was time. He would disappear in the vastness of the west and resurface in another climate as another man. He had built a prosperous life for himself by sheer force of will and he could do it again. He would do it again. They started walking and they were down the mountain and into Carolina before sunset. They kept walking through the darkest part of the night with all their senses firing. By the time the sky brightened on the next day, they had walked twenty or thirty miles. They decided to stop and rest for the day in a large stand of thick pines in a secluded area a hundred yards from the road.

The mountains of Virginia towered over the bottomland. He could see the crest of the Blue Ridge through the gaps in the pine grove that concealed his hiding place. The mountains stood like a great wall separating him from his family and from his culture. He didn't know if he would ever cross over that great barrier again. He didn't know when he would see his wife and daughters again. Tears welled up in his eyes and he let them flow down his cheeks and onto his dirty coat. He longed to hear his daughters' laughter and uncontrollable giggles as he tickled their bellies and chased them around the house. What kind of women would they become? They would be shaped by the mountain culture that they lived within. He wondered if he would ever live within that culture again. Even if he did return, the culture would change and leave him behind. He feared that their culture, his culture, would fade away forever once they discovered the wonders of the world beyond their mountains. Once he had succumbed to that same desire for the modern world. He left seeking his fortune in the Klondike gold rush as a naïve mountain boy and the wonders of the world opened his eyes. He came back a changed man. He wanted indoor plumbing and electric lights and all the new conveniences of the modern world. His new house was a marvel compared to the homes of his friends, family and customers. Others would want it too. It was just a matter of time, maybe twenty years, maybe fifty, maybe a hundred, he didn't know when but one day his mountain culture would be emulsified into the bland broth of the country, lost forever. He grieved the loss of his family, his home, and the culture he may never dwell in again.

FORTY-EIGHT

SIDNA

They rested for most of the day, waiting for the security of the night before they started walking again. The climate below the mountain was a few degrees warmer. Spring was nearing full bloom. The buds on the trees were bursting into tiny, bright green leaves that were ready to spread open and capture the warm spring sun. They foraged for more ramps and mushrooms and dandelion greens. Sidna sent Wesley out to find a large flat rock for digging. Wesley returned with a flat rock about the size of the end of a large shovel. Sidna asked him to start digging a rectangular hole. After a while, Sidna took the flat rock from Wesley and finished digging.

Sidna stopped digging when the hole was five feet wide and half a foot deep. It was the best they could do with their limited tools. He spread out one of the old dirty quilts that they had been using to keep warm. He placed his two rifles in the middle of the quilt and folded the quilt around the weapons. He'd taken much pride in those guns. He'd hoped to pass those guns down to his grandchildren. Now he'd lay them to rest in the soggy North Carolina soil and try to leave behind all the violence and turmoil that men wrought with those loathsome tools. Sidna cradled the quilt of guns in his arms and placed them in the brown dirt. He used the rock to push the dirt over the quilt and then patted it down with his feet. He gathered some dead branches, small rocks, and several handfuls of pine needles and covered the disturbed ground until it appeared natural again. He marked the spot in his memory, just in case he ever made it back, about one hundred yards to the east of the main road and about five miles north of Mount Airy. He wasn't sure that he ever wanted to return to dig up those guns that he had once considered some of his prized possessions. Now they were nothing more than hollow instruments of destruction that had accompanied his downfall. He knew that in this country it was impossible to live a life without the secure burden of guns, especially while being a fugitive, but he wanted to try.

"We better get some good rest today," Sidna said. "We've got a long walk ahead of us. We can't take the train out of Mount Airy. It is too close to home and too risky to step foot in that city. We are going to have to walk to Winston."

"How far is it?" Wesley asked.

"'Bout fifty miles."

"At least it's the piedmont. Should be some good flatland for walking through," Wesley said.

"Let's get some rest before we start walking," Sidna said.

Sidna settled down on his back with his head resting on his pack and covered his face with his hat. The high sun was just starting to hit its peak for the day. It warmed him through to the bone.

FORTY-EIGHT

MAUDE

Maude stared out of the window above the kitchen sink with a rag in her right hand and her left hand submerged in the hot soapy water searching for the next dirty dish. Her mother swept the day's dirt from around her feet and her sister was out back tending the chickens. There was a knock on the front door and then the voice of an unknown man talking to her father. She didn't pay it much mind and thought it was just one of her father's friends coming around for a chat. The low pitch of the man's voice carried down the hallway and through the gap around the kitchen door. The voices stopped and she heard footsteps down the hall. Her father opened the door.

"Maude, there are some men here that want to ask you a few questions about Wesley. Can you please join us in the front room?"

She grabbed the dishcloth and started drying her hands as she walked through the door and into the front room. The man had a friendly face and the nicest-looking suit she had ever seen.

"Miss Iroler, my name is Dan Baldwin. I'm the Founder and President of the Baldwin-Felts Detective Agency. I'd like to ask you a few questions about your sweetheart, Wesley Edwards."

That was the first time anybody had called Wesley her

sweetheart and she balked at the suggestion. They weren't really sweethearts. There had been a spark with Wesley, but it hadn't been cultivated and had fizzled down into a dying ember. She hadn't seen Wesley since before the shootout. She would lie awake most nights thinking about him and what he had done, trying to resolve the feelings for him against the violent act that he had participated in. It was hard to reconcile after the misery she had witnessed at Betty Ayers' funeral, and she didn't know if she loved Wesley anymore. She almost blurted out, "He's not my sweetheart."

"When was the last time you saw Wesley Edwards?" Baldwin asked.

"A few weeks before the shootout. He came to visit me on the farm after he got out of jail."

"You haven't seen him since the incident?"

"No."

"How would you describe your relationship with him? Did you intend to marry him before this incident?"

"We're friends and he was trying to court me."

Maude's father spoke up. "She never considered it seriously. He came here to call on her one day back in the winter, but I ran him off. She has several suiters and I'd say that Wesley Edwards was never considered a serious candidate. There is a fine man from just down the road named Ken Marsh who has come calling for her several times. He's from a prosperous family and has made it known that he is interested in Maude."

The detective stared at her like he was waiting for her reaction to that declaration. It was true. She liked Ken and she could see herself with him, maybe forever. Ken had agreed to allow her to enroll in Radford Teacher's School, but only if she found a way to pay on her own way. She didn't know how she would afford it on her own, but the concession on his part had softened him a little in her eyes. She knew it was more than most other suitors would allow.

"That's true. I never thought of Wesley as a serious suitor," Maude lied.

"Do you think he would try to sneak around and see you if he was still in the area?"

"I don't know. He hasn't yet."

"Where do you think he is now?"

"I don't have any idea. He is probably far away from here. Why would he stay around here with your men chasing him? I swear I haven't seen him, and I think if he had stayed around here then he would have tried to visit me. That's just his personality."

"That boy is wild headed like his Uncle Floyd. It's hard telling where he is," her father said.

Baldwin turned to address Maude directly. "You know that it is very important for us to capture Wesley and Sidna, right? We can't let people go around defying the laws of the Commonwealth of Virginia. It is very important that you let us know if you hear from him, okay, Miss Iroler? There's a big reward, five-hundred dollars for Wesley and a thousand for Sidna. That is life-changing money for you people around these parts. Please let us know if you see him." Baldwin paused, and his open face turned to a scowl. "And if we find out you have seen him and didn't tell us...well, then you have a problem."

Baldwin stared her down in silence for an uncomfortable amount of time and then turned to her father.

"Mr. Iroler, you mind stepping out on the porch. I need to speak with you in private."

Maude took some deep breaths to calm her heart and went back into the kitchen with her mother. They did the dishes and finished cleaning the kitchen in silence. Her sister Elizabeth walked in through the back door with a basket full of eggs from the hen house.

"What's wrong? Y'all look like you seen a ghost," Elizabeth said.

FIFTY

SIDNA

They ended up in Salisbury after hopping a freight train just outside of Winston-Salem. The Salisbury train station bustled with activity. Sidna stood in the center of the main platform looking at the schedule posted on a sign that hung from the ceiling. People pushed past him, oblivious that they were shuffling past one of the most wanted men in the country. He rubbed the tickets that he had just purchased between his thumb and index finger and wondered what they would do for the next thirty minutes before boarding their train to Asheville. He walked across the platform, away from the train tracks, to where Wesley stood studying a large bulletin board that was covered with flyers and posters pinned up haphazardly.

"Looky here," Wesley said.

Wesley pointed up to a poster pinned right in the middle of the board. It was their wanted poster. The poster was the biggest one on the board, about ten inches wide and fourteen inches long. The poster was printed by the Baldwin-Felts Detective Agency and announced a significant reward for the capture of members of "The Allen Clan" and included their pictures and a brief description. Sidna's picture was on top, and he commanded the highest reward amount. Claude and Friel were below Sidna's with the word *Captured* printed over their faces. Wesley's picture was at the bottom below Claude's. Sidna frowned and shook his head as he read the descriptions knowing that he and Wesley were the only ones still on the lam.

One Thousand Dollars ($1,000) Reward—Dead or Alive
Sidna Allen*. Age 46. Height 5 feet 9 or 10 inches. Weight 145 to 155 pounds. Light-brown hair, mixed with grey. Blue eyes. Long hatchet face, long nose. Complexion rather sallow. Smooth shaven. Very large mouth. Left-handed. Reported shot through the muscle of left arm, and slight wound in left side. Two gold bridges in the upper part of his mouth, one with four teeth, and the other with five, and both running back from the two eyeteeth and anchored by hoods and crowns.*
Sidna Allen was the leader of the gang, consisting of Claude Allen, Friel Allen, Wesley Edwards, and Floyd Allen. Sidna is not as heavy now as when photograph was taken. He is very resourceful, has traveled widely, and may try to make his way out of the country on horseback or in a wagon. He may undertake his way west or may possibly go to some seaport town with the view of sailing to some foreign country.

Eight Hundred Dollars ($800) Reward
Claude Allen*. Son of Floyd Allen. Age 22. Height 6 feet. Black hair, ends slightly curly. Smooth face. Dark complexion. Gray-bluish eyes. Good teeth. Long, black eyebrows that connect. Large, round face, very prominent cheek bones. Rather good-looking, but features a little bit rough. This man has a two-year college degree in business,*

but has traveled very little and may undertake to make his way west or out of the country via some seaport.

Five Hundred Dollars ($500) Reward

Wesley Edwards*. Nephew of Floyd and Sidna. Age 20. Height 5 feet 7 or 8 inches. Weight 160 to 170 pounds. Stock built. Dark hair, slightly curled on the ends. Gray eyes. Features regular. Face always flushed. Complexion dark. Smooth shaven. A bad and dangerous man.*
This man is illiterate, and he spent most of his life operating illicit distilleries in the mountains of Virginia and North Carolina.

Five Hundred Dollars ($500) Reward

Friel Allen*. Son of Jack Allen and nephew of Sidna Allen. Age 18. Height about 5 feet 7 inches. Slender build. Light hair. Blue eyes. Fair complexion. Regular features.*

These men are members of the gang who murdered Judge Thornton L. Massie, Commonwealth's Attorney W.M. Foster, Sheriff L.S. Webb and others at Hillsville, Carroll County, Virginia, on March 14th, 1912. This was the most brutal murder ever committed in the United States, and we appeal to all officers and citizens to assist us in apprehending these murderers. These men may undertake to leave together or may separate and may be traveling on horseback or in wagon through the country.

"Wesley Edwards," Sidna read aloud. "A bad and dangerous man. That's quite a description. I'd better keep my eye on you. Are you reading this right now?"

"Yes, sir. I've read it a few times."

"But how is that possible? According to this you're illiterate."

"That picture hardly looks like you. Hatchet face?" Wesley said, looking sideways at Sidna.

"My wife must've given them the worst picture possible. That's all I can figure. Bless you, Bettie."

"At least they got the illicit-distilleries part right about me," Wesley chuckled.

"If you are the bad and dangerous one, then why is my reward higher and I'm the one they will take dead or alive? It's no wonder their grand posse hasn't been able to catch us. I feel better about our odds after seeing this ridiculous poster."

They kept their conversation to a whisper so they couldn't be overheard, but there was really no danger of them being recognized. People were going about their day and many of them looked distracted by something. There was a buzz flowing across the platform, like something noteworthy had happened. A crowd gathered at a newspaper stand and men walked by trying to read folded-up newspapers while they walked to and from their trains. They both stood and watched as people continued to pass by, paying them no attention.

They had spent the previous two nights on the outskirts of Winston-Salem and were in rough shape when they arrived at the four-room inn that was attached to a small tavern. Sidna was terrified that the old man running the establishment would ask too many questions and figure out their story, but the clerk paid them no mind. The old man had been happy to take their money and Sidna figured that he must have offered up his rooms to worse-looking men than he and Wesley before. They got some much-needed rest after three nights of walking across North Carolina. The hot bath and clean clothes had rejuvenated Sidna and made him feel like a respectable-looking man again.

Wesley was still gawking at their wanted poster. Sidna swiveled his head back around toward the crowd. An elderly woman hobbled down the platform laboring to drag a large suitcase behind her tiny body. She looked directly at Sidna and started walking toward him. Wesley turned to look at him, laughing, almost hysterically.

"That damn poster says I'm two inches shorter than you."

"Settle down, someone is coming this way," Sidna said.

The old woman eased her way across the platform and stopped on Sidna's right side. Her thin gray hair was tied up under a white bonnet with a blue bow on top. She was hunched over at such an angle that Sidna thought she would topple over. Her breath was heavy, and he could tell that she was struggling with the suitcase. She craned up her neck and head towards the board and began studying the posters and pictures.

"I hope they catch those murderous hillbillies," she said, looking up through round glasses.

Sidna turned to her and smiled his wide, disarming grin.

"Me too, ma'am. I'm glad I know what they look like now. I'll certainly keep my eyes open for them. Do you need help with your suitcase?"

"Oh yes. Thank you so much."

"Where are you traveling?" Sidna asked.

"I'm visiting my daughter and her family in Asheville. Her husband will be away on work travel for some time. She has two small children. I'm getting too old to chase those young 'uns around, but I'll try to help where I can."

"I have two young daughters myself. They can wear you out."

Wesley snuck off covering the side of his face from the old woman and Sidna started dragging her heavy suitcase across the platform. He was immediately impressed that the old woman had moved the heavy suitcase as far as she did.

"Where are you and your associate traveling?"

"We are just passing through on our way west to Cincinnati on business. Asheville is a nice little mountain town. I've been there a couple of times."

A loud hiss from a steam engine filled the platform. Sidna escorted the woman to the car printed on her ticket. He walked past a newspaper stand with people waiting in a long line. A large group of people were huddled off to the side of the stand chatting over their newspapers. He wondered if it was news about "The Allen Clan." He continued across the platform with the old woman behind him and he heaved her heavy suitcase up the three steps into the train car.

"Have a nice trip, ma'am."

"Thank you, sir."

Sidna went back to the newspaper stand and got in line. The line moved quickly as one after another grabbed their paper and moved on. He caught a glimpse of the front page.

TITANIC SINKS!

He reached the head of the line and handed the salesman a nickel in exchange for a newspaper. The salesman handed him a rolled-up newspaper and two cents change. He stuffed the paper in his pocket to be read on the train. He went back down to the platform to find Wesley. He didn't see him and went on down to their assigned carriage. He scanned the platform and started to panic when he didn't see Wesley. Then he heard pecking on the train-carriage window and peered up at the train. He spotted Wesley with his face pressed up against the window. Wesley motioned with his hand as if to say hurry up or you'll miss the train. Sidna climbed the stairs to their train car and took his seat next to Wesley. Wesley acted giddy. Sidna felt a rush as well. He felt like they were finally in the clear. After weeks of hiding in the woods and only moving at night and going days without food or adequate shelter he finally felt like they were putting some real distance between themselves and their troubles. He pulled out the newspaper and pointed at the headline.

"What's the *Titanic*?" Wesley asked.

"A supposedly unsinkable ship."

FIFTY-ONE

PAYNE

"These are some of the best pickles that I've ever eaten," Payne said.

"I agree. You know, I have always wondered why they call pickled cucumbers pickles, but everything else that gets pickled must be called by its name. Pickled carrots, pickled eggs, pickled pig's feet. But cucumbers are just pickles," Phaup said.

Payne chuckled and acknowledged that he didn't know. He didn't care to contemplate the naming of pickled foods. Payne and Phaup were out in the county a little east of Fancy Gap wandering the roads and looking for signs along the wooded patches and pastures that dotted the rolling plateau. They had stopped for lunch along the side of a sun-drenched green pasture. Ham sandwiches and pickles again, but Payne didn't mind. A little general store in Hillsville had been supplying lunch for the detectives and eating the huge whole cucumber pickle had become one of the highlights of his day. It was sour and salty with subtle hints of dill and garlic. He was bored. Had been ever since the trail on Sidna Allen and Wesley Edwards dried up. Sidna and Wesley disappeared on that foggy morning with the dogs running, and the agency hadn't received a tip or seen any sign of them since. Payne knew they had gotten close with the bloodhounds. He didn't know how close, but later that day they found tracks that went in the opposite direction of where the dogs led them. Sidna and Wesley had somehow slipped through their search lines and evaded the noses of the bloodhounds.

"Sure are a lot of people out and about. You think it's the warm weather?" Phaup asked.

"They are long gone, and these people know it. They know they can leave their houses without getting caught up in any trouble with us or our fugitives prowling around. We haven't received a single tip since that foggy morning when we had the bloodhounds after them. It's like everybody around here knows they are gone. Everyone but us."

Payne took his time on the ride back into town. He rolled up his sleeves and felt the warm spring sun on his bare arms. He had been so wet and cold and miserable over the past month while crisscrossing the narrow mountain roads to hidden farms and small homesteads that he had almost forgotten what it felt like to be warm. People were talking about how that March had been one of the coldest on record and he believed it. He had lost weight and felt like he had aged ten years. He had also gained a respect for the local people and that was unexpected. He rode up main street and turned his horse over to the stableman outside of the hotel where they had been staying. Three couriers were milling about in front of the hotel and a dozen horses were parked in the hitching lot. He recognized Thomas Felts' regal black horse. It stood four hands taller than the other horses. He went inside and was immediately accosted by Elmer Brimm.

"Felts and Baldwin are looking for you. You better hurry. They have been meeting in there for over an hour and I was supposed to meet with them at four. It's already half past and I'm still waiting," Elmer said.

"Alright. Which room are they in?"

"Baldwin's room."

Payne walked down the wood-paneled hallway and stopped in front of Baldwin's room. He could hear them talking through the door. He took a deep breath and knocked. They stopped talking and the door cracked open. Luke peeked through and motioned for Payne to come in. William Baldwin and Thomas Felts were seated around a small table that was covered in correspondence and maps and half-empty coffee cups. Luke walked back over and took a seat in the third chair alongside Baldwin and Felts.

"You mind standing, Ed? Or you can sit on the edge of the bed there if you like," Baldwin said.

"I'll stand. I've been riding all day."

Felts stood and looked at Payne. "Well, I'll just cut right to it. There is trouble in the coal mines with the unions. We are going to send you back up there to help get things under control again. We have been neglecting our duties in the mines and there has been a surge of union activities. The miners at Paint Creek mine in West Virginia went on strike and the company has hired us to break them. The company is not budging on their demands, neither are the miners. We need all hands on deck up there. We want you to leave first thing in the morning. You and I will head to headquarters in Bluefield for a day or two and then ship out to the mines."

Payne tried to hide his disappointment. He gazed over their heads at a painting of a little house with a wraparound porch and a big tree in the front yard. He stared at the picture and Baldwin broke the silence. Luke kept his eyes down and started reviewing some of the papers in front of him. Payne knew that Felts was irritated with him, and it was just a matter of time before Felts tore into him for pursuing his theory about Goad. Maybe being sent back to the mines was part of his punishment. It was clear that Baldwin and Felts were not interested in the truth, and he accepted his banishment.

"I'll happily go back to the mines. Thank you for the opportunity."

"Good man," Baldwin said. "We are promoting Luke. He will stay here and lead the search with me. We are changing strategy and cutting back on the number of agents here. Fewer agents and more clandestine tactics. We are going to have to broaden our search for Sidna and Wesley. We think they have escaped from this area. Felts is going to shift to coordinating our men with you and his brother Lee in the mines."

"That will be all, Ed. You can go ahead and get packed up and get some rest. We leave tomorrow," Felts said.

Payne turned to walk out of the room and stopped in the doorway. He turned around and asked, "Do we still have that note that I found on the judge? Did we keep that as evidence?"

"Yes," Felts said. "Why?"

"Where is it?" Payne asked.

William Baldwin walked over to the side table beside of the bed and picked up his brown leather briefcase. He pulled the note out from a folder and handed it to Payne.

"Thanks," Payne said.

Payne grabbed the note and turned to leave the room.

"Where are you going with that?" Felts asked.

Payne did not answer the question. He left the room and went back down the hallway with the handwritten note in his hand, walked out of the front door, and sat on a bench on the sidewalk in front of the hotel. He stretched is long legs halfway across the sidewalk. He had finally accepted the kind of man he was, and he didn't like it. He thought about what being a detective with the Baldwin-Felts Agency had done to him, how it changed him. The Baldwin-Felts Agency had grown accustomed to skirting the edges of justice for money and recognition. They were not traditional detectives. Some called them the Gun Men of Capitalism. Others called them the Pinkerton of the South. They were more like mercenary henchmen. That had bothered him in those first years as a detective, but he loved the title and the power that came along with being a Baldwin-Felts detective. He had protected the Norfolk Western Railroad for most of his early years as a Baldwin-Felts detective. He had played along and ignored their unethical practices. When they couldn't find the cause of the train wreck, they would find a scapegoat. They would always find someone to blame train wrecks on, black people or poor whites living in isolated communities near the crash. The cause of the crashes would be filed as tampering with the railroad or leaving something on the track. There had to be a cause of each train wreck to ensure that the train company got their insurance money and Baldwin-Felts always found a cause.

He watched people going about their day on the busy main street. Women in their bonnets and cotton dresses walked by carrying baskets and dragging little children behind them. Men walked by in their suits and hats going about their town business. The courthouse towered over the town with its Greek columns and the Confederate soldier stood his ground in the middle of the road. He pulled out the crumpled note in Dexter's handwriting from the day when Dexter's daughter had dictated his answers. He read the note that he had pulled off the judge's body and compared the handwriting. The similarity was inconclusive, maybe because Dexter was half lit on morphine when he wrote the second one that Payne had swiped off his bed. Payne stood and crumpled the two pieces of paper up together and tossed them into the muddy street. He walked back into the hotel to call his wife.

A phone box hung on the wall behind the registration desk. He still hadn't spoken to his wife since he arrived in Hillsville. Either he hadn't had time or when he did have time he was in the middle of nowhere and miles away from a phone. It was probably best that he hadn't been able to reach her because she would babble away for minutes on end without even giving him a chance to speak and make him feel guilty for being away. Her loneliness broke through every time, and it always dampened his spirit to hear that longing in her voice. His job paid for the nice house in Bluefield, and it paid for her loneliness. She didn't know the man who protected the trains and evicted miners, didn't know the man who had killed other men, and didn't know about the list of the men he had beaten that he kept in his little notebook. His life as a Baldwin-Felts detective had often taken him away from her for months at a time and he had gotten used to the distance. When he was there with her for those insufficient moments, he couldn't tell if he was happier there or happier away. He picked up the phone and gave the little handle one long crank and waited for the operator to answer.

"Operator," a woman said.

He stated the number and then said, "Edwin C. Payne of Bluefield, West Virginia."

"Just a minute," the operator said. He waited and then her sweet voice cut through the static.

"Hello."

"Hi Rose, it's Ed."

"Ed, I've been worried about you. Are you alright?"

Payne paused, he swiveled his head around the room and down the hallway towards the lower-floor rooms and then peeked up the stairwell, making sure no one was within earshot.

"Honestly, no. I'm exhausted."

"What do they have you doing, honey?"

"I'm coming home tomorrow. They are assigning me back to the mines to deal with a labor strike."

"That's great. Did you capture the rest of them, then?"

"No. The trail has dried up and they are changing direction here. They need me back in the mines."

"I've been following it in the newspaper. I'm proud of you for what you are doing. I love you."

He could hear the excitement in her voice.

"I don't know how much longer I can do this, Rose."

"Do what?"

"My job. I love my job but between being stationed in the mines and being stuck in this backwater and...."

"And what?"

"I'm tired of having to look the other way. There is more to it than you think. The Allens aren't the only bad guys here. Hell, I may be one of the bad guys. Sometimes I wonder."

There was a long pause and she started talking. He thought while she was talking and missed most of what she said. He couldn't stand being cut out of the decision-making process. He'd exposed his body and his life to danger by leading the manhunt and wouldn't get any credit for it, just pushed aside during Felts' desperate attempt to change things up and catch the outlaws before they slipped away forever. Of course, it was Luke who was filling in the leadership space vacated by Payne. He couldn't hate Luke for it though. Luke was just doing what he thought was best to climb up the ladder and help the agency complete its mission, but it was still galling to be pushed out of the leadership team.

"Ed. Ed. Are you still there?"

"I'm here. I've got to pack. I'll see you tomorrow."

"Okay. Love you."

"Love you too."

FIFTY-TWO

MAUDE

She didn't know why they called them Lazy Wife Beans. They were easy to grow and easy to harvest, hearty in the ground, and hearty in the belly. Those qualities didn't sound lazy to her. She thought the greasy-bean variety should be called Smart Wife Beans instead because they allowed time to be spent on other chores instead of having to finesse the fussier varieties. She placed the large, white beans in the hole under the wooden trellis and used a rusty hoe to smooth out the topsoil over the seeds. Her back ached from squatting and bending and digging all morning. She pulled a handkerchief from the front pocket of her dress and wiped the sweat from her forehead. She placed her hands on the small of her back and arched towards the sky and examined the row. Four more to go with beans planted on each side of the A-framed trellises.

"Maude," her mother called from the back porch. "Can you please carry this out to John Crowder? I'm sure he is getting hungry by now. I think he is out plowing the top field."

"Why don't you get Elizabeth to take it today?" Maude asked.

"I put your lunch in the basket too. Elizabeth has already eaten lunch. Why don't you just eat with him?" her mother asked as she handed Maude the picnic basket.

Maude frowned. She propped the hoe up on the trellis and grabbed the basket from her mother. It was a two-hundred-yard walk to the top field. She ate her sandwich as she walked through the baby alfalfa that had recently pushed its way out of the ground. John Crowder had been working as a farm-hand for a week and it was the fifth day that her mother had made her take him lunch. He was plowing a thirty-acre field where they aimed to plant tobacco. The oxen were stopped in the middle of the field, and he was fiddling with the chain attached to the arm of the plow disc. He had his shirt off and she thought maybe this wouldn't be such a boring lunch after all.

"I brought you some lunch," Maude said.

He jumped at the sound of her words.

"I didn't mean to startle you. What happened to the plow?" Maude asked.

"I think I hit a big rock and the disc got thrown out of place. I'm having a right hard time getting it back on."

"You want me to send Daddy up here to help?"

"Yes. I think I'm going to need some help."

Maude sat the picnic basket down and opened the lid. He left the plow and sat down in the dirt beside of her. She handed him the salt-ham sandwich and a jug of water. He tore into the sandwich. She studied him as he ate. There was something queer about him that made him seem phony. He was in his early thirties. Older than the typical farmhands her father hired. He was handsome and had a not-from-around-here accent that she couldn't place and he didn't know a lick about farming. A man his age who had worked on farms his whole life, as he claimed, would be more autonomous.

"It's getting hot out here today. Hope you don't mind that I am shirtless."

"Not at all. Feels good after that unusually cold winter we had."

He turned up the water jug and took a long drink. She watched his thick Adam's apple pulse as he drank hard from the jug. Brown stubble grew out of his sharp jaw. Her eyes wandered down his shirtless torso. He may not have been very knowledgeable at his job, but he had the strong look of a farmhand. He stopped drinking and caught her looking. He scooted closer. She turned away.

"You're about the prettiest thing I've seen around these parts," John said.

"Where are you from again?" Maude asked.

"Dobson, North Carolina. I've got family up here though."

"Who's your family?"

"The Smiths from over around Ararat."

She didn't know of any Smiths from Ararat.

He took a bite of his sandwich and spoke while he chewed. "I heard that you are Wesley Edwards' sweetheart."

As soon as he said sweetheart, she knew. The only other person who had ever called Wesley her sweetheart was the head of the Baldwin-Felts Detective Agency when he visited her home a few weeks prior. She felt the anger and shock hit her like a sledgehammer and she blurted out a response.

"That is none of your business," Maude said as she stood.

"Well, I think what happened to him and his kin is awful. The way they have been treated like criminals and fugitives. Everybody knows that it is not a one-sided affair. Bad ones on both sides, I figure."

She didn't respond and he continued.

"If you ever see Wesley, then let me know. I can give him some money or supplies or even give him a place to hide. I'll do whatever he needs to help. You just tell me where he is if you hear from him. Okay?"

"I have to get back to work," Maude said.

She walked back across the field. She turned her head back when she was a hundred yards away. He had put his shirt back on and she watched him kick a clump of dirt that busted into dust.

PART III

CARRY ME BACK TO VIRGINIA

FIFTY-THREE

WESLEY

Wesley climbed down from a ladder in the dining room of the large Victorian house where he had been nailing ornate crown molding. He unfastened the thick leather tool belt from his waist as he walked out into the side yard and placed it in the back of the tool wagon.

"Hey, boss," Wesley said.

"What can I do for you, Joe?" the foreman asked.

"I need to take next week off. Is that okay?" Wesley asked.

"Well, I guess it would be okay. We are about finished with this job, and we will be prepping the next house across the city next week. Your timing is good."

"I know. That's why I asked now."

"Where are you going?"

"I have some family things I need to tend to back in Virginia," Wesley said.

"Have a good trip, Joe."

"There anything else I can help with before I leave for the day?"

"Nope. See you week after next."

It was a fifteen-minute walk from the house he was working on in Sherman Hill down Locust Street to the small boarding house where he and Sidna had been staying. It was a nice day and he decided to walk instead of taking the streetcar. After living in Des Moines for five months, Wesley still marveled at the sights he encountered when walking through the growing city. He walked under power lines and phone lines and streetcar lines that hung slack in endless connection. The street was filled with motorcars and horses and wagons and people all sharing the same busy roads that ran in straight lines through the city. He had only seen a handful of motorcars in his life before he left Fancy Gap and had never ridden in one. Living in the city was like living in a different time. He couldn't ever live in Virginia again. Not because of the terrible act he'd been a part of, that was another issue. He couldn't live in those mountains again because it would be shifting his life into reverse. Way he figured, those five people dying in the courthouse, seven if you count Floyd and Claude who would soon fry in the electric chair, might be the best thing that ever happened to him, and he would never be able to reconcile that shift in direction in his conscience.

The train from Salisbury had taken them to Asheville and from there the Carolina Special carried them to Cincinnati and then to Chicago and finally down to Des Moines. Wesley had wanted to stay in Chicago and try to blend in, but Sidna convinced him that Chicago was too cosmopolitan for them, said they would be better off in a smaller city somewhere in the Midwest. They arrived in Des Moines on a Friday, rented a room in Mrs. Cameron's Boarding House on a Saturday and they both had jobs as carpenters by Monday. Sidna used his knowledge of carpentry and his smooth tongue to land them the jobs. Sidna kept that job for a month and then he got work with a different outfit so they would not be seen together for extended amounts of time in public. Wesley had never lived so well. Mrs. Cameron and her maids kept up their room and washed their clothes and fixed their meals. It was an epic turnabout from scrambling around atop the freezing rocky outcrops of the Blue Ridge or hiding out in people's filthy barns.

Being on the run was always in the back of his mind. The flatland of Des Moines and the busy city streets made him feel exposed and anxious. The wide-open sky that stretched out over miles and miles of flat cornfields made him feel like an exposed baby rabbit with hawks circling overhead. The only things he missed about Virginia were the security of the mountains, his mother, and Maude. They had been living and working in Des Moines for five months and he had money in his pockets and a promising career in the booming Des Moines construction industry. He had already bought an engagement ring for Maude. The ring was stashed deep in his travel bag in the boarding room. It was a little white-gold band set with a half-carat emerald. He had been planning the trip back to Virginia all summer and he couldn't wait any longer. The only thing left to do was tell Sidna and that made the fifteen-minute walk from Sherman Hill to their boarding house slow to twenty minutes as Wesley's pace dragged with the anticipation of telling Sidna that he was going back to Virginia. He finally ambled up to the corner of Eleventh Street and Locust Street and into Mrs. Cameron's Boarding House. It was a three-story wood brick building with a front porch that wrapped around the right corner of the house on the Eleventh Street side. Wesley walked across the front parlor and nodded to Mrs. Cameron who was reviewing books behind the small registration desk. She had her gray hair pulled up in a large bun and shifted her eyes up at him over the small round spectacles resting on the tip of her nose.

"Good evening, Mr. Jackson," Mrs. Cameron said.

"Good evening."

He kept going up the open stairs to the second-floor landing and opened the first door on the left. Sidna was sitting at the tiny desk in the right corner of the room beside of the door. The room was all dark-wood paneling with a single window set high across from the alley to the brick building next door. Wesley walked past Sidna's bed and set his hat and wallet on the little wooden table between the beds and sat on his bed.

"Hello, Joe. How was your workday?" Sidna asked.

"Good, Tom. I'm exhausted. We finished remodeling that house over in Sherman Hill. Starting on another one next week in the same area," Wesley said.

Wesley stretched out on the mattress and closed his eyes. He didn't know how to tell Sidna that he was leaving for Virginia in the morning, but he had to tell him. He couldn't just sneak off and not say where he was going. Sidna would think that he had been captured or gotten scared and run off by himself. He just had to go with it, Sidna's reaction be damned.

"I'm going back to Virginia tomorrow. I already bought the ticket."

Sidna didn't say anything and stopped reading whatever it was he was reading and took off his glasses and rubbed his forehead.

"Why don't you wait just a little longer? It is too soon to be going back. It might be safer to wait and go back next spring," Sidna said.

"I can't wait, Uncle Sid. Summer's almost over and they keep saying that the winter's here are pretty rough. I don't want to wait that long and, honestly, I'm not sure that Maude will wait that long for me. I miss her and I'm gonna miss my chance with her if I wait. Might already have."

Sidna stood and paced back and forth in the small space between his bed and the desk and the closed bedroom door.

Wesley sensed that Sidna was restraining himself. Sidna stopped pacing and took a deep breath.

"Don't you think I miss my family. I have two little girls that I haven't seen since March, and I miss Bettie more than you could possibly understand. I don't dare even write her letters because they might be traced back here. And here you are saying you are going to go back into the thick of it."

"I'm going. I'll be cautious. I have to try, or I think I'll regret it forever."

"We are doing well here, Wesley. You need to forget about Maude and build up some money and find another woman out here or wherever we go next. That's what I did. I waited to get married until I was thirty-five. I know that sounds crazy to you, and most people where we come from, but it made all the difference in my life. It allowed me time to grow and know myself and build a nice little life. You are young and you've got plenty of time, son."

Wesley wanted to scream, *I'm not your son*. He held it in and held his voice down against the thin walls of the boarding house. "And look where you are now. You lost it all. You lost all that wealth that doesn't mean anything in this life anyway. You lost your family, and you aren't even doing anything to get them back. You are scared. I'm going."

"You're damn right I'm scared. You should be too. They've already sentenced Floyd and Claude to death in the electric chair. You will share their fate if they catch you. Are you willing to risk that for this girl of yours?" Sidna asked.

"It's decided. You can't stop me."

Sidna stared off out the little window above Wesley's bed. Wesley didn't say anything. He could see that Sidna was chewing on his decision. Wesley had made up his mind. He was prepared for Sidna to kick him out right then and there. He reckoned that he might never see Sidna again. If he was Sidna, he would leave in the morning and try to start over again somewhere else. It was a good chance that Wesley would bring the Baldwin-Felts detectives back with him and if Sidna was smart he would save himself and move along without Wesley.

"This will be the end of us. If they catch wind of you there, then they will track you back here and arrest us both."

"I'll be careful. I'd understand if you want to part ways with me here and move on out West."

"I'm not going anywhere. I expect you to be back here as soon as you've done what you need to do. What's your plan?"

"I've already bought the train ticket to Mount Airy and I guess I'll walk home from there."

"Go see your cousin Victor when you get there. He will make sure you get to Maude safely. Don't visit your mother or anyone else, okay?"

"Okay."

Sidna stood, put on his hat, left the room, and walked down to the parlor of the boarding house. He could hear Sidna talking to one of the maids in his usual charismatic tone like everything was fine. Sidna told the maid that Joe Jackson was leaving in the morning and would be gone for a week or so. Sidna told them Joe's going home to Virginia to visit family. Wesley started packing his bag.

FIFTY-FOUR

MAUDE

It was two hours past midnight. The bright moon stretched her soft shadow down the road to Victor Allen's house. Her mind fired from one thought to the next so quickly that all of them wound together in one anxious knot. She had been trying to forget about Wesley and then her friend Alice came calling. Alice was friends with Victor Allen's wife and Alice had a message. Wesley was at Victor's house and wanted to see her.

She stopped in front of the house and stood behind a tree trunk across the road for fifteen minutes. She peeked from around the tree and saw a man blocking the front door, his silhouette framed by the light from inside of the cabin. He looked out for half a minute, swept his head from left to right, and ducked back into the house. She thought about turning around, thought about going home and never worrying about Wesley again, but something kept pulling her towards him. She couldn't turn back. She took a deep breath and walked across the road. She knocked and Victor opened the door. He placed his large hand on her right elbow and ushered her inside.

"Do you think anyone followed you?" Victor asked.

"No, I don't think so."

He pushed his head out of the door and looked up and down the road and across the yard and then he shut the door.

Victor pointed to the door off the little kitchen. "He's in the back room there."

Her heart pounded as she walked across the front room and opened the door. Wesley was sitting there in a chair in the corner of the small bedroom. His face lit up with a smile and she couldn't help but smile back. He walked across to her and touched her hand that was still on the doorknob. He closed the door. He stood there beside of her looking at her and she felt his energy again like that night at the corn shucking and that night in the backroom of the orchard shed. She had forgotten what his presence felt like. She had started courting Ken Marsh over the summer. The people who knew would say that he was her boyfriend, she wouldn't disagree. But what she felt now, with Wesley, was not how she felt with Ken. This was different. Something deep down in her brain was pushing her toward Wesley. He left his hand on hers and they kissed and then they were on the edge of the bed and then they were in the bed.

"Wait," she said as she pushed him away.

She sat back on the edge of the bed and straightened the shoulders of her dress. Wesley squinted at her with a confused, disappointed expression. Wesley stood and walked over to the corner. He dug around in his bag, moved clothes to the side, found what he was looking for and turned back toward her holding a tiny brown box.

"I know that you need to get back up the road, but I've got something to ask you first. I wish I could stay right here in this room with you forever. You are enough to make me a happy man for good."

She knew what was coming and she almost said, *Don't do it, don't complicate it for me*. But she kept quiet and let him continue because she hadn't made up her mind yet. He bent down on one knee and opened the brown jewelry box to reveal a ring with a thin white-gold band set with a small emerald.

"Will you be my wife?"

She hesitated.

"Come back to Iowa with me. We could change our names and start again. I'm known as Joe Jackson now. We can leave the violence behind and start again out West."

"I don't think I can."

"I know this has all happened fast. I just didn't know how else to do it and I've missed you so much. I want to spend the rest of my life with you. Just think about it. Don't say no yet."

Wesley hung his head and kept hold of the ring. He went back over to his bag and pulled out an envelope. He handed it to her. She opened the envelope and removed the contents, fifty dollars and a note. The note said Mrs. Cameron's Boarding House, corner of Locust Street and Eleventh Street, Des Moines, Iowa.

"That will be enough to get you a ticket from Mount Airy to Des Moines if you change your mind. Me and Uncle Sid are staying at a boarding house. That's the address. You wait for when the time is right and come join me. But please don't wait too long."

They both stayed silent for a while. Wesley waited for her to say yes, she could see the anticipation in his expression. She wanted to say yes but there was too much to consider, and she couldn't convince herself to say it out loud.

"I need to get going."

They kissed again and then he quietly escorted her out of the house. The eastern sky brightened through the deep blue of early morning. The birds sang their first songs of the day through the canopy of trees above the dusty road. A large bird startled her as it flew from its perch. She froze. The sky was bright enough to watch the black shape of an owl fly off silently into the damp air. A thin strip of sunrise appeared over the horizon and the wispy clouds grew pink in the east and lavender above. She didn't pass a single soul on the walk home. What would a new life with Wesley be like in Iowa? She knew she would be happy with him, but for how long? His Uncle Floyd and cousin Claude had already been found guilty and given the death penalty. Would he share their fate? It felt like only a matter of time, either he would eventually get caught and she would be worse than a widow. Widows can get remarried. Divorced women whose ex-husbands were in jail didn't stand a chance and she would be trapped in the loop of endless chores at her parents' house her whole life. She turned left off the road and walked down the rutted dirt path through the orchard and up to the house. The house was dark, and the wavy glass windows reflected the pink glow of the sunrise. Her father was sitting on the front porch steps with both of his hands cupped around a coffee mug. Her heart felt like it was going to jump out of her chest when she saw him there. She had spent too much time with Wesley, too late, now too early. She slowed her pace and took a deep breath to steady her nerves. Then she remembered Wesley's envelope, which she still held in her hand. She tucked the envelope into the inside pocket of her jacket and continued up to the house. Her father took a sip of coffee, steam evaporated into the morning air from the tin mug. He narrowed his eyes.

"What are you doing out?"

"I…" Maude stuttered. "I couldn't sleep. The upstairs room was stuffy, and I needed some cool air."

"What was in your hand?"

"Nothing."

"Don't lie to me."

FIFTY-FIVE

SIDNA

It was half past nine in the morning when Sidna sat down to write his first letter. He addressed it to a local construction company and dated it, September 14th, 1912. It was exactly six months to the day from when his life changed forever on that tragic morning in the Hillsville Courthouse. He paused writing and thought about how far away from home he was. His old life had vanished, and he was working to build a new one as Tom Sayers in Des Moines, still holding out hope that one day he would be reunited with Bettie and his daughters. Wesley had brought back news of his family's well-being and it wasn't good. Their magnificent house was gone, confiscated, and sold off in May along with his general store and sawmill and over a thousand acres of land to raise money for the victims of that horrible day. Bettie was forced to move to Hillsville with the girls. Apparently, she was living with her sister and working as a housekeeper and laundress in town. It made him sick every time he thought about it. Those thoughts fueled his desire to find a way to provide for his family again.

He turned his attention back to writing the letter. He had just quit his job as a carpenter to start a new venture with a man he had met in the Carpenter's Union. The man's name was Mason Sellers and he installed acetylene generators for lighting homes that did not have access to electricity. The lights in Sidna's former house had been powered by an acetylene generator and he was familiar with the setup. Mason Sellers was to handle the distribution and installation and Sidna was to oversee sales. This was the first of many letters he planned to write to all the major construction businesses in Des Moines soliciting in-person meetings.

It was hot in the small room. Sweat beaded on his brow as the summer heat held on right up until fall. He had left their room door open to get a cross breeze from the small window over Wesley's bed. He heard the soft steps of Mrs. Cameron walking up the stairs. A man was with her, asking about a room. The sound of the man's heavy boots echoed down the hallway. They stayed down the hall for a few minutes while Mrs. Cameron gave him a tour of the small boarding room that was available.

"I'll be back presently with my trunk," the man said.

He stopped and had a look-see inside of Sidna's room. Sidna made brief eye contact before the unknown man hurried back down the stairs. His boots moved quickly down the steps. Sidna started another letter and was interrupted a few minutes later by more quick steps up the stairs. One of the maids stuck her head through his doorway.

"Joe Jackson's girl is here on the porch waiting for him."

Sidna jerked up from the desk and walked out onto the landing above the stairs. Just then the man who had been asking about a room came running back up, two stairs at a time, with a gun pointed in Sidna's direction.

"Sidna Allen, put your hands up."

Sidna froze and kept his hands by his sides. Another man came running up the stairs with a gun and yelled, "Sidna Allen!

You're under arrest. Baldwin-Felts Detective Agency. It's over, put your hands up, now!"

Sidna didn't comply. He stared over the men's heads. They shouted at him again, "Put your hands up."

They shook their guns at him. He barely heard their barking. *I can see my girls again. I can go back to Virginia and put my fate in the hands of attorneys and jurors who may be lenient.* He raised his arms and smiled. The heavy burden of the deception that accompanied a man on the run was lifted from his weary mind. They handcuffed him and led him down the stairs. The maid looked astonished.

"Lordy, this is not Sidna Allen. This is Tom Sayers. I've read about the Allen outlaws and Tom is a good and civilized man. Nothing like the newspapers say."

"No, ma'am. I am William Baldwin of the Baldwin-Felts Detective Agency. You have been unwittingly aiding fugitives."

Sidna saw a young woman sitting in the corner of the parlor. She had a stoic look on her face like an atheist trying to make it through a church service. The man who introduced himself to the maid as William Baldwin looked at Sidna and asked, "Where is Wesley Edwards?"

"He is at work," Sidna said.

"When does he get back?" Baldwin asked.

"After quitting time," Sidna said.

"Where does he work?"

"I don't know. He works construction and they have him going all over town doing various jobs. I honestly do not know where he is right now," Sidna said.

Baldwin looked satisfied with Sidna's answer and walked over to Mrs. Cameron who hadn't moved from behind her small registration desk.

"Where does Wesley Edwards, or uh, Joe Jackson work?"

Mrs. Cameron quickly shook her head. "I don't know where he is at this moment. He usually returns by 5:00 or 6:00 p.m. every day."

"You have a phone?" Baldwin asked.

"Yes," Mrs. Cameron replied and pointed her head up to the wall near the hallway.

Baldwin turned towards the other detectives. "Call the police and get the chief of police over here. We need help looking for Wesley Edwards and we need him to lock down the city."

Sidna turned to the detective who had first rushed up the stairs and confronted him. The detective's badge identified him as Hugh Lucas.

"Y'all followed her here?" Sidna asked.

"Oh no, we accompanied her."

"So, she knew what she was doing?"

"Oh yeah, her family is getting a nice payday for leading us to you. Fifteen-hundred dollars will go a long way in Carroll County."

FIFTY-SIX

WESLEY

A streetcar lumbered down to its next stop on West Ninth. Wesley boarded and walked to the back. The carriage was packed with men returning home at quitting time. There was an open seat in the middle, but he kept going and gripped the brass pole in the aisle at the back of the car. The streetcar took off again and he swayed in unison with the other standing passengers as it cornered to the right. Two men stood between him and the back exit. He was tired from working a ten-hour shift replacing the roofing shingles on a house in the West Ninth neighborhood. His stomach growled and he wondered what was for dinner at the boarding house. It was the same mundane day over again for the last five months. Work all day, go to the room, and eat and listen to Sidna scheme new ways to make money to regain the status and wealth that he had lost.

It had been a week since he had returned from Virginia. He wished Maude was in Iowa. Every day that she wasn't there meant it was another day that she had waited, hesitated. Maybe Maude would be sitting on the front porch of the boarding house when he walked up the stairs. The move to Iowa had opened opportunities that he would never have had back home in Virginia. He was a member of the Carpenters

Union, learning a trade that could become a career. He could provide for a family now. What if she was there waiting? She could change her name, Mrs. Jackson. They could get married and she could get a job, maybe as a maid in Mrs. Cameron's Boarding House while she went to teacher's school, and they could rent a house with Sidna for a while and save up for their own house. He liked the houses he had been working on over in the Sherman Hill and West Ninth neighborhoods. They could save for a house and raise a family and live a more convenient, more comfortable life than they could have ever dreamed of in Virginia.

The streetcar slowed to the next crowded stop. A single man boarded the car first. Another man stayed on the sidewalk and held back all the other people waiting to get on. The man who just boarded immediately started swiveling his head back and forth, intently looking at each passenger as he made his way down the center of the carriage. The man was not dressed like a policeman, but wore a shiny bronze badge on his left breast. Wesley turned around to hide his face. The man couldn't be looking for him on a random streetcar. He never expected to be tracked down while riding a crowded streetcar. He always reckoned that they would track him down at the boarding house or at work. He was always cautious when approaching the boarding house or a new jobsite because those were the places where he spent most of his time. The man continued working his way down the middle of the car and Wesley turned his head to see how close the man was out of the corner of his eye. The man shifted his head down slightly and squinted at Wesley. Wesley froze and turned back toward the exit door.

"Wesley Edwards," the man shouted. "Don't move. You're under arrest."

The man started pushing his way down the crowded aisle.

Wesley turned and shoved the man between him and the exit out of the way and reached past the other man standing in front of the exit. He grabbed the handle, pushed it open and jumped out. He jumped into two police officers who were waiting in the street. One policeman tried to grab him around the waist, but he twisted away and tried to run. The other policeman wrapped an arm around his neck and dragged him down into the dirty street. Another policeman jumped on him. It was over.

FIFTY-SEVEN

WESLEY

The platform for the 7:00 p.m. train to Chicago was crowded with a mass of people. Wesley figured it was just a busy train depot when they first pulled up in the back of the police wagon, but there was something different about how the crowd moved. They were not moving about like train passengers. They were all standing and facing away from the train looking in the direction of the police wagon. An armed group of policemen and Baldwin-Felts detectives pushed the crowd down the platform away from Wesley and Sidna. Then when a path had been cleared, they pulled Wesley and Sidna out of the police wagon. The crowd hollered and hooted at them from down the platform. Cameras flashed and reporters dressed in fine suits with sharp fedoras holding notepads and pencils shouted questions in unintelligible unison. Wesley and Sidna kept up with the quick pace of their escorts across the platform to the train. It was raining and the smell of the clean rain mingled with the fumes from the burnt coal. Wesley carefully stepped on the wet grated-metal steps and up onto the train.

The engine hissed and the whistle blew. The large carriage was empty except for the five detectives from the Baldwin-Felts Agency and Maude. They put Wesley and Sidna in the middle of the carriage in the aisle seats across from each other and handcuffed them to the armrests. One detective guarded the back exit, and another was stationed at the front exit. The rhythmic chug of the engine increased as the train eased down the track. The detectives started celebrating as soon as the train started moving forward. They whooped and howled and hugged each other and smiled the wide smiles of men who thought they had just done something great. The train picked up steam and when it was up to speed the guards came and removed the handcuffs from the armrests and told Wesley and Sidna to get up. The guards shuffled Wesley and Sidna down the aisle to the back of the carriage. He set eyes on Maude sitting by herself in the back of the carriage. She looked up at him with heartbroken eyes and lowered her head back down to her lap as he walked toward the exit. They crossed the gangway into the next carriage and the guards put Wesley and Sidna into a small sleeping compartment.

"This door will be under constant guard. Knock if you need anything," the detective said as he locked the door.

The small sleeping quarters had two bunk beds and an empty wardrobe with a pull-down desktop and a small chair in the corner. Wesley took the top bunk. They lay there in silence for a long while. Wesley lay on his belly propped up on his elbows and stared out of the small window at the end of his bunk. The pancake-flat cornfields blurred past. It was a long journey back to Virginia, but not long enough. The train felt like purgatory roaring across the countryside. He wasn't in hell yet, but he was on his way.

"You awake?" Wesley asked.

"Yeah," Sidna replied.

"I'm sorry, Uncle Sid. It's all my fault. I can't ever be patient and I can't ever listen."

"Partly. It's partly your fault. There was a lot of history there with Floyd that you couldn't help. The decisions that you made were peripheral things that just made it worse. This is a family tragedy, not yours alone. She sold us out, Wesley. Maude intentionally brought the detectives here so she could get the reward money."

"How do you know that?"

"One of the detectives told me. She came here with them, and they were going to use her as bait, if need be."

"No, she didn't. I don't believe you."

"That's what they told me and I believe them. I guess you'll have to ask her yourself if you get the opportunity."

Wesley couldn't bring himself to believe that Maude would lead the detectives to him. They must have followed her without her knowledge. Sidna got out of the bed and knocked on the door.

"What?" asked the guard through the flimsy door.

"You got any reading material?" Sidna asked.

"Let me check."

The guard returned a few minutes later. He cracked open the door and slid two books through to Sidna. "Straight from Mr. Baldwin's suitcase. Enjoy."

"What'd they give you?" Wesley asked.

"Detective novels. You want one?"

"No thanks."

FIFTY-EIGHT

WESLEY

A day of travel and they were in Cincinnati. The platform of the station was packed with people, ten times more people than had seen them off in Des Moines. Wesley couldn't figure why so many people cared about catching a glimpse of him and Sidna. The noise from the crowd swept through the train carriage when they opened the door, a mixture of boos and cheers. Wesley felt a moment of panic and thought what if some crazy son of a bitch was out there with a rock to throw at them, or worse a gun.

"We've got to change trains here," Baldwin shouted. "Stay close to us."

Wesley nodded and they got off the train. Three Baldwin-Felts agents led the way followed by Maude and Sidna and then Wesley and then two more agents behind. He walked past a mother with two little children. She grabbed her children by the shoulders and held them back against the bad men. He could see it in the mother's eyes. They were devil men. He knew there was no way that mother would ever trust him or Sidna with her children even though Sidna was a kind and gentle father to his own little girls. He and Sidna were nothing more than villainous outlaws in a sideshow.

The train from Cincinnati was smaller than the train they

had taken from Des Moines to Chicago, and it did not have separate sleeping quarters. He and Sidna were handcuffed to their armrests in the middle of the carriage again and Maude was in the back seated by herself. He obsessively turned his head around to watch her, just to catch a glimpse of her eyes to see if he could find the answer in her downward gaze.

It was dark when they crossed into West Virginia. Wesley had spent most of the ride staring at the same spot on the back of the seat in front of him. He was beginning to doze off when Maude walked up the center aisle. She didn't look at him and kept walking to the front of the carriage. She started talking to Baldwin and the other detective they called Luke. Baldwin turned and looked in Wesley's direction and then nodded his head like he was agreeing to something with Maude. She said thanks and started walking back down the aisle. She stopped at his seat and slid by him and sat down in the window seat next to him.

"Hidey," she said.

"Hidey."

She gave him a solemn look. His heart was crushed, and he could see that hers was too. They were both beaten and battered by circumstances out of their control, people out of their control.

"Why?" Wesley asked.

She looked at him with pity. "What am I supposed to do at this point? I can't abandon my family and my place in the world. And I can't be a prisoner's wife."

"I wasn't a prisoner until you ratted me out."

"I didn't rat you out."

"Sure the hell looks like it."

"I didn't have a choice. My parents found out. They found the envelope with your money and address in Iowa."

Wesley believed her. He had to because the alternative was too tragic to consider.

"Will you wait for me? I'm innocent until proven guilty, right? There is still going to be a trial. We might still have a chance after the trial."

"Well, they found Floyd and Claude Allen guilty and sentenced them to death. Why would you be any different from them?"

He found the reasoning in her words. They sat there for a little while longer, neither of them wanting to speak. Eventually, she turned and looked at him with teary eyes.

"I'm sorry," she said. "I have something else to tell you." She paused like the words were hung up in her throat. Like the words and the tears had gotten all mixed together and she sobbed and finally she blurted it out. "I'm engaged to Ken Marsh."

Wesley looked at Maude's left hand and saw a ring. A modest diamond that dwarfed anything he could have given her. There was nothing else to say. The tears streamed down her face. She stood and slid past him. Wesley turned toward the window and wanted to disappear into the dark night that encased the train, but the yellow light from inside the carriage prevented him from seeing past his own reflection.

Epilogue

PAYNE

1926

Payne and his wife dawdled down the middle of main street in Winchester behind the large crowd at the annual Shenandoah Apple Blossom Festival. He followed his wife as she perused the various booths set up on both sides of the street. She slowed as they walked past a booth filled with apple-themed artwork. Oil paintings of apple orchards and apple trees in bloom and apples sitting on tables in bowls. Another booth was filled with hand-thrown cups and bowls and mugs. He followed dutifully not really paying mind to the contents of the booth. His wife stopped in front of a booth filled with handmade jewelry. She ducked inside the tent. He spotted a stand across the street selling hot apple cider.

"I'm going to get some cider. You want any?"

"Sure," Rose said.

He cut sideways across the slow-moving mass of people and got in line at the cider stand. Payne and his wife had made the trip up from Bluefield. His wife had been wanting to visit the Apple Blossom Festival ever since it started back in 1924 and she had convinced him that a trip up through the wide valley would do him some good. Since his retirement from the agency, she complained that all he did was sit around. Most days he never left the house. He would spend all day in a chair in the parlor or on the back porch, reliving the violent scenes of his past. The more he sat around with nothing to do the more the past returned. Suppressed memories of violence seeped out from the darkest corners of his brain. He had nightmares about the mine wars that drenched him in sweat and made him flail himself awake. The rednecks returned in daydreams and marched outside of his window. The Battles of Paint Creek and Cabin Creek and Blair Mountain and Matewan became as real as ever.

He waited in the cider line and pulled a crumpled flyer out of his pocket and scanned the schedule and the list of vendors. He couldn't believe his eyes when he read the name Sidna Allen on the exhibit list. It was pure coincidence that they had ended up there that day and there he was in the same place with his old nemesis. The festival flyer described Sidna's booth as a display of the artwork that he made while incarcerated. It had been a year since Sidna Allen and Wesley Edwards had been pardoned by the governor. Payne remembered being dumbfounded when he read the news that Sidna Allen had been pardoned. He read all the newspaper articles on the unusual pardon and read about the grassroots campaign led by average citizens that eventually got the attention of Governor Byrd. Thousands of signatures were collected, and hundreds of letters were written, some by very prominent Virginians, asking for Sidna Allen's pardon. Floyd and Claude Allen hadn't been so lucky. They were both executed on the same day in March 1913, a year after the tragic shootout.

Payne made it to the front of the line and ordered two cups of hot cider and one apple fritter and walked back to the jewelry booth where his wife was buying a bracelet with apple charms dangling from a cheap-looking chain. He found a bench, waited, and sipped from the cider and finished off the sweet cinnamon-spiced fritter. Rose finally walked out of the booth and showed off her new bracelet.

"That's nice," he said as he handed her the other hot cider. Steam rose from the cup into the crisp evening air.

"Thanks. Let's head on down that way. I want to see the booth with the candles."

"Let's split up. There's a booth up the other way that I want to see."

"Really?" Rose asked.

"Meet back here in an hour?"

"Okay."

He walked in the opposite direction from Rose toward the town's center following the numbered map on the back of the festival flyer. The sun had just set, and the streetlights burned against the dying light. Up ahead a crowd of men and women were gathered around in a half circle, four or five deep. His height gave him a clear view over the crowd. Sidna Allen was standing on a chair in front of five delicate-looking tables and two intricate trunks on display behind him. Sidna had the quiet crowd's full attention. Payne listened.

"Shortly after my incarceration I became the foreman of the prison woodshop. My significant expertise and experience as a carpenter, even though it had never been my chief vocation, made me a good fit for the job and I quickly turned it into an efficient and productive enterprise. My nephew Wesley became an apprentice with me in the prison woodshop. Wesley is standing right over there," Sidna pointed to a man standing behind him.

Payne instantly recognized Wesley Edwards. Wesley removed his cap and revealed a face much older than Payne expected. Wesley was probably somewhere in his middle thirties, but his balding hairline, weary eyes, and pudgy waistline made him look much older. Sidna continued.

"We made desks, chairs, pews, pulpits and other furnishings for public buildings. At first, I was not allowed to make things for myself, but I quickly ingratiated myself to the prison officials by making them beautiful wooden novelties such as puzzles or small woodcarvings. Eventually, they allowed me to stay in the shop after hours to work on my personal projects. I took the broken pieces and scraps from the woodshop and put them together to make these beautiful and intricate pieces displayed here for your enjoyment tonight."

Sidna pointed to one table behind him that had a square top with tiny pieces of wood inlaid together in a circular pattern. Payne didn't have an eye for such objects, but he was impressed.

"My first work of art is the first table on the right. It is made from seventy-nine different varieties of wood. I started it in March of 1916 and finished in August of 1917, taking almost a year and a half to complete. I call the last table over on the far left my masterpiece. It contains seventy-five thousand individual pieces of wood, and it was the last table I made before I was pardoned almost a year ago today. No paints or stains were used in finishing any of the furniture. I cut, finished, and polished each tiny scrap by hand. Please feel free to walk over and view the pieces from a respectful distance and I will answer any questions that you may have. I consider them almost priceless, but I would part with one or two for the right price. Now, people often ask me about my time in prison and the tragic circumstances that led to my incarceration. Earlier today I had the honor of finally meeting Governor Byrd, the man who pardoned me and my nephew. He is from right here in Winchester, as I'm sure many of you know. He was the Minister of Crown at last year's Apple Blossom Festival, and he filled me in on the history of this great festival. I think he is about as fine a man to ever be governor of this great Commonwealth. I spoke with him for a piece this afternoon and I'll tell you what I told him about the tragedy. For a long time, I was bitter and angry and distraught at my situation. I discovered that one's enemies can inflict untold harm. My life was destroyed. I lost everything except my loving wife and sweet daughters. My brother and his son were wrongly executed, and Wesley Edwards and I were wrongly imprisoned. However, now I have no enemies because I reconnected with God while I was incarcerated. I read the Bible every night for the final ten years of my sentence and it taught me to forgive my enemies and love them because in the end what they do does not matter. Now I am at peace and the happiest I have ever been. I picked up the shattered remains of my old life and put them back together again and built a new life. Just like the works of art before you. I have put my life back together from the scraps and made something beautiful out of shattered little pieces of hope. Reunited with my loving wife who waited for me all those years and my now grown daughters who are building lives of their own. Thank you all for listening to me. Again, please let me know if you have any questions."

The crowd clapped and then most of the people scattered into the street. A handful lingered and formed a line to admire the furniture on display. Payne waited for the line to dwindle and considered whether to approach. He kept back and watched Sidna interact with the others. He always knew that Sidna was intelligent and articulate and charismatic, but it was eye opening to witness it firsthand, seeing Sidna there talking with his broad smile and easy laugh. He could hear the intelligence when Sidna spoke, could see it in his eyes and in his demeanor. Payne figured that Sidna would still be on the run if it wasn't for his reckless nephew. He would still be out in Des Moines living under the name Tom Sayers and living the good life. He would probably have another house bigger than the one he lost. It appeared that he was on his way towards regaining that status again after all those years in prison with his fascinating display of prison-made furniture. So fascinating that even the Governor of Virginia couldn't resist taking part. Sidna was the type of man who rose to the top like the cream. He was always going to find a way to be successful because it was built into him like his blue eyes. Payne knew that he had never had that kind of grit. He had always been a follower. He couldn't hack being a leader during the search for Sidna and was relegated to follower for the rest of his career in the Baldwin-Felts Detective Agency. When the mines in West Virginia were set ablaze during those violent years following the search for the Allens, he did what he was told and endeared himself to the bosses of the agency as an enforcer who was loyal and willing to kill for the agency. He never rose above the equivalent of a lieutenant in the agency. Taking orders from the top and relaying them down with bloody results against the unionized miners and not thinking about the consequences, not thinking about right and wrong.

The line diminished and the last person shook Sidna's hand. Sidna and Wesley started packing up the display booth. Wesley started dismantling the large canvas tent that covered the booth. Payne stepped forward. He felt compelled to talk to Sidna. Sidna raised his head up in a nod and smiled.

"Feel free to come over and look at the pieces," Sidna said.

Payne didn't answer and walked over to where the furniture was on display. He pretended to inspect the different tables and chests, but his mind was working on what to say. Sidna walked over and picked up the chair he had been standing on and loaded it into the back of a Ford wagon parked in the grass behind the exhibit.

"You need any help?" Payne asked.

"Sure. My wife Bettie usually helps us load up, but I think she is wandering the street, looking for bargains," Sidna chuckled.

"My wife is too," Payne laughed.

Sidna walked to one of the small tables and grabbed underneath the top and motioned his head for Payne to come over. Payne walked over and grabbed the other end of the table and lifted with Sidna. It wasn't heavy, it had a delicate feel, and Sidna shuffled back gently toward the Ford. They loaded the first one and walked back for the other pieces.

"I'm Sidna Allen," Sidna said, extending his hand.

"Edwin Payne," Payne said.

Payne extended his own hand and Sidna gripped down and held on.

"Payne. That name sounds familiar. You from around here?"

"No. Just visiting. Up from Richmond."

"It was a good crowd today. I appreciate you stopping by and helping me load up," Sidna said.

Sidna flashed his broad smile as they loaded up another piece. "You need a job? I'm going to be hiring a man to help me unload and load the art and be my driver. My nephew is just helping us for this show. He has to get back home to his fiancée in Richmond tomorrow."

"No thanks," Payne chuckled. "I'm retired."

"What are you retired from?"

"I retired from law enforcement a few years ago."

"What agency were you with?" Sidna asked.

"Baldwin-Felts," Payne said.

Payne noted a spark of recognition in Sidna's eyes.

"So, are you taking these pieces on tour?" Payne asked, trying to change the subject.

"I've been on tour for the last month. I'm going all over Virginia and North Carolina. This is as far north as I've been. The governor's friends invited me and made sure it was worth my time. They paid me a flat fee. I usually charge an admittance fee at most venues."

They finished loading the rest of the furniture. Rose was waiting for him on the sidewalk. He waved her over.

"Thanks again for your help," Sidna said.

"You're welcome. Nice to meet you," Payne said.

The crowd had moved out and the other vendors were packing up their booths. Payne walked over to where his wife was waiting in the street.

"Who was that man?" Rose asked.

"Sidna Allen."

She turned to him with wide eyes. "Really?"

His wife stopped and turned back around to look at Sidna Allen again.

"He's looking back at us," Rose said.

Payne turned around and Sidna was staring back at him with a sour look on his face. A sturdy woman with a round face veered off the street and into the grass toward Sidna. The woman walked up beside of Sidna and all four stood there staring at each other for a quarter of a minute. Wesley continued packing, unaware of the queer reunion.

"You almost had us on that foggy morning with the dogs running," Sidna said.

"I know," Payne shouted back.

Payne turned and started walking up the street with his wife. He felt Sidna's eyes on his back until he and his wife vanished into the crowd. He stopped when they were out of sight and reached into his breast pocket and pulled out his little notebook, crumpled and frayed at the edges, with all the names of men he had fought. He kept it for all those years, more out of habit than anything else, but also as a reminder of a prowess that he no longer held. He hadn't added a name in over a decade. He pulled out the little pen that was clipped inside of the notebook and added another name: Jeremiah Sidna Allen. He wrote one word beside the name: *worthy*. It was a word that, up until then, was missing from his little notebook. Sidna had beaten him. Payne never laid eyes on Sidna during the manhunt and Payne's career with the Baldwin-Felts Detective Agency had hinged on that failure. He tossed the notebook into a trashcan on the edge of the sidewalk and kept walking.

AFTERWORD

A Bad and Dangerous Man is a novel based on the tragic true story of the Carroll County courthouse shootout in 1912. I grew up three miles from Hillsville, Virginia surrounded by the stories, legends, and rumors of what happened on that terrible day.

Historical fiction tries to understand the emotions associated with past events and the people who experienced those events. I have taken great liberties in the writing of this novel. The dialogue, thoughts, and feelings of the characters, who were real people, are a product of my imagination based on reading period newspapers, memoirs, historical non-fiction, and scholarly journals. I compressed the timeline of events to create a more compelling narrative and some of the people involved in the events before, during, and after the shootout have been left out, consolidated, changed, and artistically interpreted. However, the overarching sequence of events in my novel remains unchanged. Wesley Edwards got into a fight with the boyfriend of a young woman he kissed at a corn shucking. Wesley was charged with assault and fled to North Carolina before being captured and then illegally rescued by his uncle, Floyd Allen. Floyd's arrest reignited an old political feud with the politicians who controlled the county court. Floyd was put on trial and refused to accept his guilty verdict. The courtroom erupted with gunfire and five people were killed: Judge Thornton L. Massie, Commonwealth's Attorney William M. Foster, Sheriff Lewis F. Webb, Betty Ayers, and Andrew Howlett. The Governor of Virginia called on the Baldwin-Felts Detective Agency to lead the manhunt for the Allens. Floyd Allen, Claude Allen, Friel Allen, and William Sidna Edwards were captured within weeks of the shootout. Sidna Allen and Wesley Edwards avoided capture for six months. They made it as far as Des Moines, Iowa before eventually being apprehended after Wesley briefly returned to Virginia to visit his girlfriend, Maude Iroler. Maude led the Baldwin-Felts detectives to Iowa, probably against her will, and married another man soon after Wesley was captured. Floyd Allen and his son Claude were executed for their participation in the shootout. Sidna Allen, Wesley Edwards, Friel Allen, and William Sidna Edwards were sentenced to long prison terms but were all eventually pardoned by two different Governors of Virginia.

Certain details have been lost to history. People directly involved guarded their secrets tightly, in some cases only revealing the truth on their deathbeds. Various details of the shootout itself have remained shrouded in the gun smoke that never settled from the stale air inside the courtroom. Rumors and legends persist. In 1912 Carroll County, the heroes and villains of the shootout depended on people's perspective. Lies, grudges, strong family bonds, political differences, and false reporting perpetuated rumors and legends. Over the years it became hard to distinguish fact from fiction. All those facts, legends, rumors, and lies converge creating fertile ground for a novelist to explore the human condition.

FURTHER READING

In researching the events of the Carroll County courthouse shootout, I relied on the following resources:

Allen, J. Sidna, *A True Narrative of What Really Happened at Hillsville, Virginia*. Cana: Rufus Gardner, 1929.

Bowman, Rick, director. ***Hillsville 1912:*** *A Shooting in the Court.* Lethal Sounds, Inc. and Backyard Green Films, 2011.

Hall, Randal L. "A Courtroom Massacre: Politics and Public Sentiment in Progressive-Era Virginia." *The Journal of Southern History*, Volume LXX, No. 2 (May 2004).

Hall, Ronald W. *The Carroll County Courthouse Tragedy: A true account of the 1912 gun battle that shocked the nation; its causes and the aftermath.* Hillsville: Carroll County Historical Society, 1997.

Payne, Edwin Chancellor. *The Hillsville Tragedy: Story of the allen clan.* Edited by Edward Boyle Jacobs. M.A. Donohue & Co., 1913.

Rountree, Travis A., "Hard to see through the smoke : remembering the 1912 Hillsville, Virginia courthouse shootout." *Electronic Theses and Dissertations.* Paper 2620 (2017). https://doi.org/10.18297/etd/2620

Williamson, Seth. "*The Hillsville Massacre.*" The Roanoker, November 1982.

ACKNOWLEDGMENTS

Thank you to my wife, Abby Whittington, who encouraged and supported me throughout the writing process and provided valuable feedback as my first reader. Your love, support, and understanding have been invaluable.

Thank you to the beta readers who helped make this novel better: Charlene Bell; and Kevin Whitten.

Thank you to my parents for a lifetime of guidance and love. Thanks to my grandmother for keeping a copy of J. Sidna Allen's memoirs on her bookshelf.

Thank you to Ron Phillips and Shotgun Honey Books for getting this novel into the hands of readers.

Brett Lovell lives in the Blue Ridge Mountains of Southwest Virginia with his wife and two young children. He grew up near Hillsville, Virginia a few miles from where the events chronicled in his debut novel, ***A Bad and Dangerous Man*** took place.

ABOUT SHOTGUN HONEY BOOKS

Thank you for reading ***A Bad and Dangerous Man*** by Brett Lovell.

Shotgun Honey began as a crime genre flash fiction webzine in 2011 created as a venue for new and established writers to experiment in the confines of a mere 700 words. More than a decade later, Shotgun Honey still challenges writers with that storytelling task, but also provides opportunities to expand beyond through our book imprint and has since published anthologies, collections, novellas and novels by new and emerging authors.

We hope you have enjoyed this book. That you will share your experience, review and rate this title positively on your favorite book review sites and with your social media family and friends.

Visit ShotgunHoneyBooks.com

Printed in the USA
CPSIA information can be obtained
at www.ICGtesting.com
LVHW031121301123
765241LV00092B/3516